Periphery

by

AA Dasilva

Cover Art by *Tina Lynn Stout*

The Wild Rose Press, Inc.
PO Box 708
Adams Basin, NY 14410-0708
Visit us at www.thewildrosepress.com

Publishing History
First Edition, 2024
Trade Paperback ISBN 978-1-5092-5771-3
Digital ISBN 978-1-5092-5772-0

Published in the United States of America

Dedication

To my family:
This book wouldn't have been possible without your love and support. I love you all beyond measure.
***
To all veterans, active military, and first responders: thank you for your service.

Chapter 1

"Reality is merely an illusion, albeit a very persistent one." –Albert Einstein

I folded my arms tightly across my chest, my hands clenched into fists. A wave of nausea rolled through me as the car slowed to a stop.

"This conversation is over, Charlotte. I am not having an affair. My father is deploying me to Virginia for a classified mission. It's my job, my duty." Jared stared at the intersection, waiting for the light to turn green, his face composed and smooth.

"But why would Kayla say that?" I gritted my teeth.

"Because her husband has affairs when he gets deployed, ever think of that? Takes the heat off him when he makes it sound like we all do it," Jared retorted.

I chewed on my lip, turning over his response in my head as I stared at the cherry blossoms across the street, buds ready to pop with the impending spring.

"Look at me, Charly," Jared coaxed.

I loosened my fists and looked over to meet his dark eyes.

He smiled widely, his face so handsome it should be illegal.

"I'm sorry, I know she's a troublemaker." I sighed.

Jared was traveling more than ever lately, but such was military life. I was going to have to approach this

1

differently after his deployment.

"It's only you, doll." He turned to watch the road as we accelerated.

I kept my gaze on his face, searching for genuineness in his reply.

A piercing screech deafened me, and the hairs along my neck prickled in response to the unexpected sound. There was no time to turn to see where it came from. Noises began to coalesce—the relentless shriek of tires attempting to stop several thousand pounds of unyielding metal, hot rubber dragging across asphalt, exploding glass.

Jared's body swung uncontrollably away from the source of the impact.

And red, so much red suspended around us just before the darkness swallowed me up completely.

****

"Blood pressure is eighty over sixty and dropping fast!" A man shouted loud enough to be heard over the chaos.

My aching head was stabilized in a collar, but my legs bounced from the hard thump as the gurney was pushed over the threshold and into the trauma bay. I tried to open my eyes, but a rush of warm blood pooled near my eyes, blinding me.

"Oxygen's dropping, pulse is weak; she's going into shock!" A voice, this time female, called out between the wailing and buzzing of machines.

Cold scissors slid across my skin and cut through my clothes. Scattered footsteps clamored around the room. There was the crinkle of packages being ripped open, metal trays clanging, the pop of a syringe being uncapped.

"Blood loss estimated to be greater than twenty percent. Page the blood bank and tell them to activate the mass-transfusion protocol, STAT!" The man shouted over the cacophony.

"We're losing her! Clearing the airway!"

The female's yelling was followed by more package-tearing, a pinprick into my hand, wheels rolling, curtain grommets sliding on a metal rod with a tinny whoosh.

"We've got to get her to the O.R.!"

I was moving, floating almost, and I could tell by the rhythmic pulse of light behind my lids that they were transporting me quickly. Something was over my face pushing air into my lungs without any effort of my own.

And then there was darkness again. The pulsing of lights overhead stopped, and for half a heartbeat, the world fell unnervingly silent. The silence faded as soft music pierced the darkness. The music encircled me like warm sunlight on a summer day.

I opened my eyes and saw a sunny road ahead. I slowed the car and lowered the radio, trying to think about where I was and where I was going. My chrome keychain swung from the ignition and reflected the sunlight across the empty passenger seat, leaving a spectacular pattern of glittering light in its wake. I blinked a few times. *Jared was driving just moments ago, wasn't he?*

I was overwhelmed with memories of the accident and trauma bay, while contending with a rush of memories that weren't mine. A foreign road lined with evergreens, a soldier I had to meet with. A nagging pit formed in my stomach, telling me I had to get to this person I'd never seen before, his face just out of reach of my memory as if formed from a dream. I needed to warn this man. Fast. He was in danger. With laser focus, the memories of the accident began to fade, and I began navigating the road with undue knowledge of how to get to him.

Time was running out.

My thoughts were interrupted by a lightning bolt through my chest—the sensation I was being ripped apart from the inside out. The road ahead became blurry, my vision glitching, as if the world before me threatened to disappear. I squinted my eyes to re-focus, gripping the steering wheel tightly while stomping the gas pedal nearly to the floor. Again, the bolt hit my chest with the strength of a hot iron fist. More beeping, unintelligible voices, shouting. And then, the blackness consumed me again.

I wasn't going to make it to him in time.

Every part of my body ached. But worse than the aching pain was the intense fire within my mind. I kept my eyes closed to untangle my thoughts before I faced the people in the room. I could tell by the echo around me that I was in the hospital—the rhythmic sound of the cardiac monitors, the hushed voices in the hall.

I could feel the presence of two, maybe three people in the room, quietly shuffling. Pages turning, someone reading, perhaps? Another movement to my right indicated someone was arranging something crinkly. Nervous movements.

Based on the sounds, the people in the hall were about fifteen meters away. My room guests were on my left and my right, and based on the speed of sound—343 meters per second— they were just mere steps away from me. Wait, what was I thinking? What did I know about sound waves and the speed at which they traveled?

And, more importantly, what the hell happened? The accident! Jared was driving, and the impact came on my side of the car. The intersection. But, what about those strange visions in the car? The foreign road, the soldier I had to warn?

And Jared! Oh, thank God he was okay. I didn't need reassurance he was fine, I was able to replay the accident in my head clearly. I could look at the acceleration on the speedometer, and judging by the sound, the impact, and the trajectory of Jared's body, no critical injury would've occurred. A head injury, perhaps. He must've gotten knocked out by hitting his head on the driver's-side window, and taken a blow to the chest from the airbag, but…he would survive that.

I needed to open my eyes, talk to the people in the room. But I sifted through equations instead. I could slow the picture in my head of the accident, rotate it and view it from different angles, and determine the impact using estimated figures. Yes, Jared would be fine. Banged up, but alive. And, here I was, intact mentally as well. My body was in pain, specifically the left side of my head that throbbed relentlessly. But it could be worse.

"Charlotte, can you hear me?" Mitch demanded.

Ugh. My father-in-law.

I opened my eyes and blinked rapidly at the unexpected brightness.

My parents jumped from their seats to hurry to my side. Everyone tried speaking at once.

A soft knock, and a man in a white lab coat entered the room.

The drab olive-and-yellow curtains revealed my

location. I was in the VA Hospital close to home.

My father squeezed my hand gently.

My mother dabbed at her tears with a wrinkled tissue, and her mascara left black streaks along the lower rim of her eyes.

I tried a half-smile and croaked, "I'm okay."

"Charlotte—" Mitch cleared his throat and sat in the vinyl chair near my bed.

He was wearing his green service uniform adorned with a plethora of colorful ribbon bars and metals.

The man in the lab coat stepped forward.

Tomas Gustav, M.D., his lab coat embroidery indicated.

"General, I'm going to need a moment with the patient before you proceed," the doctor interjected.

I inhaled sharply when Mitch, my parents, and the doctor began speaking all at once.

Mitch didn't appreciate being interrupted. Typical.

My head ached as I recalled the memory of the accident again. Jared's head shattered the driver's window, his large brown eyes were wide with shock, and a rivulet of blood streamed down his cheek.

I was startled back to the present when the doctor placed his hand on my wrist.

My visitors exited the room while I was examined.

The doctor performed a neurologic exam and gave me a rundown of the accident—which I didn't need— and the extent of my injuries—which I did.

Not good, but not bad. Survivable.

The room filled with my guests again. The medications were wearing off, and with that came an increase in pain but also mental sharpness. In fact, my mind felt sharper than it'd ever been. Strange.

The hospital sill was filled with baskets, colorful flowers, and get-well cards. Unease settled in my chest, heavy and cold at the realization that I'd been unconscious for more than a few days.

Mitch leaned forward in the chair by my head.

My parents held my hand on the opposite side.

"Charlotte, there's no easy way to tell you this, but you need to know. Jared died." Mitch looked over at my parents, who stared at me, waiting for my reaction.

"Bullshit, Mitch. Where is he?"

My parents gasped. My mother and father tried to console me.

I shook off their hands. "Mitch! I know he didn't die. What are you, preparing me for the worst? The head injury won't kill him. The impact wasn't enough to—"

"Enough, Charlotte! I am burying my son! You have a long road of rehab and recovery ahead. Get a grip on what I'm telling you, so you can deal with it appropriately."

My father flew to the other side of my bed, and Mitch stood to meet him.

"You watch how you speak to my daughter! How dare you—"

"You just take care of your daughter. Clearly she's going to need more than just physical help." Mitch towered over my father, took a deep breath, and smoothed his uniform.

"General, I'm sorry for your loss, but Jared was also her husband. Have mercy, for God's sake!"

I listened to my father and Mitch bicker and slowly tuned them out.

My mother was mopping her tears again.

Mitch returned to the chair beside me.

I stared at him blankly while he spoke.

"Charlotte, we'll have a memorial service you can attend once you're recovered. Full military honors, of course."

Impressed. That's the word I was looking for. Mitch looks impressed that I'm not crying.

And I'm not crying because he's wrong.

The room fell quiet as a matronly nurse bustled in and replaced my IV bag.

A rhythmic clicking signaled fresh medications dripping into my vein.

She smiled and put the call button within reach.

I nodded thankfully as she left the room, closing the door behind her.

One of the baskets on the window sill held an array of self-care items—face wipes, towels, aromatherapy oils, and a leather-bound journal.

"Hand me that, please." I motioned to the basket behind Mitch.

"That's from Jess—" my mother started.

My father put his hand on her shoulder and watched me curiously.

I pulled the journal from the crinkly cellophane wrap, and my father placed the basket back on the sill. Everyone watched as I opened the brown, leather-bound journal.

My father handed me a pen.

Moments passed in lovely silence except for the sound of the pen scratching along the stiff new pages of the journal.

Equations—acceleration, velocity, impact, trajectory.

After several pages worth of calculations and a few

sketches of the accident, I closed the journal and rested my head back against the pillow with a satisfied sigh.

I closed my eyes.

Definitely not dead. Mitch is wrong.

The journal was gently pulled from my hands as my body went slack. My consciousness drifted while pages were riffled. Then, a soft thump where the journal was tossed lightly to my side.

"She's going to need help. Dr. Gustav is a great neurologist, I'll make sure she gets the best care," Mitch spoke to my parents.

I felt the journal leave my side again and heard stiff pages being turned.

"What the hell is all this?" my mother asked.

"She's traumatized, in denial," Mitch replied to my mother.

And you're wrong! I wanted to scream, but the medications flowing into my vein made me unable to fight the heavy weight of drowsiness. My awareness drifted, but I was certain that I was right.

Chapter 2

Four years, twenty days. Or, one thousand, four hundred eighty days. More precisely: thirty-five thousand, five hundred forty-three hours since the accident.

I stared down at the brown journal, now well broken in and with nearly every page filled. Equations, sketches, and ramblings of words all meaningless now, so many years later.

I was wrong.

Jared did, in fact, die.

I pulled at a loose thread that held the binding of the journal together and twirled it around my finger absentmindedly. I could understand physics since my accident and calculate things with scary accuracy, something I never could've done before.

But what did it matter? When it really counted for something, I was wrong.

I flipped to the page where I'd sketched the accident, marked by the neatly folded police report. I unfolded the report—now tearing at the seams from years of folding and unfolding—and laid it side-by-side with my drawing. Uncanny how I was able to recreate the accident I viewed from inside the car long before I ever saw the police report.

But I did.

The neurologist said I'd developed acquired savant

syndrome after the injury to the left anterior temporal lobe of my brain. But the damage didn't matter, just the death. And nothing, not the damage or the journal or the guilt, could bring Jared back.

I folded the report and used it to mark the page. I closed the journal and drummed my fingers on the cover. Stillness settled into my marrow as I counted higher and higher with each thump of my fingertips connecting with the soft leather. I folded my arms on my desk and put my head down.

The screeching table saw woke me. My long hair spilled over my face when I turned my head, partially blocking the sunlight shining through the slats of the blinds. Another wail from the saw caused me to groan as I lifted my head off the desk. I hesitated before rising and lifting one blade of the blinds, scowling at the construction truck parked outside my neighbor's house. I let the slat fall back into place and headed toward the bathroom.

After a long shower, I took my time getting dressed and drinking coffee. I stared at the clock until I was left with just enough time to arrive at work just past eight. I didn't want anyone questioning my sleeping patterns— *again*—by arriving obnoxiously early.

I paused on the front porch, inhaling the unmistakable smell of spring. Petrichor and lilac. Heading toward my car, I winced when the saw raged once again.

"Good morning," a construction worker boomed. He tipped his head toward me courteously while balancing a long beam of wood on his shoulder.

The tall, muscular man's dark hair was caked with sawdust and sweat, and his arms were littered with fading black tattoos.

I didn't have a chance to respond as he walked around the side of the house, keeping his gaze on the destination ahead of him.

Several other men were unloading the truck, yelling to each other over the sound of the saw and clanking boards of wood.

"And it's going to be 80 effin degrees out!" another man bellowed and abruptly stopped.

His shoulders hitched when his profanities echoed throughout the neighborhood as the saw stopped in poor timing with his announcement.

Our gazes met, and he looked embarrassed.

"Sorry about that, ma'am." He smiled broadly, his lips surrounded by a black goatee and eyes hidden by dark sunglasses.

I laughed at his poor timing, something I could relate to wholeheartedly. I smiled back and held my travel cup up to him in a half-wave.

I slid into my car and pulled the door shut, grateful the sounds of construction were muted in the sanctuary of my sedan. I backed out of my spot slowly.

I stopped at a red light and tinkered with the radio. I took in a sharp breath when a quick vision of a car barreling toward the passenger side of my car flickered into my mind's eye. Just as quickly as the memory came, it disappeared, leaving me scowling at the car behind me impatiently blaring its horn.

The light had turned green.

Traffic crawled along, lines of cars attempting to merge onto East Main from the sprawling New England neighborhoods. Tourist season was just beginning to ramp up in the bustling ocean town, adding to an already hectic commute each morning.

It was unseasonably warm for April, and the scent of the ocean swept into my car when I powered down the window. I glanced at the large VA hospital, spanning high above the maples and pines in the distance. I took a sip of my iced coffee as I reached the gate to the base.

"Good morning, Charlotte. Badge, please." Pfc Goodman in his army fatigues greeted me at the gates to the base.

I hung my badge out the window.

He passed the scanner over my badge and waved me in as the striped barricades slowly lifted.

****

I pushed hard on the heavy steel door to make my way into the building.

The clinic was connected to the emergency room, allowing walk-ins for urgent care, mostly for the military and their children.

We did occasional sutures and wound care for minor injuries, treated those stricken with the flu or strep, and would triage patients to the ER for major injuries or serious illnesses.

Nelson, the security guard with an infectious laugh and smile, greeted me. He was the sunshine of the clinic, often singing or whistling loudly. "Hey, hey Charlotte, running a little late today, but beautiful as always." He chuckled and his rotund belly bounced.

"Better late than never!" I shrugged and smirked.

We both ignored the dark undertone to my statement.

"For sure, for sure!" Nelson nodded.

I opened the door to the clinical area behind triage and looked down the corridor lined with examination rooms that held only two closed doors.

Open doors were a good sign, not that the clinic had been busy as of late anyhow.

"Glad you made it," Brian teased from behind his mask and winked. The tall, middle-aged PA with kind eyes ran the clinic most days.

He wasted no time getting down to business. "We have a pediatric patient in room one who needs a throat swab, and Angela is doing vitals in room two, waiting for me to step in. Can you get the swab for me and ask the mother if the kid has any allergies?"

I opened my laptop to log in and access the patient's record.

The day wasn't busy, but steady, with the usual cases of pink-eye and suspicious rashes, diabetic wounds, and medication refills. The clinic bustled with the sound of phones ringing and indiscernible chatter behind the closed examination room doors.

Angela raised her eyebrows at me. "So, you're still coming tonight, right?"

"Of course." I feigned excitement. I would never miss drinks to celebrate Nelson's birthday.

His birthday had actually been the week prior, but tonight was the only night most of us who worked in the clinic were available.

I was never really a fan of crowded places, and bars were at the top of that list. The music and droves of drunk patrons looking for love in the worst possible place to find it caused me to loathe the establishments altogether. But while I despised the thought of going, I did enjoy the company of my friends.

When my shift ended, dread crept in. I washed my hands slowly under the hot water, debating if I could come up with an excuse to bow out.

"So, I'll pick you up at eight, okay?" Angela waited behind me to use the sink.

"Sure, sounds good." I smiled at her while drying my hands.

Angela was cheerful, ignoring the fact that she knew my smile was a façade. "You're going to have fun. We don't get you out often, but when we do, you always have a good time."

"You're right." I pulled my bag over my shoulder and tapped my badge across the reader, clocking out for the day.

****

I pulled into my driveway, and the contractors from that morning were packing their tools into the truck. *Thank God I wouldn't have to listen to that obnoxious saw again.* I headed inside to get ready for the evening ahead without another glance in their direction.

I sat on my bed and stared blankly into my closet. I didn't go out often, and many of the clothes hanging there that held any potential for a night out hadn't been worn for a long time.

I wanted more than anything to pull on a pair of sweats and curl up in bed with ice cream and Trash TV.

After several try-ons for tops and bottoms, I settled on a pair of fitted black jeans and a deep-burgundy blouse. I slipped into a pair of sneakers just as the doorbell rang. I smoothed my blouse as I walked to the front door, opening it to a smiling Angela, who looked like she'd just returned from a photo shoot.

Her golden hair was pinned to the side, and she bit her lipstick-red lip when she eyed my shoes critically. "I thought you'd need some help, so I came prepared." She walked right past me, a pair of nude strappy stilettos in her hand.

"I *like* my shoes. If I break an ankle, you'll be covering my shifts, so you might want to reconsider." I closed the door and faced her with a defiant lifted chin.

"Risk-benefit assessment says no-go on the sneaks, Charl. Sit." She motioned to the armchair near my bay window.

I plopped down and toed off my shoes. She wouldn't relent until I at least tried them on.

She dropped the pointy heels by my feet.

I bent to fasten the thin straps around my ankle. The shoes were sexy as hell. I twisted my ankle left and right, admiring the feminine look of them, but standing or walking in them would make my case. I rose from the chair and giggled as I walked with quivering ankles toward Angela. I looked like a doe learning to take its first steps.

Angela smiled and let out a triumphant sigh. "See? Perfect. Now you're ready."

"I can't even walk! I'm wearing the sneakers..." I sat to take off the shoes, but she caught my elbow and linked our arms.

"You can handle one night in a pair of real shoes, Charlotte. Now, get your stuff, we're gonna be late."

Yeah, late for sure, since my usual quick pace was replaced by slow, careful steps now that I was walking on stilts. I grabbed my purse and did a last once-over in the bathroom mirror before slowly following her out to the car, ready to get the night over with. I slid into the passenger seat and fastened my seatbelt, glad to be off my feet. How Angela managed to get around on her heels without incident was beyond me.

Angela was chatting about how she had bought her shoes from some subscription website, trying to convince me that the more I wore heels, the more I'd adjust to them.

I listened, but also got lost in my own thoughts as she turned up the radio to sing along with the song that had just come on.

I used to dress up all the time before Jared died. I studied Angela's shoes on my feet as the streetlights whizzed by and reflected off the nude patent leather. I'd attended the military ball every year, decked out in a fancy gown accented by sky-high heels and a sequined clutch, mingling with the other over-dressed wives while our spouses laughed and drank and carried on with their inside jokes. I shook the nostalgia from my mind. I stuffed the memories deep inside, because allowing myself to remember the way it was would bring me into a despair that confined me to my house for days at a time, even all these years later. Survivor's guilt was a relentless harpy.

As anticipated, the line to enter Thames Place was long.

Angela began telling me about her recent online hookup, describing in painful detail the erotic night she'd spent with a handsome stranger.

I shifted on my heels uncomfortably, hoping we'd be able to sit before I rolled an ankle. Though the other patrons in line kept their distance, their expressions made it obvious they overheard some of Angela's over-the-top details of her most recent dating escapade.

Goosebumps pebbled my arms, and I looked up to see a group of men, several patrons back, staring at us. I wondered if I knew them from years back when Jared was alive. Their appearance screamed military with their short hair and bulging muscles. A peculiar shiver made me rub my arms for warmth, or comfort. Maybe both.

"You know, you should try it." Angela looked at me pointedly, breaking me from my curious thoughts about the strange men. "It'd be good for you."

"What would?" I turned back to my friend, ashamed I hadn't been listening.

"Hello, earth to Charlotte!" Angela playfully bumped my shoulder. "Maybe that's *just* what you need. To date. To get *some*." She wagged her eyebrows.

"You get enough for both of us." I rolled my eyes and laughed.

She shrugged. "Maybe so, and maybe that's why, as a good friend, I'm recommending it. It's good for the mind *and* body."

"Yeah, maybe." I shook my head and laughed.

I'd reached a stage where I could function, and no amount of coaxing was going to get me to agree to leaving my comfort zone. Between my job, the constant upkeep of my home, and my small circle of friends who had become family, I'd found an even, comfortable pace. I wasn't looking to change that. It'd taken me four years to reach some semblance of normalcy.

I still had my rough days, but they came fewer as the years went by. Nothing stays the same for long. Life continues despite pain, loss, and tragedy. The day-to-day change from what *was* to what *is* ensured the days weren't as familiar as before the accident. This stark difference gave a clear delineation of before and after.

The world that Jared lived in didn't exist anymore.

Inside, Nelson, his wife Shonda, Beth, Brian, and his partner James had already secured a booth, so we joined them.

Angela sat with a huff. "Drinks! Lots of them!" She took in the scene, scanning the room for a guy to sink her charm into. "Time to paint the town black!"

"You mean red." James laughed.

"Whatever."

I smiled as I sat at the very end of the booth. The room was dark, and the smell of alcohol hung heavy in the air. An occasional clack from the pool table was followed by roars of laughter, giving the room a pulse of energy as unique as the exotic drink Brian put in front of me.

We laughed and enjoyed drinks and popcorn together.

Beth—as loud as she was—kept us amused as she voiced her strong opinion, in painful and insulting detail, on the latest political scandal.

Brian and James told us about their recent home renovations, and Nelson's loud laughter in between stories of James's ineptitude at home improvements kept the mood light.

Angela smiled at the stories, even as she was looking up through her long lashes, eyeing a tall, dark man a few tables away.

Nelson was the first to start the night's karaoke session. His wife joined him, gently swaying in tune as he started singing a 90's R&B tune in his rich, deep voice.

Wistful, I stared at them, both clearly so happy, so in tune with each other. Even their movements seemed in perfect timing with each other.

Angela tried to get me to work the room with her, but I refused, citing my aching feet.

"The pain is worth the reward. They're not called hump-me heels for nothing!" She winked.

"The only thing going to get screwed is my feet!" I laughed and gave her a playful push to send her on her way. No doubt she'd be headed to the tall, dark guy sitting at a pub table a few feet away.

Sure enough, Angela sashayed toward him, batting her eyelashes as she smiled and sat beside him.

Brian and James stood just below the stage, watching Nelson and Shonda perform.

Alone with Beth, I swung my legs to face out and away from the table. Beth was preoccupied, scrolling through her phone, and I was attempting to avoid any awkward conversation with her that would turn into her usual probing of my personal life.

I crossed my legs, and my shoe shin-slammed the guy sitting at the booth to my right. "I'm so sorry." I quickly readjusted my leg away from his.

He sat up straighter, making more room beside him. "My fault."

He was sitting facing out like me, but with his elbows on his knees holding a beer in both hands between his legs. His dark-blond hair was buzzed close to his head. A mosaic of tattoos trailed down from under his black shirt sleeve to his forearm, leaving no trace of flesh in the dark, intricate colors and designs.

I interlaced my fingers, squeezing my hands together uncomfortably tight to hide the unexpected shiver that made its way down my arms, leaving a spray of goosebumps in its wake. I snuck another peek at the intriguing stranger just inches away. A course of electricity ran through my hands. The odd hum of longing filling my belly, both foreign and familiar, was pleasing and terrifying at the same time.

I blamed it on the strange energy in the bar and tried to ignore the awkwardness as we sat side by side, separated only by the backrest of our booths and the glass partition that connected to the ceiling from the top of the booths.

He might've been in the crowd of men who gawked at us in line. I shrugged the thought away. I smiled warmly at Nelson as he handed the microphone to his wife and stepped aside.

Shonda chose an upbeat song, and the flat screen lit up with the vibrant lyrics. Nelson's voice had been rich, smooth. Shonda's voice was stunning, soulful, and filled the bar with a buoyant vibration.

"Can you walk in those things?"

His deep voice startled me, and I looked over at the tattooed man, whose lips curved in a downward smirk as he stared at my shoes.

"Barely," I choked, taken off guard by both his question and my quick response.

Dammit, Angela.

A wave of electricity flickered up and down my spine when he met my gaze.

"I was wondering the same thing." Beth scooted her heavy bottom along the seat to face us, injecting herself into what was already becoming a painfully awkward exchange.

I looked over to see his lips pulling into a tight grin as his gaze met Beth's.

I turned to her. "I guess I'll have to sit here forever now." I hung my head.

I stared at my over-the-top shoes, cursing Angela in my head again. My hair fell over the side of my face, hiding my now-crimson cheeks from the stranger to my right.

"Yeah, I've seen you trip in flats, no way you're getting out of here alive." Beth chuckled.

A quiet laugh came from my right. I looked over and met his gaze again, and his gray eyes twinkled with humor as they bore into mine. My whole body reacted to him. I knew this man somehow.

He was exceptionally good-looking in a rugged, sharp-jawed way. His tattooed arms were chiseled muscle, his hard chest tightening his T-shirt in all the right places. A small white scar slashed through one of his eyebrows. His stubble-laced jaw appeared clenched as he held a tight grin.

He leaned toward me, so close I felt his minty breath fan across my face.

His gaze remained locked on mine. "It's not the shoes, but those *eyes* that are going to get you into trouble." He spoke quietly, but the deep timbre of his voice allowed his words to be heard over the thrum of music.

I gaped at him. "Have we met before?"

He shook his head. "No."

I let out an embarrassed laugh, shook my head, and finally looked away.

I'd never met him before, but something about him seemed strangely familiar. He didn't resemble anyone I knew, but I was intrigued by the overwhelming feeling that this new face wasn't foreign.

My hands tried to betray me, longing to reach out and see what would happen if I touched him. An electric shock? Spontaneous combustion?

Maybe Brian's exotic drink, perhaps mixed by

Aphrodite herself, was causing me to lose it at the sight of a gorgeous man. But when I took a sip to distract myself, I tasted the tangy elixir for the first time.

I snuck a peek at him through my curtain of dark hair. He was watching, no, *reconning* was a better word. It was a word Jared often used when they were gathering intelligence for a mission. He appeared to focus on something as a concerned line appeared across his forehead.

By his poise, it was clear this guy had a military background. I inconspicuously followed his gaze, curious as to what his attention was focused on with such grave concern.

I looked over at the bar to see a large man with a dark goatee talking loudly with an intoxicated patron sporting a ragged beard. The drunk guy put the phrase beer belly to shame, and his echoing belligerent tone was causing the crowd in the bar to quiet as they turned to glare in his direction.

In between beer belly and goatee-guy sat a woman with long curly hair. The exchange heated. The steady rise of their deep voices and animated facial expressions hinted at signs of trouble.

The curly-haired woman gently put her hand on goatee-guy's muscular chest, a weak attempt to separate them.

Shonda's song ended, and a top-40 song was now blaring into the speakers, making the exchange impossible to hear. But as both men rose from their seats, something was coming.

My chest tightened with anxiety.

It happened fast—the curly-haired woman was flung to the side, and the two men were chest-to-chest, heavily breathing as their eyes pierced each other with murderous glares.

A quiet sigh to my right, and the tattooed guy calmly put his beer on the table. He rose slowly from his seat, unbothered, bored almost, and walked over to the drunken man who instigated the exchange.

The drunk guy threw a sloppy punch toward him, but he dodged it with ease. Tattoo dude grabbed the drunk man tightly by the back of his shirt, swinging his face into the plexiglass partition that separated our booths with a crash.

Blood sprayed across the unaffected partition, and drunk guy, with his bloody mouth, was now being hauled toward the exit by the calm tattooed man, while the woman and goatee-guy followed them out.

During the frightening and fast exchange, I had flung myself to the other side of the booth and was now almost on Beth's lap. I counted my breaths until the hammering in my chest slowed.

The bar resumed its electric hum of energy, the music continued, and voices erupted into chatter even louder than before.

This is why I hated going out.

My friends gathered back at the booth, James playfully teasing about my proximity to Beth.

I peeled myself back to my side of the booth.

A few hours passed.

I nodded and smiled at the appropriate times, I added to my friends' playful banter, and nursed my drink until it was mostly melted ice.

I masked my discomfort well, glancing at the time on my phone discreetly.

Angela asked, "Are you okay?"

"I'm fine," I lied.

That was the thing about Angela, she could pick up on vibes easily. She gathered her bag and winked. Soon we were saying our goodbyes to the group and walking outside to her car.

"So…the guy I met…I got his number. Did you see how cute he was?" Angela asked excitedly.

"Nice. Is he from around here?" I asked the common question, since many of the new people we'd meet at the local pub were actually military guys here for a temporary stay on base.

My body lurched to the side.

"Actually, he's not—OH! Are you ok?!" Angela caught me by the shoulders.

I grasped tightly onto her arms, thankful I didn't eat the pavement. The inevitable finally happened, I'd rolled my ankle. I swiftly straightened, laughing at my inability to walk in her ridiculous shoes. "I'm fine." I looked around to make sure she was the only witness to my near-compound fracture.

Angela raised her eyebrows at me as she opened the driver's door to her sedan.

"I saw you talking to the guy in the next booth over." She smirked.

I laughed as I slid into the passenger seat. "You don't miss anything, do you?"

"Well, he had that bad-boy vibe, pretty hot. What'd you talk about?" She tried to sound innocent as she pried.

"He actually made fun of my—er, *your* shoes, and that was before he pummeled that guy at the bar. What an ass."

"You shouldn't judge a movie by its poster. That drunk guy got what was coming to him."

"A book by its cover," I mumbled while looking out the window and remembering the sobering moment.

Angela looked at me with wide eyes.

"What?" I glared back.

She rolled her shoulders and flailed her arms, mocking my near-fall in her insane shoes. "He noticed your shoes, not your gracefulness in them. You're welcome."

We both erupted into fits of laughter as she pulled away, taking me home for the night.

Chapter 3

"In infinite space, even the most unlikely events must take place somewhere." –Max Tegmark

Saturday morning, no surprise, I was awakened by the sound of clanking boards. The saw would start soon enough. I moaned and got out of bed, ready for coffee and a day of yard work. I walked to the living room and stared out the large bay window.

Due to the neighborhood's close proximity to base, the houses that lined the street were mostly occupied by military families.

Two-story colonials and capes with two-stall garages and sprawling freshly manicured lawns lined the street. Most of the homes boasted excess, with one exception.

Mine was a decent—albeit plain—gray, Cape Cod-style home with a large lawn, a Japanese maple in front, and cherry-blossom trees that lined the drive, giving some privacy in the spring and summer.

In the years since Jared had passed, despite my attempts at landscaping, maintenance, and repair, I could no longer afford the luxury of a professional landscaper or repairman, which became evident when compared to the appearance of my neighbors' homes. My house was by no means in shambles but didn't have the same prestige as its neighbors.

I smiled and waved when I saw the mailman stuff my mailbox and drive on to the next house.

I looked down at my tank top and cotton pajama pants, cream colored and dotted with strawberries, and decided it was early enough to get the mail unseen. The saw-and-hammer sounds next door were coming from the back of my neighbor's house.

I dashed down my walk barefoot, my hair still bent in odd angles from sleep. I opened the mailbox and sifted through the typical bills and junk mail.

"Good morning," a voice boomed.

My back stiffened, and a few envelopes escaped my hands and fluttered to the ground. I turned to see the large, goateed construction worker beside his truck parked outside my neighbor's house.

He walked over and gathered the rogue mail, handing it to me with a smile.

I stared in confusion, cringing when recognition set in—it was goatee guy, who'd gotten into the scuffle at the bar with the drunk guy last night.

He lifted his sunglasses, revealing dark, friendly eyes, and then narrowed them at me. "Hey, you were at Thames last night. You were sitting with my brother…"

"Your brother?"

I looked over at the man behind him, who was stacking planks of wood in the bed of the truck. The man turned around, and it was the gray-eyed tattooed guy.

But today, in the light of morning, his eyes were ocean blue. He wore a white T-shirt, his half-sleeve tattoo visible underneath, trailing down beyond his elbow and just over the collar of his shirt, revealing a flash of dark color near his neck.

"I'm Jeff—" He waved his hand toward his brother.

"—and you already met Sy." He smiled.

"I'm Charlotte. Nice to meet you both." I pulled the mail to my chest and started to turn toward my house.

"Hello, Charlotte."

A chill walked up my spine when Sy responded, and I spun to look at him.

He balanced a row of long beams on his muscular shoulder, prompting Jeff to take the other end. With the beams balanced along their shoulders, Sy jumped down from the bed of the truck. They headed toward the back of the house.

I turned and headed back inside. I closed my front door and made sure to lock both the knob and deadbolt.

I dressed and poured my second cup of iced coffee, then looked at the forecast on my phone. Another pleasant day, 70's. Just as I lowered it, it rang.

"Hi, Mom." I pulled on my grass-stained tennis shoes.

"Hey, Charly! What are you up to?" My mother failed to hide the concern in her voice.

"Getting ready for some yard work. How are you and Dad?" I balanced the phone on my shoulder while tying my shoes.

"Oh, we're fine. Didn't hear from you last night, so just wanted to see that you were ok."

"I went out with some friends from work; it was Nelson's birthday last week." I continued making a pile of necessities to bring with me outside, keeping a mental checklist as I went. Phone. Keys. Sunglasses. Earbuds.

My mother talked about a recent meeting of the Homeowners Association. Both my parents had positions on the board since moving to Florida many years ago.

I laughed when she described some of the mundane grievances that caused an uproar in their small fifty-five-and-older community. It usually had to do with garbage pick-up or something being an inch too close to an abutting neighbor. She was passionate about her position, as was my father. When in Rome, I suppose.

I was trying to listen, inserting the appropriate mm-hm's at the pauses, hoping to get outside before the morning was over. I gathered my things and snapped upright at the loud bang followed by profanities being yelled outside. I lifted a blade of the blind, peeking into my neighbor's backyard.

"Charly, are you there?"

"I have to get outside to cut the grass. I love you, Mom." I kept peering outside as I hung up the phone and squinted.

Jeff and two other men walked hurriedly toward the back of the neighbor's house.

I let the blind fall back into place and struggled to open the sliding door leading to my backyard. It creaked and I groaned as I struggled to get the door lined appropriately on its tracks to allow me through.

I walked to the shed and retrieved the lawnmower. I filled it with gas and primed it, dusting away old scraps of grass that were piled along the front. The men were still working in the next yard over, their loud voices bellowing but indecipherable. I sighed, trying to recall if I'd locked my front door.

It took three pulls before the mower quivered and roared to life. I placed my earbuds in, stuck my phone into my pocket, and started my first strip along the back.

My thoughts wandered with the music on, sun on my back, and numbing vibrations of the mower shearing through the overgrown grass. I turned back, facing the fence that separated me from my neighbor and started along the second strip.

As usual, intrusive thoughts about the constant force of my pushing the mower and the opposing drag forces consumed me as I estimated the subtle changes in velocity while I mowed. After allowing myself several minutes of calculations, including how far I walked and how many rotations the wheels on the mower made, I shook my head to dislodge the wayward thoughts.

Instead, I tried to focus on enjoying the warm feeling of the sun on my back, the gentle breeze that ruffled my hair, and the satisfaction that would set in once the yard was cleaned up. I turned the mower again, pleased when the third strip left by the mower connected with the others, creating a noticeable difference already. I stared straight ahead, and my legs kept pace with the upbeat song I was immersed in. Turning again, I saw unexpected movement in my peripheral vision.

Jeff rounded the corner at a half jog, waving me down.

Instinctively, I reached to be sure my phone was within reach in my pocket. I pulled an earbud out and locked eyes with him as the mower shuddered to a stop.

"Charlotte? Charlotte, right? Hey, I need a quick favor. Listen, my brother's real stupid, and he, uh—" Jeff steepled his hands. "—he got hurt, won't let me take him to the hospital. I think he needs stitches, and I saw you the other day—you were wearing nurse scrubs, right?"

He looked at me nervously.

I counted my steps as I approached the edge of the yard where he stood. Sixteen, seventeen, eighteen… "Where is he?" I asked when I was within ten feet of him.

I followed Jeff as his large figure disappeared around the fence to the yard next door.

I rounded the corner.

Sy sat on the ground, pouring water over his forearm. Blood was dripping off his elbow, and the sleeve of his white shirt bore a large crimson stain.

I stepped closer while Jeff, now with two other men, backed away, allowing room for me to kneel beside Sy. "I need a clean cloth." I studied his arm closely. With all the blood, it was hard to tell how deep the gash was.

I didn't pay attention to who handed me the towel, but I took it and applied firm pressure to the wound to stop the bleeding.

Sy looked up at me for the first time.

Our gazes met, and my betraying hands tightened around the cloth I had on his arm. I loosened my grip, but he gave no indication that he felt the added pressure on his arm.

His small smile hinted at embarrassment.

I smiled in return, softened by the unexpected gentleness he exuded, despite his large, tattooed exterior. The air around us tingled with the same kinetic familiarity I'd felt when I saw him in the bar. A wave of heat coursed through me, and I struggled to ignore it.

"I'm fine, really." He spoke quietly.

"Well, let me just stop the bleeding and see how deep this thing is."

I sounded clinical, far too comfortable with the situation—one that I'd been in at least a hundred times before at the hospital. His silence perturbed me. "Are you okay? You're not going to faint on me, are you?"

He let out a half laugh at my question and looked up at me with his mouth in a tight line. "I told you, I'm fine, really. My brother needs to stop being such a—"

"What he's trying to say, Charlotte, is thank you for coming over and checking him out. Saved us a trip to the E.R.," Jeff interjected.

I was starting to like Jeff. I couldn't stifle my giggle at his infectious energy.

Sy shook his head and let out a knowing laugh.

I removed the towel briefly to assess the depth of his wound.

Jeff and the other two men groaned.

Jeff headed toward the front of the house. "I'll get the kit from the truck."

I scanned the wound again, then looked up at Sy. "I think some butterfly bandages and gauze will do the trick, but you're going to need to keep an eye out for infection. What cut you?"

"Someone left the old blade on the table, and when I went to slide the board over, I didn't see it." Sy glanced up at the table saw.

Jeff was walking back toward us from the truck, first-aid kit in hand.

"Thanks." I grabbed the kit and started shuffling through the contents, pulling out what I needed. I spoke to Sy without looking up. "You're going to need a tetanus shot within the next few days."

I turned back to him with antiseptic, gauze, and butterfly bandages in hand.

He lifted the bloodied T-shirt over his head and tossed it aside, then he rested his arm on my lap.

I tried disregarding the reaction my skin had to the heat of his arm across my legs. Goosebumps rose on my skin, despite the warm sun beating down on us, and I hoped no one would notice my reaction to his touch.

I studied his tattoos now that he was shirtless, unsuccessfully trying to ignore how well-built he was.

His shoulders were rounded with muscle, his stomach flat and defined. The half-sleeve tattoo went from just below his elbow, up his biceps, and capped his entire shoulder. A large phoenix sat at the top of his shoulder, with one wing stretching across his chest and the other disappearing around his back. A few black feathers licked toward his neck.

I was mesmerized by the shades of black and gray, all meshed together without a hint of un-inked skin in between. I repositioned myself and drew in a quick breath when I noticed the scar. It tore through the tattoo angrily, extending from his shoulder blade down his back diagonally, leaving a mesh of white-and-pink jagged skin in its wake. I couldn't fathom what would cause such a catastrophic injury, and I despondently recalled asking him about fainting.

Clearly, he'd been through something terrible.

I placed the bandages horizontally to close the wound, then wrapped his arm with gauze. I looked up at Jeff and the other two men.

"I can't thank you enough, Charlotte," Jeff said loudly. "By the way, this is Jay and Max." He motioned to the two other men. "All the brothers but one."

"You're all brothers?" I raised my eyebrows.

"Didn't you see the truck?" Jay turned to face the truck with the Donovan Brothers Construction sign.

Jay resembled Sy, light hair and eyes, and appeared to be in his early 20's. His hair was longer than Sy's, and he had a blonde beard.

Max looked like Jeff, dark hair and eyes, but without the goatee. The two dark-haired brothers looked nothing like the other two.

"And there's a fifth?" I picked up on Jeff's reference to one missing.

"Yeah, Joel's active duty," Max chimed in, smiling. "Do you work at Newport Hospital?"

"Actually, I work at the VA hospital on base. Well, nice to meet you all, I'm going to head back to mowing."

I stepped awkwardly between Jeff and Max to leave the yard.

Sy quietly lifted himself off the ground.

I turned to find him staring intently at me, his arm now wrapped in a mesh of white. I couldn't decipher the look on his face—it fell somewhere between desire and sadness.

Sy took two strides toward me, stopping when our bodies were just inches apart. He stared down at me.

The brothers began heading back to their job, and Jeff's gaze lingered on Sy before he, too, turned toward the house.

Our eyes remained locked for a long stretch of silence.

My feet were rooted to the ground. A soft breeze ruffled through my hair. It tickled, but I didn't move.

Sy finally spoke. "Thank you, Charlotte." He reached out and ran his fingers gently down my cheek, and his hand lingered at my jaw. He tucked a wayward strand of hair behind my ear.

My eyes slid closed for half a heartbeat, and I nearly trembled from the heat of his touch.

Abruptly, he turned around to start working again.

"Don't forget about the tetanus shot," I called out as I rounded the corner to get back to my own yard.

I finished mowing the back and front, weeded the

flower beds, and added mulch to the gardens. I'd just filled a watering can and was getting ready to water the young flowers in my flowerboxes when I spotted Jess walking up from her house around the corner.

That woman was one of the best human beings I'd ever met and one of the reasons I credited for my surviving the loss of Jared. She would often check on me, bringing me meals when I couldn't even stand long enough to feed myself through my grief in those early days, spending long nights holding me on my couch, asking nothing of me and just letting me cry.

Jess wore leggings and a hot-pink tank top, her red hair was pulled into a messy ponytail, and she swung a blue wristlet around as she walked toward me with a huge smile. "Hey, you sexy bitch!"

I laughed and ran to the edge of the yard to hug her. "What's up, my beautiful friend?" I grabbed the wristlet from her.

"Not much, went for a run. I think Steve might be getting deployed soon." Her brow furrowed. "I mean, you know how the rumors are. But usually they're right, and if they are, he's going to have to freeze some of his boys for me. I'm not injecting this stuff for nothing."

I unzipped the wristlet as she followed me into the house. Removing the injection pen and an alcohol swab, I dialed the dose before looking up at her. "You think he's going to get deployed? To where?"

"The border. Again." Jess shrugged. "Glad it's domestic, but still."

I put my arm around her and pressed my cheek to hers sympathetically.

She and her husband had been undergoing fertility treatments for months. This news couldn't have come at a worse time.

"Ugh, you must love that." Jess nodded in the direction of my front window where the Donovan brothers could be heard talking loudly and packing their truck up for the day.

"You have no idea." I rolled my eyes, lifted her shirt, and swabbed her stomach with an alcohol wipe before quickly injecting her fertility medication.

Jess and I returned outside and walked around the yard, watering the flowers.

Before leaving, she gave me a look of caution. "Make sure you lock your doors." She glanced over her shoulder toward the construction truck.

"Of course, Mom." I laughed and gave her another quick hug before she started the short walk back to her house.

The weekend flew by. I'd managed to accomplish a lot of yard work, and by Sunday, I was preparing my laundry and essentials for another fast-approaching Monday.

Later in the day, I walked down to Jess's house to administer her nightly fertility injection.

She had the front door open and was staring up at the sky. "You shouldn't have walked. I think the rain is going to start earlier than they're predicting. It's supposed to rain for the next few days, ugh."

I followed her into the house, and Steve called out a greeting from the couch where he sat watching a ball game. I took off my coat and rested it on the back of a tall stool, one of a row lined up perfectly along her large granite kitchen island.

The house smelled delectable, and the scents of oregano and garlic wafted toward me from the oven.

Jess casually reached into the salad bowl on the island to eat a slice of cucumber.

Her wristlet was open, and the injection pen and alcohol swabs were laid out.

She looked at me, then peered into the oven. "You're staying for dinner. I made chicken parm."

I laughed at her confident demand. "It smells good." I reached into the salad bowl to steal a cucumber slice for myself.

I washed my hands before turning back to the island to dial the dose on her injection pen. I quickly gave her the injection, and we chatted while she packed the supplies back into the blue wristlet.

Steve joined us in the kitchen. The tall, handsome man, with his stocky build and rust-colored hair, rested his hand on her lower back, and her body relaxed into his touch. The perfect couple.

I smiled at them.

Steve and Jared had been comrades, and for a flicker I longed for the past, when it would've been the four of us in their kitchen. I diverted my gaze out the window, where heavy gray clouds threatened to break open at any moment and flood the world with their tears.

We congregated in the kitchen, talking about his potential upcoming deployment while I helped set the island with plates and cutlery.

Jess bustled around, arranging the dish of chicken parm, salad, and rolls on the counter. She turned back to us, leaning on the island, staring with wet, red-rimmed eyes. She blinked rapidly. "Stupid hormones." Her voice quivered.

Steve rubbed her back. "If I have to go, you'll look out for her, right, Charly?" He swiped her ginger bangs from her eyes.

"Of course! In fact, you could even stay with me, Jess." I placed my hand gently on her shoulder.

She wiped her eyes. "It's going to be fine, really. I'm planning on staying with my parents for a while, in Jamestown. Besides, we don't even know yet if he's going. Thank you, though. This is because of the stupid hormones. I'm never like this." She straightened her back and laughed at herself.

I wanted to tell her things would be ok, but Steve quickly changed the subject to the latest neighborhood gossip—Kayla's supposed new affair down the street. This time, with a low ranking young private who'd just enlisted. Her husband was just as bad, if not worse, so finding sympathy for the dysfunctional couple was nearly impossible. The mood was light as we ate and spoke about current affairs.

When it was time to leave, it was pouring.

Steve walked toward the front door with the keys to his truck in hand. "I'll take you home."

My resistance was futile. The walk wasn't far, but the rain was relentless. We didn't talk as he drove me around the corner, only several houses down to my house. The sound of the windshield wipers swiping at the sheets of rain pelting the truck distracted from the silence.

After parking outside my house, he turned to me and said, "I'm going to tell her tonight." He was somber. "I actually got the official orders to go to the border this morning."

I didn't say anything for a long moment as the truck idled and the wipers squawked again. "When?" I ached for Jess. She would be devastated.

"Two weeks. I'll be gone three months."

I brightened. At least she'd get to finish her fertility treatments before he left.

I reassured him that I would look after her, as we often had. Three months wasn't so long. Jess and I had survived much longer deployments in the past, keeping each other company when our spouses were shipped off for undetermined amounts of time.

I was hoping and praying she would get pregnant, and envisioned her and me planning a creative way for her to break the news to Steve when he returned home.

After exchanging goodnights, I headed inside and got myself ready for an early bedtime, in anticipation of the Monday morning blues that would surely follow in the morning.

****

The next day, after clocking in at work, I plopped down in the chair beside Angela at the triage desk. It was a slow start, and between the rainy weather and fact that it was Monday, I was dragging and unmotivated.

Angela hung up the phone and swung her chair to face me with an accusing smile. "So, who's *Simon*?" she asked playfully.

"No clue." I kicked off the ground to spin my chair in a circle, gaining momentum by bringing my arms in toward my chest. I reveled in the conservation of angular momentum. The lights above me swirled as I spun faster with my arms folded across my chest. "Why do you ask?" I envisioned the forces around me that would eventually cause my spinning to slow, just as Newton's law of inertia stated. An object in motion would stay in motion until…

"Because he's coming in now, and requested *you*."

She kicked her leg out to catch mine and stop my chair-twirling.

I hadn't considered that outside source to stop my momentum. Then her words finally penetrated. I sat up, and my breath caught in my throat.

I followed her gaze to see Sy being escorted into the clinic by Nelson. My heart rate kicked up, lighting my nerves on fire. I scurried out of my seat and made myself look busy in the back hall by rearranging and counting supplies that had been thoughtlessly stuffed into the cubbies that lined the walls.

Angela escorted him to a room, and his deep voice answered her pleasantries. She looked incredulous when she returned to my side. "Oh. My. God. Isn't that the guy from the *bar?*" She leaned against the wall with her arms crossed.

"Heh. Yeah, funny story." My face burned as I pretended to reorganize a cubby filled with medical supplies. "Turns out, he's working with his brothers on my neighbor's house."

"So, you, ya-know'd him?" she whispered excitedly while making an obscene gesture.

"No! No, nothing like that. He got hurt, and his brother saw me wearing scrubs, so I helped him and told him he'd need a tetanus shot," I rambled, while the heat in my cheeks climbed to my ears and down my neck. I reached into one of the cubbies, pulling out the pack of syringe and needles I'd need for his shot.

Angela watched me closely, arms still tightly crossed, her face laced with amusement while waiting for more intel.

I walked away, and she followed me as I took a vial from the fridge. I turned around and nearly slammed into her. I laughed at her indiscreetness. "Are you kidding me right now? Can't you at least get his info up for me on the laptop instead of following me, waiting for juicy news that truly, *truly* does not exist?" I groaned and rolled my eyes.

She kept her eyes on me and wheeled the portable laptop in front of her and began whispering. "Simon J. Donovan. Age 32. Allergies, none. Born November 11th—oh, a Scorpio! Marital status, *divorced*! Enlistment status, veteran. And yes, he is here for his tetanus shot, post laceration."

I took the computer table from her and rested the vial and syringe on top. "I said get his info up, not read me his marital status or zodiac sign!" I wheeled the computer in front of me and swiftly started down the hall, trying to escape her, but I had to stop as I reached the row of exam room doors. "Which room?" I whispered loudly.

"Two!" Angela made another obscene gesture before ducking out of sight.

I stopped outside of room two and tapped my finger discreetly on the laptop. Angela's comments took my nerves about seeing Sy again to new heights. And it wasn't something I needed. I needed stability. Normalcy. I needed more time to figure out my past before I could even envision my future.

It's a normal feeling. See? You're going to be normal again. The accident didn't kill you. Only the man you swore to love until death... I forced the thoughts away, banishing the harpy to the void so I could deal with the patient waiting for me.

I took a deep breath and entered his room while staring at the laptop. I looked up, and my body relaxed ever so slightly when I met his gaze. I let out my breath and smiled.

"We meet again, Charlotte." He smiled back.

I forced myself to look away from him. I concentrated on opening the syringe packaging. "Glad you came in. How's your arm?"

My face heated. I wanted to look at him, but I wasn't able to reconcile what his stare did to me. It made me want to close the gap between us, it made me want to reach out and touch him, it made me want to see if kissing him felt as familiar as I anticipated it would somehow.

"It's fine."

He watched me draw up the contents of the vial, seeming to hold back a smile.

I wondered if his dark-blue polo shirt was why his eyes seemed more sapphire than I recalled. "No redness or pain?" I asked clinically to ensure he wasn't developing an infection.

"No." He lifted the sleeve on his uninjured arm, exposing his shoulder.

I stepped closer and wiped down his arm with alcohol. "Are you active?" I tried to avoid an awkward silence as I leaned close enough to feel his breath fan through my hair. I steadied myself and quickly shot the needle into his deltoid.

"Not anymore. Semper Fi."

"Always a Marine." I smiled.

I removed the needle from his arm and discarded the syringe in the sharps container. I held out my hand to him, gesturing for him to give me his injured arm. "Now, let's have a look at that arm."

I don't know why I did it. Maybe I just didn't know

what else to do, or maybe I was overcompensating for the discomfort I felt from the static in the air between us. But checking on his injury wouldn't hurt, and would give me a few additional moments to compose myself and my thoughts.

And a chance to touch him. I banished that thought to the void, too.

He stiffened before slowly lifting his arm for me to examine.

I gently grasped his arm and unwrapped the bandage. My hand tingled at the connection of our skin, but I focused on examining the wound.

The injury was healing nicely. Too nicely.

Perhaps my memory was failing me, but I recalled his gash being a millimeter away from needing proper stitches. I shook my head slightly, questioning my sanity for a nanosecond as I stared at the scabbed-over wound.

I pulled some fresh bandages from the drawer to re-wrap his arm. His stare never left me, but I still couldn't look up and meet his gaze while I focused on bringing my heart to a slower rhythm. I focused an exorbitant amount of energy on counting the beats of my heart and meticulously re-dressed his injury.

When I finished, he leaned back and placed his hands on his knees, slowly standing and towering over me.

Our eyes met and I froze.

"Hey, I really appreciate it." Sy paused for a moment after he spoke, then he reached out and wrapped his hand around my arm.

I froze at the touch, warmth spreading from my arm across my body in a savage mix of desire and longing. His touch sent a bolt of lightning through me. It was that *ping* of intimate recognition again. That same eerie feeling that I'd somehow known this man before. I waited for him to pull me toward him, press his body against mine, and…

"Sorry about what you saw happen at Thames the other day." He looked like he wanted to say more, but stopped.

He waited for me to say something, but I wasn't able to focus on anything but his touch. When he let his hand drop back down to his side the connection broke.

I finally responded. "Oh, hey, it's fine. I'm sure if you hadn't, someone would've had to kick that guy out." My voice came out several octaves higher than it should have been. I silently cursed Angela, certain that it was her jeering that caused me to act and feel so juvenile.

"Thanks again, Charlotte." He smiled and opened the exam-room door.

I nodded and smiled.

He seemed to use my name more than necessary. Not that I minded. But it felt so…intimate. Like he could also sense that strange magnetism, that strange recognition.

"Make sure you keep it clean and change the bandages daily." I followed him out of the room with the portable laptop. I pressed my back against the cool wall outside his room and wheeled the laptop in front of me.

When he disappeared through the exit door, I shut my eyes. I'd pretend I was charting to buy myself a few minutes before…

Too late.

I opened my eyes and Angela was already at my side, clipboard and pen in hand. Her gaze darted from me to Brian, who was staring at me, smiling from his desk across the hall, with his hand holding his chin. He let out a dramatic sigh and blinked rapidly, clearly having been informed by Angela there was a mystery man who'd come to see me at work.

Angela flipped the clipboard around, revealing a large question mark and exclamation point she'd drawn beside a poorly sketched banana.

"Stop! I can't even deal with you two right now!" I gave them both a death glare before giving in to laughter prompted by Brian and Angela's relentless gawking.

"You two are ridiculous! The poor guy needed a tetanus shot, let's not go overboard!"

The next few days rained on and off as the weatherman predicted, which meant that construction was on hold over at the neighbor's house. By Thursday morning, the ground was still wet, but the clouds were beginning to break apart, and it looked hopeful that the sun would make an appearance.

I stared out the bay window in my living room while drinking coffee. The construction truck had just pulled up for the first time that week, and I wondered about my neighbors. The house was sold a few months back, and other than the construction crew, I'd not seen anyone move in. I switched my focus to how pristine the home was. A large, classic, sand-colored colonial with stone detailing and a quaint front porch. The large oak and the rustic wooden swing hanging from it made me feel certain if you could crop my house out just right, it would be the type of home you'd see in *Newport* magazine or on a travel brochure.

My thoughts were interrupted by my realization of the time, and I headed to the bathroom to get ready for work.

On my way to my car, Jeff gave me a loud hello, and the brothers each gave a wave. I didn't see Sy—not that I was looking—though I'd be lying to myself if I said I hadn't thought about him since our last encounter. I hadn't expected him to follow through on his tetanus shot, let alone make an appearance where I worked. I kept telling myself not to overthink it, he sought VA care because he was a veteran, not because I worked there.

But he did remember me— not just from the incident at the neighbors, but from that night at Thames. *Ugh, the shoes.* I cringed internally.

Work was busier than I'd expected, and by the time I had a chance to look up at the clock, the day was half over. Angela, Beth, and Brian were bustling in and out of rooms, while I worked at the triage desk most of the day.

The phones were ringing nonstop, and when a lull finally came toward the end of the shift, Angela threw herself into the chair at the side of me with a huff.

I tried my best to listen, but as soon as she mentioned she was going for drinks with the guy she'd met at Thames, I couldn't stop myself from thinking about Sy again. Angela seemed to make the connection and was quick to add that I should talk to Sy, since he was still working next door to me. I fumbled at explaining to her I wasn't interested in dating anyone, and that things weren't like that between us. She relented faster than I expected.

"Ugh, you're so *old.*" She rolled her eyes.

"I am literally two years older than you, so what is that supposed to mean?" I shook my head in disbelief.

Angela laughed. "Let's see, you married at twenty-one. How much have you even *lived*, Charl? You don't date, and you never want to go out with us. You've developed an unhealthy relationship with Trash TV."

"*Everyone* has an unhealthy relationship with Trash TV," I quipped.

"Okay, I'll give you that. TTV does have some addicting shows. But, hello, the real world is calling, Charlotte." Angela motioned vaguely around us.

"Well, take a message for me, then." I smirked.

Behind my sarcasm I was secretly insulted. *Move on!* I knew they all wanted to scream—it practically oozed from their pores. *Stop being the broken widow! You're still young!* Angela was right about one thing though. I hadn't *lived* much before the accident. I got married young, and Jared handled everything once I was his wife. After the accident I lived even less. Sure, now I'd been through something, experienced an unthinkable tragedy to taint my innocence. A young widow, obsessed with mathematics, physics. An oddball, a recluse. A misunderstood sadness bubbled up in me, but I quelled it with a quick shake of my head.

"I'm just saying. TTV can't give you *everything* a woman needs." Angela wiggled her eyebrows.

The subject was dropped abruptly when she noticed the time.

I encouraged her to get home so she'd have time to prepare for her date. I was going with Jess for a run and didn't want to be late, either. I always took the chance to spend time with Jess, now even more so, with everything she was going through. I grabbed my bag, swiped out for the day, and headed home to change.

Once home, I pulled on a pair of black leggings and a sweatshirt. I stuffed my pockets with my keys, earbuds, and phone, and headed out the door. I turned to lock the door, and my phone vibrated in my pocket. It was a text from Jess:

So sorry, I have to cancel our run. I'm sure you're heartbroken...ha-ha...doctor's appt tomorrow, wish us luck.

Just as I looked up from my phone, a wasp flew into my face. I shrieked and stumbled back, waving frantically, unsuccessfully searching for the banister. My foot missed the concrete stair beneath me, and I accepted my fate— I was about to break a bone without having run a foot.

I braced for impact, my face scrunched and eyes squeezed shut, while estimating the distance to the ground and the speed at which my head was moving toward it. The concrete wouldn't be forgiving...but my body fell into two strong arms instead. My shock and fear melted into confusion.

I opened my eyes and looked into Sy's blue eyes. I stared into them, dazed.

"In your defense, it was a pretty big wasp, he was going straight for your jugular." Sy smiled and slowly helped steady me upright.

"It's like it was waiting for me." I shook my head.

"Definitely a premeditated attack." He raised a brow. "Did I catch you on your way out?"

I laughed at his pun and was thankful he'd stopped me from splitting my face open. "Actually, I just got ditched." I held up my phone with Jess's text still on the screen.

He scanned the message.

I fumbled as I swiped the text away and stuffed the phone into my pocket.

"How about you let me take you down to the cliff

walk? I could use a good run, and I can make sure you don't break anything." He smirked.

I nodded. "Thanks for the offer. Accidents stalk me."

If only he knew.

"Accidents and wasps are no match for me."

"Old blades?" I teased.

"Touché." He shrugged his broad shoulders.

"I forgot my water bottle, come in for a sec." I walked back up the stairs and unlocked my door, holding the screen door for him to enter.

Sy hovered at the doorway, hands in his pockets, large arms tightening the sleeves of his gray T-shirt. He slowly walked over to the side table in the foyer, gazing at the photos lined neatly along the length of it while I headed to the fridge to grab a water.

Upon my return, I stood behind him, staring at the same photos he seemed to be engrossed in. My wedding photos revealed a different version of me—rounded cheeks, lighter hair, and softer arms, smiling uninhibitedly with my handsome husband by my side. I was more lean muscle and sharp angles now, my hair back to its natural espresso brown, my eyes never quite sparkling like they did before. In the last four years, they'd somehow darkened. My wedding photos sat alongside other photos of Jared and me, my parents, and pictures of my friends and me.

His voice pierced the silence.

"Deployed?"

"No."

My voice gave it away immediately.

"I'm sorry."

Sy turned to me, and I couldn't meet his eyes. I

wanted no pity, no condolences. Jared died, I didn't. Life wasn't fair. The end.

Sy immediately dropped the subject when he saw my unease. "I have my car with me today." He pulled his keys from his pocket and motioned to his jeans. "You don't mind coming with me to my house, do you? I have to change."

"Sure." I nodded. "But I have to ask, though I'm thankful you prevented a head injury, what brought you over?"

Sy held the screen door for me and spoke while I turned to lock the door behind us.

"I wanted to see you again," he said simply.

I silently followed him as he made his way down my lawn and toward his car. Sy's brothers were outside packing up the truck, and I could feel their eyes boring holes through us as we got into Sy's sleek black car. I gave a quick smile and wave when I caught Max's eyes. His brothers were talking loudly, and though I couldn't discern what they were saying, I knew it was about us.

Jeff looked up from the tools he was loading into the truck. He stared in shock as we drove away.

"Don't worry about them." Sy seemed to read my thoughts.

On the way to Sy's we made small talk. He asked me about my family, and I told him about growing up in Massachusetts, and my parents' move to Florida after I'd married Jared. Then he asked what it was like to work at the hospital, and I told him stories of fear, of illness, of death, and of miraculous recoveries I'd witnessed, when all the nurses had to rotate through the ICU and ER during the first years of the pandemic.

Sy told me about how Jeff and Max were actually

his cousins-turned-brothers when he and Jay were adopted by their aunt. He told me how close they all were, having taken over his uncle's business several years after the man's death, with the exception of Joel who chose a full-time military career and was stationed in Fort Dix, New Jersey.

Sy's aunt, whom he referred to as Mom, lived a few towns over in Tiverton.

I didn't ask what happened to his parents, but I wanted to. I wanted to ask him about his scar, about his time in the service, and about his divorce that I had no business knowing about—thanks to Angela noticing it in his chart. But I didn't. I kept it light and watched his face as he spoke, evaluating his strong jaw, well-built arms, and another discreet scar over his left ear, the same side as the scar on his eyebrow where the hair no longer grew.

As we entered Portsmouth, the sun was sparkling on the nearly still water of the Mount Hope Bay, interrupted only by the gently rocking boats in the water, a sign of the impending summer ahead. We turned onto Bayview Avenue, and the road hugged the bay, allowing a perfect view of the Mount Hope Bridge spanning above the quiet waterfront road.

Sy's house was a two-story white cottage, and the location and design of the home made the value of it ostensible. I stared at the gorgeous house, admiring the wraparound farmer's porch and magnificent views of the bridge and bay. A wooden swing hung from chains on the classic porch, and an American flag was hanging from a post on one of the banisters.

Sy noticed my ogling and invited me inside with a proud smile. "Unless you want to wait here." He assessed my face.

"I'll go in." I smiled, my curiosity getting the better of me.

I exited the car and followed him in.

The house's open layout—from the living room to the kitchen and the entire back wall, lined with glass sliders—allowed for a panoramic view of the bay. The blue-painted walls featured several built-in shelves. The kitchen had light granite counters, with glass cabinets and a center island. His living room furniture was all white, punctuated with navy pillows, giving it a nautical theme to match the views that could be seen from any position on the first floor.

Sy dropped his keys on the island and headed upstairs to change.

I walked over to the slider, gazing out at the rustic white deck that held a fire pit and circle of chairs. The grass in the small backyard was delineated by crumbling concrete stairs leading down to the rocky shore below.

Mesmerized by the beauty of the location, I didn't hear when Sy came up behind me and rested his arm on the edge of the slider frame. When I caught a glimpse of him in my periphery, my skin tingled where we were almost making contact. My pulse quickened. "I've always wanted to live on the water. This is breathtaking."

"It's ok." He shrugged. "We'd better get back to Newport, unless you want to run in the dark." He picked up his keys from the kitchen island, and we headed to the car.

The cliff walk was dotted with runners, couples jogging, and people congregating at the banister edge to watch the undulating waves crash below.

I zipped my hoodie up as the wind sent a shiver through me.

"Ready?" Sy smiled, and we took off running.

The rhythm of our feet hitting the pavement was calming, synchronized, making counting the paces a relaxing refuge instead of an intrusive thought.

We found a comfortable speed along the cliff walk, and the water glistened below us.

I focused on the perfect pace we were keeping together; my skin tingled where we nearly touched, and I could feel the heat of him on my side.

My mind wandered beyond counting paces without the effort it normally took. How did he feel like home even though I'd just met him? A memory of his arms wrapped around me flashed in my mind. He'd caught me from falling. Kismet. Although he was in the right place, right time, with the wrong girl.

My future consisted of surviving only. I deserved no more in this life than the mercy bestowed upon me by death itself. Was Jared the payment I unknowingly offered in lieu of my death? And if so, how could I ever atone for that?

Still, my betraying hands longed to touch Sy, and my face heated at the thought.

We ran past scores of people of all ages—teenagers lounged on blankets in the grass, parents chased their wobbly toddlers, and elderly couples sat on wooden benches facing the ocean that seemed to stretch on forever.

Jared had never found time to run with me. He was always just out of reach, just on the outskirts, of our life. He was deployed often, and when he wasn't, we spent time learning how to be together again after building lives for ourselves while apart. His service took priority, but in his defense, perhaps I didn't try hard enough to *be* in his world, and instead, just *waited* for him to come back to mine.

I didn't want to feed the witch, the guilt that threatened to pull me under and drown me. But sometimes I examined her, trying to make sense of why she was so unrelenting. Maybe, if I'd not asked about the affair, he would've been more attuned to his surroundings, braked a moment sooner, avoided the crash altogether.

I asked him about an affair that day because it wasn't uncommon when someone was suddenly traveling so often, and Kayla's husband was living proof of that. And maybe I *was* jealous. Not of another woman, but over how secretive Jared'd get when deployed to Virginia with his father, the general. He had an excitement about these trips I'd not seen before. He wasn't dreading the suddenly too-often travel. Jared became more confident, but also more withdrawn and controlling than ever. He couldn't tell me anything about his deployments, dubbing them *highly classified.*

But that was enough feeding the witch for one day. The only guarantee in a complex system is that the unexpected is, in fact, a variable you have to account for. Chaos theory. A butterfly batted its wings halfway across the world, causing the tsunami that killed unsuspecting villagers thousands of miles away. Or, in our case, the hit-and-run accident that ripped our lives apart, leaving only damage and death in its aftermath.

I looked over at Sy and smiled when he looked down and caught my stare.

He smiled in return.

I breathed in the salty air while listening to the rustle of the waves in the distance. I tried to steady my breaths.

Perhaps I wasn't in the best shape for running alongside a Marine. I tried counting our paces, but it became impossible.

My legs are shorter; that's why this is getting difficult.

I increased my speed to keep up with Sy. Faster and faster, I tried to compensate, attempting to close the gap in stride length by increasing my speed to regain the synchronicity— but then realized he was messing with me. I slowed to a stop and put my hands on my knees, panting.

"You jerk!" I laughed and gave him a playful shove.

"I wondered how long it'd take you to catch on," he said, breathless and smiling. "What were you thinking about?"

"Oh, nothing." I shook my head. "Just in the zone, trying to keep up with *you*."

He laughed and playfully bumped my shoulder with his.

His touch ignited fireflies in my stomach.

The sun began to set, and we turned to walk back down the length of the cliff walk to his car.

Sy asked so many questions, and the more I answered, the more questions he had, insatiable to know about my life. I tried asking him questions, but he was able to flawlessly answer and immediately use it to question me about something else in my life. Once we could see the end of the trail, Sy walked over to the barrier on the cliff's edge and rested his elbows on it.

We looked at the white-capped waves below in silent wonder of the ocean and setting sun before us. The seagulls cried overhead, the choppy waters splashed the serrated rocks below, and the sky boasted a fiery palette of colors as it bled its goodbye to the sun.

On the ride home I talked about my co-workers Angela, Brian, and Beth, and our workday shenanigans. He vaguely remembered them from the bar.

Sy asked the typical questions about where I'd grown up. I told him about my childhood home that sat deep in the woods, and how my favorite pastime while growing up was to get lost in the forest with a backpack full of books.

"So, no crazy teenage years? No drinking or smoking cigarettes in the woods?" He raised his eyebrows.

"Nope." I laughed. "I was fiercely introverted, and I got married by twenty-one. I guess I skipped over the reckless years." I shrugged.

He nodded. "You didn't miss anything. Your world sounds much better, anyway."

I smiled. "It was a good time. Sometimes, I wish I could go back. There was this tree I'd climb—it wasn't tall by any means, but in the center, there was a spot where I would fit perfectly. It was a magical place to read or journal or just…escape."

He smiled wistfully. "I had a place like that, too."

When he pulled into my driveway, I stared at my house, silently vowing to paint the shutters if the weather allowed over the weekend. We were silent for a moment, with the radio playing a popular angsty rock in the background. I reached for the door handle and stopped when Sy began to speak.

"I hope you don't mind my asking, but how'd…."

I knew what was coming when Sy chose his words carefully.

"…was it during a mission?"

"A car accident." I answered the questions I knew were coming next. "Four years ago. Right here in Newport. We were only five minutes from home. I died on the table from blood loss, but somehow, they got me back."

"Sorry." He sucked in a breath, then clenched his fist around the steering wheel, and the muscles on his tattooed arm flexed from the pressure.

"Don't be. It is what it is. I have come to realize there is no reasoning with what happened, life just sucks sometimes, and you deal with the hand you're dealt."

He appeared deep in thought. His knuckles were white as he clutched the wheel, then he dropped his hand to his lap abruptly, as if resigning himself to something unsaid. "I was married a while back, too. Divorced now. She left after I got injured in Afghanistan. I was in the hospital for weeks; she never even came to see me. She didn't care whether I lived or died. Took off with some asshole from her work, so I know what you mean about reasoning and dealing with the hand."

I immediately thought of the scar across his back, and the small silver scar above his ear and through his eyebrow. I tried to picture Sy lying in a hospital bed, broken, but the image was impossible to find in the presence of his strong, capable body and calm manner.

"What happened?"

"Our helicopter was taken down just outside base. The pilot died at the scene along with another one of our men. They were our friends, damn good soldiers, and just like that, they were dead, taken out by terrorists that'd ambushed us. Jeff was with me, and he's the reason I'm alive. He dragged me from the ruins to safety. I ended up dying for a few minutes before I was resuscitated. I was in a coma for a while."

Wow. Figures we'd happen to have the most unlikely thing in common— surviving death.

"Oh, my God. I'm so sorry." I reached out and touched his arm.

I'd initially found it odd, Jeff panicking over a surface wound the day he'd called me over to help Sy. I'd wondered if there was an ulterior motive. But now I better understood the bond between him and Jeff. The protectiveness Sy felt in the bar that night for his brother who'd saved his life, and the minor injury he'd sustained the other day that caused Jeff to panic.

He turned to face me, and his gaze went from my eyes down to my lips. "I believe everything, no matter how painful or tragic, happens for a reason. Whether we like it or not, we have to go out and find our own healing, our own happiness, down whatever path the universe opens for us."

I nodded, his statement resonating deeply with my own tragic story. "So, what'd you do?"

He looked away and shrugged. "I was honorably discharged after that, and Jeff's now in the reserves." He laughed. "Now I'm stuck working with him and nearly cutting my arm off in the process because he's a slob, and forgets to throw away old blades."

He lifted his arm, now un-bandaged and scabbed over, a far cry from the angry wound I'd cared for last week.

"Wow, Sy. You're lucky to be alive."

"I don't believe in luck."

"What do you believe in, then?"

"Destiny." He winked at me and smiled.

This time, it was my gaze that dropped to his lips as

he spoke. I took a deep breath, then looked up at him.

He leaned toward me, and I grasped the door handle. "Thanks for today." I quickly opened the door and nearly stumbled out of the car.

He leaned back into his seat and chuckled. "Anytime, Charlotte."

After he left, I showered and put on my pajamas. I snuggled into bed deliciously sore from the run. I hugged the covers tight around my body, and fell into a deep dreamless sleep, the type of sleep that had eluded me for the past several years.

Chapter 4

A couple of weeks had passed since our run, and I wasn't sure I could define normal any more. I wasn't sure what to make of Sy and all that I'd learned about him, about us both being resuscitated, about how I felt when I was near him.

And, most importantly, we hadn't gone out again. Had I said something that spooked him, or was he also mystified by the coincidences we shared? I was curious as to why he'd even bothered taking me to the cliff walk, and I finally reasoned it was his gesture of thanks for wrapping his wound and giving him his tetanus shot. Bizarre.

And while we hadn't gone out after that run, I was seeing Sy often, which made it impossible to *not* think about him or the information about his life he'd divulged to me. Or the fact that he admitted—when he caught me falling from the steps—that he *wanted* to see me.

The construction truck parked outside made his close proximity impossible to ignore as he worked with his brothers on the house next door a few days a week. We had a couple of very short conversations on the few occasions I went to get my mail and ended up close enough to him that avoiding an exchange would've been awkward.

When I did see him, he would nod politely while I jabbered away about the news or something nonsensical.

I knew when to stop, when his large arms crossed in front of his chest and the corner of his mouth twitched into an amused smile. He was being polite, simple as that. I'd always regret my impulsivity after chatting with him, wishing I'd just let it be awkward and get my damn mail without acknowledging him, but there was something about his stance, the way he faced me in expectation, that forced me to make a fool of myself. Every. Damn. Time.

And he knew it, that damned tight smile he'd hold while I rambled about the weather, or when I'd explain the latest house project I was tackling that he didn't ask about—but his eyes did—when he'd scan my front lawn strewn with garden tools or the old rusty toolbox that housed Jared's old tools.

A few times I caught him glancing over at me as he grabbed supplies from the truck. He'd acknowledge me with a tip of his head and smile. One time, I caught his shoulders shaking in what appeared to be stifled laughter as I waged war on a wasps' nest just outside my front door, shrieking in between sprays of bug killer— complete with full-on sprinting away when I'd gotten the wasps angry enough to come after me. Luckily, I managed to kill them off that time without getting stung.

On a warm Saturday morning, I went to the garage to roll out the dirty old toolbox and a can of black paint. I dragged the ladder, drill, and paint to the front of the house. The neighborhood was vivid in the morning sun, the birds were singing their summer songs, and I stopped to admire the row of cherry blossoms in full bloom that lined my driveway. The bright-pink flowers twinkled to the ground like snow in the soft breeze, leaving a fluffy blanket of petals on the grass below.

At the end of my driveway, just barely in view due

to the cherry blossoms, a black SUV with deeply tinted windows was parked between my property and my neighbors'.

I stared curiously for a moment, then decided to tackle the task at hand.

Removing the shutters wasn't nearly as difficult as I'd anticipated, but the wasp nests hidden beneath them was an entirely different story. I struggled to keep steady as I unscrewed each shutter and threw them one by one to the ground with a clatter, hoping I wouldn't get stung by the increasingly angry yellow jackets.

When I had all the shutters off the front of the house, I piled them up in twos and carried them around back to paint them. They'd dry fast in the sun that was slowly starting to warm up the morning. I kneeled beside the can of black paint, prying it open with a flat headed screwdriver. One at a time, I counted swipe by soothing swipe, and the shutters shone slick with fresh black paint. I stepped back to admire my handiwork. This small project would give the front of my humble home a desperately needed facelift.

When I thought I heard the doorbell through my open slider, I lowered the music on my phone and peered through the slider to the front door. Someone was standing on the porch, and I assumed it was the package I'd ordered being delivered. I struggled to open the slider farther to enter the house. It was jammed on the track, and I tried squeezing my body through the small opening. I was stuck half outside as I used my hip to attempt to buy myself at least another inch to squeeze through.

"Leave it on the porch!" I called out, struggling to get free.

The front door opened, and Sy looked in shock at my current predicament. He walked over to the slider, put a hand on either side, and aligned it on the track to free me from the grips of the faulty door.

"Couldn't decide if you wanted out or in?" He laughed.

"Apparently, I'm bigger than I thought."

"There are a lot of words I'd use to describe you—" He stepped closer. "—but big is certainly not one of them."

My face flooded with heat, and I let out an embarrassed laugh. I looked down at the worn wood frame of the slider in disgust. "I hate this door!"

"Ya know, this is a really easy fix. Two hours, tops. Get a new door, pop it into place, couple of screws and caulk...." Sy was mostly talking to himself as he examined the doorframe. He looked down at my paint-stained hands and sweatpants with raised eyebrows.

"The shutters." I waved my hand out the back door, proudly showing off the gleaming black shutters. I eyed him suspiciously, then I glanced down at the familiar set of keys in his hand.

"I was leaving and noticed you left these out front." He handed me the keys.

Once again, just an informality brought him over—in this case, my negligence about my own personal safety. "Is the door really an easy fix? I can pay you when you have the time."

"Don't be ridiculous." Sy unclipped the measuring tape from his waistband and pulled it along the bottom of the door. "I'll use Jeff's truck to go grab the door while he's still here. I'll be back in an hour."

I was awestruck. Now? He had the time right now?

The day had certainly taken an unexpected turn. "I really don't want to put you out. You've been working all day." I looked at the broken door wistfully.

"No trouble at all, gives me an excuse to be here."

My gaze snapped to his. "An excuse? You've been avoiding me," I accused.

"Avoiding you? I've wanted to see you again, I just…figured you needed space after learning about…everything."

"Coincidences don't scare me. Plus, I've had a lot of space, maybe it's time for something different." I shocked myself with that statement.

"Well then, I'll see you in an hour." He reached out and grazed my cheek with his fingertips.

"SY!" Jeff's voice boomed.

Sy rolled his eyes and headed out the front door in the direction of his brother's voice. "One hour. Don't try escaping, or I'll tell the wasps!" he called over his shoulder.

I laughed and ran to the bathroom to scrub the paint from my hands. I groaned at my reflection. Wisps of dark hair matted around my face, falling from my loose ponytail. A streak of black paint was smudged across my cheek. I scrubbed my cheek viciously with a towel and combed roughly through my hair with the brush. I pulled my hair back into a neat bun and sighed at my reflection. I tossed the towel aside and headed back outside to check on the drying shutters.

When Sy returned, he and Jeff carried the brand-new slider to the back of the house.

Soon, my old wooden slider was history and a gleaming white metal-framed slider was in its place.

Jeff was loud and animated while he helped Sy,

cracking jokes as they worked. Max and Jay had joined them, and their laughter echoed into the house through the open door.

I stood in the kitchen, pouring glasses of lemonade for the guys. I enjoyed watching them joke and tease one another, sweat beginning to gleam on their foreheads in the noontime sun.

Jeff often referred to Sy as *Simon* when he was teasing him, eliciting an angsty reaction that was amusing to anyone watching the exchange.

Max and Jeff had both asked to use my bathroom, and I motioned toward the second door on the left in the hall. What I did notice, however, was the quick stop they each made after I told them where to find the restroom. It wasn't lost on me that Max stopped a half-pace as he walked by my sofa table that held the same photos Sy stared at the first time he came in—my wedding and family photos.

Jeff wasn't as discreet on his way to the bathroom; he actually bent forward and lifted his sunglasses to squint at the photos.

Jared was a presence. He'd been in the service since he'd turned eighteen and seemed to know *everyone*. I wondered if the brothers somehow knew him from their time in the service, and if they did, why wouldn't they mention it to me? Was the topic of being a widow off-limits? These guys were seasoned veterans. It wasn't likely they felt the need to tiptoe around anything, let alone a fallen comrade who had died outside of the service.

It dawned on me that they were likely just recognizing him from the heavy news coverage of the accident, the accident that shook the small ocean town when everyone learned the general's son died and his wife almost did, too.

I was about to question Jeff when he noticed my stare.

His back straightened, and he let his sunglasses fall back into place. "Sorry, just being nosey." He ducked into the bathroom.

Jay, Jeff, and Max, after being thanked profusely by me, took off in their truck, and Sy stayed behind. He stepped closer to the opening of the slider, with him standing outside and me just inside the door. "You have your keys, right?"

I nodded and glanced in the direction of the keys on the counter.

"You should be more careful. Anyone could've noticed them out front like that and taken them." He crossed his arms over his chest and kept his wide stance just outside the door.

I didn't hide my annoyance at his semi-lecture. "Yeah, I was in and out all day. I was going to go back out front to get them," I lied.

He stared at me with an amused look. He knew I was lying. "Why don't you give me your number in case there are any issues with the door?" He scanned the frame and back to my face. "Not that there should be, but…"

"Yeah, of course, here, let me put yours into my phone, then I can text mine to you." I pulled out my phone and added his info.

Sy starting gathering his tools and packing them up.

I stood just inside the slider watching him.

The doorbell rang.

I darted over to the front door, assuming it was one

of his brothers, but when I opened the door, my smile rapidly faded. I stiffened when I saw Jordan staring at me, glassy-eyed. He reeked of cigarettes and whiskey as he clung to the doorframe to steady his swaying body. I recoiled when the humidity of his breath wafted toward me.

"Hey, Charlotte," he slurred, leaning toward me uncomfortably close. "Need help with those shutters? Looks like shit with them all pulled off the front of the house like that…"

Jordan. Kayla's husband. The cheater who made me question my own husband's fidelity. He lived two streets over, and last I'd heard, he was still in his dysfunctional marriage.

At one time, Jordan and Kayla were considered our friends. After Jared died, Jordan helped with a few repairs around the house. Until the day he pushed me against the wall in an attempt to kiss me.

I shuddered at the memory and how disgusted I was with myself, and him, for allowing him to take advantage of my situation.

I'd kicked him that day, yelled at him, and pushed him off me multiple times. After I'd thrown him out of my house, he walked shamefully home to his wife. He twisted the story to make his wife jealous, and thwart any attempt I might make to tell her what he really did. He told her he wasn't going to help me around the house anymore, and that I'd thrown myself at him. I'd endured months of stares and looks from our friends and neighbors who ate up the untruthful gossip. *Desperate widow*, I was sure they all thought. *Going after her friend's husband.*

"You need to leave," I told Jordan sharply.

I began to shut the door on him, which abruptly stopped when he jutted his boot out to catch it. I jumped backward as he pushed the door open with enough force that it slammed into the wall with a loud crash.

He was inches from my face, seething with anger. "Not feeling like being a whore today?"

"Leave. *Now*." I backed away from his swollen, twisted face.

He looked up and past me, then abruptly turned and left, letting the screen door slam behind him.

I closed the front door and rested my hand on it for a moment to gather myself. I swallowed hard, begging the tears not to escape.

No, no, no! Please, don't let Sy have heard! I begged the universe.

I went out the slider and saw Sy locking up his toolbox. "Hey, thanks again, I really appreciate it." I scanned his face for any hint he'd heard the horrific encounter.

"Don't mention it." His jaw pulsed.

But something sat in the air between us. I attempted to write a check for his services, but he sliced his hand through the air, waving away my attempt. I insisted, and followed him to his car with my checkbook in hand as he opened his trunk and dropped the heavy toolbox inside. He waved me away again, and told me the only payment he'd accept was my agreement to not leave my doors unlocked or my keys out front.

I stopped and laughed at him.

"I'm serious, Charlotte."

Okay. The protective type or a chronic worrier? I didn't blame him for seeing the world through a darker lens; he'd seen some evil during his tours of duty. I relented and nodded at the only form of payment he agreed to accept. That I take my safety more seriously. Ha. If only he knew my level of anxiety was enough to both save me and kill me, given how paranoid yet scatterbrained it could leave me in its wake.

Sy gave a halfhearted goodbye, and my stomach dropped. I thanked him again, and dashed up the walk. After closing the front door, I rested my forehead upon it and my shoulders wilted. *Scumbag Jordan, I hate you!* Heat and sweat prickled the back of my neck, and I let out a loud sigh before lugging myself into the shower.

I took a long, hot shower and considered the day. Sy most definitely heard the exchange between Jordan and me, and that's why he insisted I be more careful. Did he think I was a desperate widow hustling her way through town in exchange for favors, after hearing Jordan offering to help with my shutters and exploding when I shut him down? Sy and his brothers installed a new slider for me free of charge, door and all. My pride came up with the only solution that made sense—I *had* to pay him. I wasn't desperate, or pathetic, even if I felt that way, alone in the shower with my thoughts.

Afterward, I lay in bed in my towel and cried—tears of anger and embarrassment—until I fell asleep.

When I woke up, the sky was dark. I checked my phone to see it was nine in the evening, and I had a few missed messages from Jess. I wouldn't sleep that night, so I texted her back, hoping she'd be up for a chat. In typical Jess fashion, she sensed the tone of my text and immediately responded with a simple:

Coming up now, open the door for me.

I hopped out of bed and threw my towel into the hamper. I pulled on a fresh pair of pajamas and waited for Jess at the front door. I felt guilty, since by now, Steve had broken the news to her about his upcoming deployment. She'd had her insemination at the doctor the other day. All these things considered, I didn't want to bog her down with my bad day, too, but it was too late.

Jess came in, holding a tall gift bag.

"What's the occasion?" I eyed the bag suspiciously.

"It's just a little something from me and Steve. You've helped us out so much, especially since I'm a big baby about needles and doing my meds. It's just a little something for you to—" Jess shrugged. "—enjoy yourself". She flitted over to the dining table and sat.

Something about my dull world seemed to disappoint my friends and family. I wished for a way to reassure them that I wasn't unhappy with the mundane. I thrived on the constants in my world. My mind didn't work the same as before, constantly engrossed in the invisible yet incredible forces of nature. Physics in every movement and expenditure of energy. Physics in every invention of consequence. The numbers and invisible forces that kept us tied to the Earth and to each other.

And now, the impossible. A man I'd just met was teeming with a familiarity that I couldn't wrap my mind around. A familiar stranger, how odd. I knew if I ruminated on it long enough, there would be an answer. Some magnetic force or…

I pulled a bottle of spiked iced coffee from the gift bag.

"I know you don't drink much, but you love your iced coffee. This is iced brew with a little kick of alcohol."

"Perfect. If it's got coffee, count me in, thank you so much, Jess."

I popped the bottle into the fridge and started to ask about the deployment, but turned to see her staring at me expectantly.

"So, are you going to tell me what's up? Doctor's appointment was fine, deployment happening in less than two weeks. Now, I want to talk about you," she demanded.

It didn't take much, and the floodgates opened. I told her about Sy. The chance encounter at the bar, his injured arm, and then seeing him again at the clinic. The run at the cliff walk, and him fixing my slider.

Jess smiled and nodded for me to continue.

I looked down at my feet when I revealed the unbelievable coincidence that we'd both died and been resuscitated.

Jess gasped. "You're kidding. That *is* a coincidence." Her eyes widened.

Then I told her about Jordan's unexpected visit, and my sobbing afterwards.

"So, you really like this guy, huh?"

"Of everything I told you, that's your takeaway?" I shook my head in disbelief.

"I don't see the problem. We already *knew* Jordan was an asshole. So, the real question is, why is that so embarrassing to you? You afraid of what Sy thought? If anything, I wish he'd have come right to the front door and pummeled Jordan's ass for you. The fact that he didn't tells me that he probably didn't even know anything happened at all. I mean, he was out back, right?"

Jess stopped for a minute and her eyes lit up. "I bet that's why the police were there today! I bet Kayla already did it!"

I whispered, "The police?"

"Yeah, the police were at Kayla and Jordan's house today, sometime around three or maybe four. If he went home trying to make her jealous again, I bet she beat his ass and had a domestic called!" She hooted.

"You're probably right." I shook my head and laughed at the thought of Kayla and Jordan's dysfunction.

Jess eyed me suspiciously. "So, you *don't* like this guy, huh?

"No, I mean, yeah, he's a good guy. I find him…interesting, but—"

"Interesting?"

"Well, yeah, he's got an interesting past, and he's been through a lot, so I guess I'm a little intrigued because…never mind." I trailed off, trying to make sense of my thoughts and words.

"Oh. So that's the draw, he's been through hell too?"

"Maybe. I don't know, it's just he's different from anyone else I've ever met, yet something about him is…familiar," I replied.

"Familiar?"

"I can't explain it, I know it sounds strange, but I feel so…*drawn* to him. Like I've known him before. It reminds me of the theory of quantum entanglement…"

"Quantum what?" Her eyebrows shot up.

"Entanglement. It's this theory that two things, be it people or particles, can impact each other even if separated by great distances if they've somehow connected before."

"Charlotte, hold on, stop." Jess put her hand up and sighed. "I get it. You're gifted after the accident. This physics thing, it's cool, it really is…but what the rest of us would call this is *attraction*. I'd love to understand what you're trying to tell me about the theory, but most of us"—she motioned vaguely around herself—"can't grasp those theories." She smiled, attempting to soften the blow.

"This guy sounds like exactly what you *need*, Charlotte. I know you've been through a lot, but there's a future waiting for you too, you know."

"I'd love to know about this future you speak of, but how am I supposed to do that when I can't even make sense of my past? I *died*, Jess. And yet, here I stand, resuscitated, moving on. But Jared is gone, forever. And I don't know if any of that will ever make sense to me." I shook my head and blinked rapidly.

"Charlotte"—Jess took my hands in hers as she spoke—"you survived for a reason. The universe doesn't make mistakes. Jared died, and while that is a tragedy, you are a person without him. Always have been. I know grief. I know sadness. But what you're doing isn't healthy."

"You sure about that, Jess? Did I survive? Look at me. I haven't moved on, and I'm not sure I ever will. And I know what you're thinking, that I glorify the past, and I acknowledge that, but sometimes not knowing is worse."

"Yes, you do glorify the past. I will not speak ill of the dead, but Jared was far from perfect. In fact, I always hoped you would—" She shook her head. "You know what? Never mind. You take all the time you need to heal, and I'll be here for you, no matter what."

"Say it, Jess. Please."

"I always hoped you'd leave him, okay? There, I said it. Happy?"

"Why, Jess?" I was begging.

"Charlotte, are we really doing this now? Why?" Jess looked down at her hands.

"Please. I just need to hear you say it." My begging intensified.

She sighed and squared her shoulders. "Because you were too good for him, and he wasn't good for you. That's all I'm going to say about it. I know you wish you could see if things would've changed, and I'm sorry you didn't get that chance."

"Thank you, Jess." I refused to entertain the harpy cackling in my head, insisting there was a minuscule flicker of relief when I learned he was gone. *Only evil people would feel that. It was a small, fleeting feeling, but it existed! You know it! Admit it!* she crooned.

"No!" I shocked myself when I realized I'd spoken aloud.

"What?!" Jess glanced around the room wide-eyed, seeking the source of my outburst.

"I meant, oh, no! I thought I was out of popcorn, but remembered I bought some…" I scurried out of my seat, hoping she believed my lie and didn't suspect I was as crazy as I was beginning to believe I was.

"So, what does Sy look like?" She kept her eyes on me as I went to the cabinet and fetched a bag of popcorn.

I turned to put it in the microwave, and while it heated, I kept my hand on the handle. I didn't look at her when I responded. "He's tall, like a lot taller than me, maybe over six feet. He's blond and blue, a pretty big guy…" I watched the bag of popcorn inflate as it turned and began popping.

"Is he good-looking?"

I nodded. "Exceptionally."

Jess bounced up and down in her seat, unable to contain her excitement.

"Stop! Please, don't make it weird," I hissed. I pulled the bag from the microwave and poured a bowl for us.

"Well, I'm just saying, this might be a really good thing for you. It's not like you need to marry the guy. But sometimes a healthy distraction—" She popped a kernel into her mouth. "—can be healing, too. You gonna see him again?"

"I was supposed to text him my number, but then Jordan showed up and I didn't, and now it's too late, so it'll be weird, so…just forget it." I turned to the fridge to grab us bottles of water, and found myself struggling with the plastic packaging.

Jess giggled at my plight. "Need scissors in there, Charlotte?"

I dug my fingernail into the plastic to tear the packaging of the 24-pack open. "I'm ok, I got it," I called out from behind the refrigerator door.

I finally pulled two bottles of water out and sat back at the table.

She flinched, and then smiled in such a way that I could see every tooth in her mouth.

"What did you *do*?" I gasped.

"You know better than to leave your phone unattended. He has your number now. Let the chips fall where they may." She popped another kernel into her mouth and grabbed the bottle of water.

Jess ended up leaving around eleven and, despite her hijacking my phone, I was glad she'd come over. Hashing things out with her always gave me clarity that I often struggled to find on my own. After she left, I hopped into bed and pulled my journal from the nightstand.

My phone buzzed.

I reached over, expecting to see a text from Jess, but to my surprise, it was Sy.

There you are. Around tomorrow at 11?

Hi, I'll be around. I want to pay you for the door. I insist.

OK, I'll pick you up. Hope you don't get seasick.

Only if I can pay you for the slider, cash or check?

We already settled this earlier.

No, we didn't. I love the water. See you tomorrow.

My stomach was in a knot, and I hadn't planned on getting a whole lot of sleep before receiving his text, but after this exchange, I was certain I wouldn't.

After approximately three hours of sleep, I pulled myself out of bed, anxious about Sy's arrival. It was only nine, but I needed coffee and extra time to see if any of the clothes in my closet were fit for an outing. I settled on a pair of jeans and a striped shirt.

When Sy arrived, I had him come in while I packed up some things.

He stopped at the sofa table of photos again.

I slid my sandals on and looked up at him, and he was staring at me.

He ran his fingers through his short hair and looked away, shaking his head.

"I'm ready." I slung my bag over my shoulder and stepped beside him, looking down at the photos again.

Sy pointed at a photo of me and Jared. "Where was this?"

I picked up the frame. In the photo, I held Jared's face adoringly, my hand obstructing just one side of his face, but his wide smile was visible as he gazed at me. "Heritage Park, Fall River. It was the night he proposed." I smiled at the memory, then put the frame down and looked at him questioningly.

Sy's brow pinched. "Ah, I thought I recognized the area." He smiled. "I'm ready."

He headed out the door, and I followed him to his car.

When we got to Sy's, we went to his backyard and down the crumbling concrete stairs to the rocky shore below. The old wooden dock there led to a large white-and-midnight-blue cabin cruiser boat that had the name *Silence on the Sea* painted near the bow.

The water was choppy, and the air crisp and filled with the scent of the briny water.

Sy jumped into the boat in one easy launch.

I struggled, afraid to fall, frozen with one foot on the dock and one on the rocking boat.

Sy laughed, reached over, and effortlessly pulled me into the boat with him.

There was a pause when he held me, our faces just inches away, and my heart skipped a few beats.

Does he feel that? What is that?

I had calculations that could help me determine buoyancy and momentum. I could estimate kinetic energy and torque, but I didn't have a calculation that helped me figure out why I reacted to his touch, his gaze, his voice. It wasn't *just* attraction, as Jess surmised. It was something more, of that I was certain.

Sy turned and fired up the motor, ready to cruise through the bay.

The ride was exhilarating, the sky cloudless and blue. The wind whipped through my hair, and I was in awe of the sights flying past.

People walked along the beaches, and boats were filled with people cruising or bobbing in place fishing.

Sy took us down the Mount Hope Bay, slowing past beaches with black sand that glittered like diamonds in the sun.

Cattails grew along the water's edge, dancing in time to the constant ocean winds.

We went from Rhode Island into Massachusetts and past the old Battleship Cove. The old WWII warships, a proud landmark, were scarred with rust and barnacles but stood tall despite their age.

Sy pointed to the *USS Massachusetts* and told stories of the soldiers who inhabited the ships during WWII. He watched me with a smile as I stared at the old warships, now retired and forever anchored in place. The secret horrors of war and joys of return remain trapped within the decaying metal.

When we finally pulled back up to his house, Sy tied the boat to the dock and helped me out.

"That was amazing."

Sy grinned. "I'm glad you enjoyed it. Can you stay longer?"

I nodded, a thrill running through me. I didn't want the day to end.

Sy fired up the grill, and I sat on an Adirondack chair on the back deck watching him. We talked more about his time in the service, and I told him more about my family. When the conversation moved to our jobs, his tone changed slightly.

"So, all five of the brothers own Donovan Construction?" I wondered about the brother I hadn't met.

"No, just the four of us. Joel wanted nothing to do with it."

"How much time does Joel have left in the service?"

"He's a lifer, he'll never retire. I planned on doing the same until the crash."

"Do you see him often?"

"I try not to."

"Ah, now *that's* a story I want to hear." I crossed my legs.

"What family *doesn't* have drama?" He poked at the charcoal in the grill.

"Humor me." I smiled sweetly and rested my chin on my hand.

He sighed. "I was offered a private military contract position after my injury in the Marines. Joel didn't want me to accept the offer, but I did anyway."

Sy was interrupted by the sound of loud bellowing voices followed by laughter and jeering.

Max, Jeff, Jay, and a curly haired woman I recognized from the bar rounded the corner to the backyard.

Sy rolled his eyes.

Jeff looked gravely at Sy, then turned and smiled at me. "Charlotte! Fancy seeing you here. Simon, where have you been? Tried calling you."

Sy didn't look up from the grill. "We were on the boat. Didn't hear the phone."

I was introduced to Jeff's wife, Linda, and liked her immediately. She was outgoing and friendly and offered to help cook, so I joined her in the kitchen.

We chatted about the brothers while we chopped vegetables for a salad. Linda, I learned, was an interior decorator who took great credit for making Sy's house the nautical beauty it was. I filled a pitcher with water, ice, chopped lemon, and orange slices and set it on the patio while Linda scraped the colorful vegetables into the salad bowl.

Jeff, Max, and Jay were laughing and carrying on at the table, engrossed in debating the latest political gossip.

Sy walked up behind me.

His stubble tickled the back of my neck when he leaned down to whisper an apology for the arrival of his family. I turned to him, our faces just inches apart, and I ignored the butterflies in my stomach long enough to tell him it wasn't a problem.

He reached for my waist, fingers curling around my hip as he brought his body closer to mine. His gaze dropped to my lips.

"You two must be *starving*. Please, join us," Jeff called out, interrupting our moment.

The others laughed, and I stepped back abruptly from Sy. We joined his brothers and Linda at the table to eat.

The atmosphere was easy and laid-back. We laughed and joked and talked until the sun began to set across the bay, ready to disappear beyond the horizon.

The lights on the Mount Hope Bridge lit up, twinkling as the silent, distant cars drove over it. A bonfire could be seen on the shore across the bay, and the sunset shone like orange fires in the windows of the shoreline properties.

I walked over to the edge of the yard to admire the view over the water and was joined by Sy's younger brother, Jay. The guy looked strikingly similar to Sy, albeit several years younger. His hair was much longer, but they shared the light hair and eyes. They both had a perfect blade of a nose, but I noticed that despite their similarities and Jay's pleasantness, I didn't react to Jay the way I did to Sy.

"Charl?" Jay offered me a smoke.

"No, thanks."

"Do you ever get out of this postage stamp-sized state?"

"I used to visit my parents a lot in Florida, but I haven't in some time. Do you?"

"Mostly deployments." He shrugged. "Me, Max, and Jeff are in the reserves and run the business with Sy, so I rarely get to travel recreationally." He took a long pull off his cigarette. "Do you have any family here?"

"No," I replied.

Sy stood behind me, his wide eyes boring into Jay furiously.

The younger brother put his hands up in the universal symbol of submission.

"Does Sy always materialize that quietly?" I asked Jay, trying to soften the tension that hung between them.

"They don't call him *The Silencer* for nothin'."

Sy shot Jay another warning look.

I was curious, but based on Sy's face, this wasn't the time to ask.

Sy chided Jay for being so juvenile.

Jay gave me a secret wink and walked back to the group, flicking the remnants of his smoke to the shore below.

"Do you have to work tomorrow?" Sy asked quietly.

"I'm off for the holiday." I smiled at him.

His eyes lit up. "I have to take Charlotte home, guys, lock up when you leave."

I was confused as he reached for my hand and we sprinted to his car.

"I'm sorry they're so intrusive." Sy was watching the road, glancing at me and then back to the road as he spoke. "Where would you like to go?"

I thought hard for a moment. The fact that he didn't want us to hang out with his family all night hinted that his intentions were to be with just me, but I stopped that thought in its tracks when a wave of anxiety hit. He always seemed to have a logical reason as to why we were together, and it never involved anything more than him lecturing me about safety or me dressing a wound of his. The run, that was payment for my nursing services. The slider, that was done out of…pity? I mean, he did see me literally stuck in the door. I couldn't fathom that he felt the same strange magnetism I did. Was it possible?

I didn't want to go to a bar. We'd already eaten, and I wasn't sure what to suggest, until I remembered the bonfire I'd seen across the water. "Come to my house, and we can light the fire pit."

"Sounds good." Sy smiled a wide grin and shook his head.

When we got back to my house, Sy went into the backyard while I pulled the bottle of spiked iced coffee from the fridge and thumbed through my phone for music. I stared at Sy from the kitchen window as I mixed the beverages with ice before joining him outside, where he was lighting the thick branches in the fire pit. Soon, we picked up our conversation over the drinks with our faces glowing from the flickering flames.

Our conversation flowed with the help of the drinks, the warm darkness, and the crackling fire. We discussed the pandemic, politics, our lives before and after our injuries, and our hopes for the future. In what felt like mere minutes, hours passed, and we were pouring our last drinks from the nearly empty bottle. I'd have to remember to thank Jess again for that later.

"So, the contract, you didn't finish telling me about it," I prompted.

His face darkened while he stared into the fire, flames dancing in his clear-blue eyes. "I have one job left," he answered without looking up.

"How many have you done so far?"

He looked at me and said, "Too many."

"Just one left, then? A deployment?"

"Yeah. I work as an intelligence agent of sorts. I can't talk about it too much, really; it's classified." He looked back into the fire.

"Like a *spy?*" I asked dramatically, trying to ignore the eerie similarity to Jared's highly classified deployments. The hairs on the back of my neck stood on end.

"You could say that." Sy looked up at me. "If I knew then what I know now, I wouldn't have signed. Sometimes I regret it, but then I think about all the positive things that have come out of it. I was able to help my brothers save the company, I was able to buy a home and a boat and enjoy my life after my injury instead of being confined to a wheelchair. If I hadn't signed, I wouldn't have been able to afford the surgery on my spine. I wouldn't have been able to do all the things that have made the last few years of my life…the best years."

"The VA wouldn't pay for the surgery?"

"No. It was considered experimental at the time." Sy looked up at me. "The contract pays unbelievably well per job completed. But now that I'm older, I realize there's a cost that is not financial that I have to deal with."

"You regret it?"

"When you always have to be ready to travel at a moment's notice, it's tough to put down roots. I just want to be done with the contract. The mission I went on in Afghanistan almost took my life, and until I finish this last job, I feel like I'm still tied to it. To that part of my life."

I drew in a sharp breath. "I'm sorry. It's like you had no choice."

"Yeah, it felt that way at the time." Sy looked intensely at me. "Meeting you was one of the things that made it worth it. I would have never met you if I hadn't had the surgery."

My face heated.

I leaned my head against the back of the chair and stared up at the infinite sky speckled with billions of stars. "Even the smallest choices we make can significantly change the course of our lives. I mean, are choices really half-chance? Or are there bigger components at play, like fate or chaos theory?" I stopped and internally reprimanded myself for coming a little too close to discussing my obsessive theories. Jess would be disappointed.

"Yeah, I think about it too." Sy picked up where I left off without missing a beat. "One small decision has such a substantial impact on where you are now. The missed encounters, the close calls, it makes me wonder, as you said, 'What if'? If I'd never enlisted, or signed into the contract, or …."

"If I hadn't gone to college in Rhode Island, or gone

with Jared the day of the accident…"

We began listing events in our lives, big and small, that led to us being there at that moment, by the fire.

Sy looked thoughtful and turned to me. "Do you ever wonder if there's another chance? That maybe somewhere out there, a place exists where you made different decisions and were living the consequences of them?"

"I think about it all the time…choices and chances. What lies beyond this life, or exists parallel to it, if you will. Einstein, Greene, and Hawking hypothesize that there is…"

"The multiverse," Sy answered for me.

"Yes! The theory of the multiverse—that multiple realities exist, that there could be different versions of you and what your life could be, based on different choices out there, somewhere." I stopped and closed my eyes, then continued speaking. "I can't help but wonder, are we given different scenarios, different choices, and ultimately different outcomes, that test our character, our strength, our virtue, all during a set of lifetimes within a multiverse?"

"I know that theory." Sy leaned back and looked up at the stars. "I know it really well."

"Reading those theories helped me stay sane after the accident, I guess I became a bit obsessed with the idea after what I'd been through. I wish there was a small window we could peer through, to see what life would look like if we'd made just one or maybe two different choices."

"A window," Sy repeated, considering my statement. He reached for my hand, then stopped, holding my gaze intensely.

It wasn't every day two people who'd experienced the trauma of a near-death experience got to talk about it with someone who could truly relate to surviving against the odds.

"Sy, did you notice anything about yourself change after being resuscitated?" I sat up and leaned toward him.

"Yes. It's very hard to put into words, but… my intuitiveness has improved. I can *see* more…as if a bridge was built inside me, connecting me to parts of myself I couldn't access before."

I thought for a while about what he said. He seemed to have a better grip on himself after the accident, while I had a better grip on a hard-to-grasp science to help explain my life and internal changes. I wondered if there was any meaning to it all, or if dying just awakened parts of us that were always there but lying dormant.

"And you, Charlotte?"

"No gifts here, just the curse of savant syndrome involving lots of numbers and physics."

"Gifts can feel like curses until we learn how to harness them." He brushed the back of my hand with his fingers.

I closed my eyes and focused on the pleasantness of his touch. Had I given too much away? I opened my eyes to find him staring at me, and I had a sudden urge to ask him if he felt the strange familiarity I felt. Was it the resuscitation? The near-death experience that drew us together?

I decided to break the strange magnetism that loomed between us by grabbing my journal. Maybe if I showed him some of the equations, the impossibilities that occurred… no. Maybe I'd just show him my uncanny sketch of the accident. Maybe if he could see how hard I worked to make sense of everything, maybe he'd mention the magnetism first. As I got up, my footing gave out, and I stumbled.

Sy hopped out of his seat and caught me by the waist before I could hit the grass.

"I'm sorry! I never drink, I was sitting the whole time, I didn't realize…" I grasped his arms to steady myself.

Sy's arms remained around me, and I looked up to meet his blue eyes, the fire reflecting and dancing in them.

He brushed my cheek lightly to remove the wayward hair from my face. "You amaze me, Charlotte—" He drew a deep breath. "—I wasn't expecting *you*."

I stilled in his arms.

"Not merely a theory, *you* are my chaos," he whispered.

"I-I'm not sure if that's a compliment?" I held tighter to him, a little dizzy from the intensity of the moment.

He cupped my cheek. "Oh, most definitely a compliment. Who knew it'd be you? Not the deployments or the accident or even death. It's you that'll be my undoing."

He stared at me, letting out a low hum as he ran his thumb along my cheek.

I leaned in to his hand as he caressed my cheek. I turned his words over in my head. They made no sense, but somewhere deep within me I understood.

The witch, the harpy of guilt and trauma grinned silently within. *Of course you'll be his undoing* she'd say if I let her speak. But I didn't.

My eyes fluttered shut as he closed in, two hands on my face now, tracing his thumbs along my jaw, as he slid his fingers into my hair.

He leaned down and kissed me, gently at first, then with more hunger and increasing want.

He delved his tongue into my mouth, and I reveled in the taste of him. The elements of earth, wind, and fire held no power against the fury of his kiss, which I returned fervently with my own burning desire. His body crushed against mine, causing my body to ache with need for him.

His rough hands fell to the small of my back, then wrapped around each hip to pull me against him.

He was intoxicating, all-consuming. His heat. His smell. His touch. His strong hands pulling my body impossibly closer.

Our extraordinary kiss wasn't as *familiar* as I was expecting. It was unexpectedly, deliciously new. It was beyond satisfying, knowing how his lips felt on mine, revealing how badly we both needed each other in that moment. I surprised myself when I clung to him, wrapping my body against his and drinking in the moment. It was more than I'd imagined, kissing him. Now, my thoughts wandered to how much more I wanted from him.

He pulled back abruptly and muttered something under his breath. "I'll come back tomorrow, let you sleep on the idea of kissing me without a drink in your system."

"You think I won't want to?" I locked my hands behind his neck and pulled him toward my lips again.

He kissed me softly, pulling away slower this time.

I unhooked my grasp on him and he interlaced his

fingers with mine. His hands were rough and had swollen abrasions along the knuckles.

Worker's hands.

"I just want to make sure. You are so beautiful, but you don't realize that, do you?"

I tried to look down but he pulled my chin up to face him.

"Tomorrow?"

"Tomorrow."

He kissed gently along my lower lip and then put his face into my hair, breathing in heavily, seemingly to restrain himself.

He pulled back. "I'll see you tomorrow, okay?"

I couldn't help but wonder if the idea of *sleeping on it* was for him or me, because he seemed so torn, but I couldn't deny the way he looked at me, like I was beautiful, and that I was more than just the trauma I used to define myself after the accident. But there was something else, too. A look that lurked in the shadows of his eyes— a look that felt like he found me forbidden, but he wanted to claim me for himself, anyway. My body heated at the thought.

After he left, and against my better sober judgement, I texted Jess:

I think you were right about Sy. Maybe this is *what I needed. Need to thank you again for the bottle. Have a lot to fill you in on.*

I expected her to be at my door within minutes of my text, but to my surprise she called instead, and I answered before the first ring even finished its jingle.

"I need to know *everything.*"

"Your self-control shocks me," I teased, avoiding the question. "I expected you to bust through my front door."

"I honestly would have, but Steve wouldn't let me walk to your house in the dark. I found out why the police were at Jordan and Kayla's the other day. Turns out, he got attacked on his way home!"

"Attacked?"

"Yeah, the day of the incident at your place, he got jumped on his way home. Serves him right."

"Is he okay?" I whispered.

"Just a busted lip and black eye or two. I forget. He obviously has a lot of enemies, so I'm not surprised, could've even been one of Kayla's boyfriends."

I closed my eyes while she continued talking, envisioning Sy's swollen knuckles.

"Charlotte? You there? So, tell me…" Jess's voice interrupted my thoughts.

I told her about the boat ride and his house, about the dinner with his family, and about the kiss. I wasn't sure if her excitement was because it was a sign I was beginning a new chapter after Jared, or because she truly wanted me to be with someone and not alone any longer. She worried about me a lot despite my constant reassurances that I was fully capable of living—and being happy—alone.

As I drifted off to sleep that night, the only memory that replayed itself in my head was Sy and his amazing, breathtaking, mind-blowing kiss.

Chapter 5

"We each exist for but a short time, and in that time explore but a small part of the whole universe." – Stephen Hawking

It was almost four o'clock in the morning when my eyes popped open and my body stiffened. I lay in the silence for a few moments, wondering what woke me, as if my body knew something my mind didn't yet realize. I tried to ignore the feeling, tossing left, and then right. I put my leg outside of the blanket and listened to the heavy silence.

My heart beat viciously in my chest, and I wracked my brain to determine if I could remember having had a dream, but my mind came up blank. I got out of bed and made my way to the living room, counting my steps along the way, an attempt to shake away the ominous feeling. I counted paces over the beige shag rug in the living room, each fiber feeling like grass beneath my bare feet. I concentrated on my breathing, hoping to slow the pounding in my chest.

I plopped down on my sofa facing the bay window and rested my head against the plush cushions. I squeezed my eyes shut and took another deep breath. Just as I exhaled, I heard a car door outside. I lifted my body from the sofa and made my way to the window.

Probably just a neighbor, my brain tried to reason

with my fears. The street was dark, illuminated only by the weak streetlights casting yellow circles just below and leaving all else blanketed in deep shades of charcoal and black. The tree branches clawed at the inky sky like the black arteries of a corpse. No lights were on outside or inside any of the homes lining my street. I started to relax, taking in the serenity of the darkness and quiet, until I looked down the driveway and just past the row of sepia cherry blossoms that lined it.

There, in the dark, just barely noticeable in my line of sight, was the black SUV. I'd seen it parked in the same place before, the day I'd removed the shutters from my house. I stared at it curiously and leaned closer to the glass, my hot breath creating a patch of fog on the window.

I jumped back from the window and presumably out of sight when I saw movement behind the windshield. Someone was in the car, someone *saw* me, I could feel it in my bones. I scurried to my room, grabbed my cell and quietly ran back to the window. *Who would I even call? The police? And say what?* The car wasn't on my property, and I had no reason to be panicking the way I was, except for the feeling of dread that sat itself in my stomach like a brick set ablaze.

I squinted at the windshield of the SUV and saw the orange glow of a cigarette. I was momentarily blinded when the headlights turned on, and the vehicle sped away.

I sat back on the sofa until dawn started to break, allowing my fears to dissolve as the sky turned from black to navy blue, to a fiery orange and red, then slowly to lavender that melted into blue. I pulled myself into the shower and scolded myself for being so paranoid.

But, if someone was indeed watching me, who and why? Jordan was an asshole but never struck me as the stalker type, unless he felt I had something to do with his attack the other day.

Sy? I scolded myself harshly for that thought. He did show up the day with the shutters, the first day I ever saw the SUV, but he came in his car. I couldn't recall if the SUV was still there when he helped me with the slider.

By the time I was showered and dressed, I decided I was being unreasonable, despite the fact that every cell in my body reacted the way it had that morning, from the moment I woke to the moment I spotted the SUV. I sat at my desk and cracked open my journal. I wrote the names of those close to me, and drew lines connecting each to the day I first saw the SUV. I made columns and listed each person and their potential motive, whether it was protective or sinister.

After several pages of suspects, timelines, and equations, three things became abundantly clear: Simon definitely attacked Jordan, Jordan and/or Kayla were likely pissed, and finally—this journal was all the evidence someone would need to commit me to a psych unit. I slammed it shut, stuffed it into my desk drawer, and stomped into the kitchen to grab my keys.

It was only seven, but I needed to get out of the house to clear my head. I pulled out of my driveway, unsure where I was headed but determined to leave the early morning memory behind.

I drove by Jess and Steve's and Kayla and Jordan's. All their cars were parked in their driveways, no SUV in sight. I drove out of the neighborhood and onto the main road, where a few cars idled at the red light. I drove by the base and down through Middletown and straight into

Portsmouth.

I neared the Mount Hope Bridge with my window down, and I could smell the salty air from the bay. I drove through the winding roads of Portsmouth and without thinking, right down Bayview Avenue.

I pulled up to Sy's house, not sure what the hell I was thinking, but there was no one else I wanted to see more. I got out of the car and slowly walked up the large wraparound porch, stopping at his front door. I hesitated before knocking, my loose fist hovering inches away from the door, and I considered sprinting back to my car like a coward.

In for a penny...

The door opened before I could knock, and I stepped back with a gasp.

Sy leaned on the doorjamb casually, then crossed his large arms over his chest. The tank top put his toned, tattooed biceps on full display.

I gulped.

"You're looking for trouble awfully early, aren't you?" He stared at me with smoldering blue eyes. A feral smile broke across his face, revealing perfect white teeth.

"Trouble is my middle name, and I slept on it—"

Before I could finish my sentence, he swooped down, flinging me over his shoulder with ease.

I shrieked at his sudden movement, and he kicked the door shut behind us. I wriggled and squirmed, howling with laughter and weak protests. "*Simon!*"

"Yes, Charlotte?"

I couldn't see his face, but I could hear the amusement in his voice.

He headed toward the stairs as if I weighed no more than a sack of potatoes.

"Put me down!" I kicked and laughed, weak and breathless.

"As you wish."

He bounded upstairs and flung me down onto his unmade bed, a sea of light-blue sheets and white down comforters.

I gaped at the view. His bedroom was the entire second floor, and like the first floor, his room also had a panoramic view of the bay with several large windows facing the ocean. The sun was rising above the water, casting an amber glow across me as I lay on his bed, still laughing and breathless.

He pulled his tank off, the shapes of his chest and stomach delineated in the bright morning light. He pounced on me, kissing me senseless like he had the night before.

He buried his hands into my hair, and I wrapped my arms and legs around him. I ran my fingers down his back and over the raised, jagged skin of his scar as I parted my lips, deepening our kiss.

He pulled away slightly. "Am I being too presumptuous? You only get one chance to escape."

My chest heaved with breathlessness, desire lighting my body on fire. I was certain if he let me go, I'd burn to ashes right where I lay. "Don't let me," I nearly begged.

He let out a low growl and kissed me again, this time with nothing but absolute recklessness.

Every cell in my body screamed for him, begging to be impossibly closer to him, without limits, without separation or questions or clothes. I was tired of the coincidences, of the longing and inexplicable magnetism between him and me. Years of grief and loneliness and what-if's combusted in that electrifying moment.

I dragged my lips across the exposed skin of his neck, and then his chest.

His hands ran along my soft curves with deliberate care.

He grasped my tank top in his fist, and in one quick movement, tore it right off me.

I shuddered when he wrapped his arm around me, pulling me closer. Our chests pressed against each other as his lips found mine once again.

Without breaking our kiss, he pulled at the waistband of my pants, and I lifted my hips, allowing the garment to be pulled free. An involuntary sigh escaped my lips when my bare skin connected with all of him.

Pulling away to admire my exposed body beneath him, he caressed my chest and stomach slowly, his lips making his way to each area he touched with tenderness. "You are fucking incredible." He spoke against my skin.

I ran my hands along the hard planes of his chest and abs. The last of the clothes keeping our warm skin apart fell away, along with every coherent thought I'd ever had. Inhibitions, memories, intrusive thoughts and numbers, all vanished.

It was the first time I'd made love to anyone in over four years. The way he did it, the way he made me feel, the way our bodies molded together, fitting perfectly and completing one another, was new and undeniably incredible. Better than incredible, absolute nirvana.

I wrapped myself in his light-blue sheet and nuzzled up to his chest as I looked out the window at the bay. He took a deep breath, and I looked at him. He wasn't watching the sunrise or the bay, he was watching me.

He smiled and kissed my forehead, his eyes heavy while holding my bare skin up against his. "If I told you that I've been waiting for you for a very long time, would you believe me?"

"With your improved intuition, didn't you see me coming?" I teased.

"You seem to throw off my new powers a bit, admittedly. I question myself when it comes to you." He chuckled.

"Oh?"

"I want to make you happy," he said.

"You already do."

He was the first person I'd been with since Jared, not that I hadn't had opportunities—I just never had the desire for anyone—until now. I interlaced my fingers with his, and rubbed my thumb across his still-swollen knuckles.

"What happened?" I stared at his hand.

"It's just from work." He looked out the window as he spoke.

I let it be. If he did beat up Jordan, it was well-deserved, and he did work with his hands for a living. The scar across his forearm was living proof of that.

I dozed and woke up around noon to Sy standing over the bed glistening from a shower, a teal towel wrapped around his waist. He smiled at me as I lay there, still wrapped in his light-blue sheet with my dark hair spilling around me on the pillow. I noticed another scar on his upper left shoulder, just near his collarbone. I sat up while holding the sheet around me and ran my fingers over the raised, discolored skin of the round scar. "Gunshot?"

"Yeah."

"Afghanistan?"

"Iraq."

Without engaging the conversation about his scar any further, he grabbed my waist, and in one quick movement, laid me back on the bed. He was on top of me trailing soft kisses down my neck as I inhaled his sweet scent, a mix of soap and peppermint. I ran my fingers through his hair and pulled him back toward me so I could kiss him. I went to pull the towel off his waist, and he stopped me.

I pouted and he laughed.

"You're going to be the death of me," he growled into my neck.

"Are you sure about that?" I teased, ready to have him again.

"We have somewhere to be."

"The shower is a good place to start." I giggled.

"I knew I should've woken you. The shower it is."

He swooped me off the bed and carried me toward the bathroom. And he worshipped every inch of my body in that long, hot shower.

After getting dressed, I asked, "Where do we have to be?"

"Lunch." He winked.

Somehow, I knew it was going to be a little more complicated than that.

Sy held my hand as we walked to his backyard and down the crumbling steps to the shore below. We walked down the mossy dock, where he lifted me into his boat, launching himself in after me.

"Where are we going?"

Sy flashed a quick grin at me and turned to fire up the motor.

"For you to meet the rest of my family…" He glanced at me over his shoulder and turned to navigate us out into the bay.

The boat slowed as we pulled up to a long wooden dock. The ride had only taken about twenty minutes or so, and silence surrounded us once the motor was off.

The wind had died down, and I walked over to Sy nervously.

"Charlotte, I'm taking you to a cookout, not a haunted house." He helped me out of the boat and followed me onto the dock.

"Ah, Memorial Day." I recalled.

I still hadn't processed our passionate morning together, or the incident with the SUV, which felt like days ago as opposed to just earlier that morning, and now I was going to be surrounded by his family. I smiled as he grabbed my hand, and I struggled to keep up with his stride as we walked uphill toward a modest gray house.

Loud voices and laughter echoed before I could see where they came from. As we approached the top of the hill in the back, I realized the family was congregated on the deck ahead of us. The air was filled with the smoky barbeque aroma wafting outward from the sizzling grill.

One by one, as each family member noticed our presence, the voices and laughter died down. Our approach was met with stares of silent astonishment.

I recognized Max, Jeff, Linda, and Jay, and I smiled at them, a little relief running through me when I realized I knew a good portion of the family that was there.

Sy squeezed my hand and casually made his way up the stairs to the deck.

The silence was only broken by the sounds of our feet on the wooden planks of the deck steps.

Linda noticed my discomfort and immediately hopped up from her seat to greet me and usher me to one of the patio chairs beside her.

Jeff, Max, and Jay nodded their hellos, and Max introduced me to his girlfriend, Andrea.

Sy introduced me to his mother, and then he put his arm around her, giving her a quick peck on the cheek before looking over my shoulder at the man sitting a couple of chairs over.

He was tall, with a shaved head and dark features.

Sy nodded at him stiffly, introducing me to his eldest brother, Joel.

I shook Joel's hand, and the crowd fell silent again.

Joel tried to return my smile, but it didn't reach his eyes.

It was hard not to relax once the family resumed their normal loud banter as plates of food were being handed out.

Linda placed one in front of me, and I listened to her stories about her latest renovation job intently, noticing out of the corner of my eye how hard Sy and Joel were working to actively avoid one another.

I followed Sy's mother into the house to put my plate into the sink. I offered to help clean up, but she shook her head and quietly motioned for me to follow her to the living room. We stopped at the large wooden mantel above the grey-slate fireplace.

At least a dozen frames, pictures of Sy and his brothers growing up, were displayed. A photo of Sy and his brothers around the age of nine, with dirty knees and rusty bikes, making peace signs with their fingers, tongues out, and eyes crossed. Photos of them opening gifts in front of a large colorful Christmas tree, photos of them as teenagers sitting atop an old Chevy pickup, the brothers in a line dressed in tuxedos at what appeared to be one of their weddings. Single photos of Joel and Jeff in their military blues; Sy, Jay, and Max in uniform in front of an American flag backdrop.

Sy's mother stared at the photos, and her mouth curled into a loving smile before she spoke. "Simon is an incredible man. He's been through a lot in his life, but refuses to acknowledge the effect his past has had on him."

"He told me about the attack. His recovery is remarkable." I smiled at the photos of Sy and his brothers.

His mother looked up and met my eyes. "His injury was the culmination of a series of unfortunate events in his life. My sister, his mother, never had good taste in men. Simon never knew his dad, and his stepfather was an abusive drunk. Simon took a lot of beatings to protect his little brother, Jay. I offered to take the boys away from the turmoil when I saw just how volatile Simon had become from what he was enduring at home. He is extremely protective of those he loves. The military was the best thing he ever did. Even despite the injury."

"Wow. I didn't know…"

"But he's on a good path now, and I hope that doesn't change. For any reason." She stopped speaking and looked behind me.

It took me a moment to realize Sy was standing behind me.

He had his cheek packed as he chewed, and he let out a grumbly laugh at the photos. He put his hand on my waist as he leaned over and examined the photos while his mother and I looked on.

I knew she wanted to talk more with me, and thinking back to his history with his ex-wife, I understood her caution.

"Simon, I'm so happy you came." She smiled warmly at him.

He broke his gaze from the photos to look at her. "I wanted you to meet Charlotte."

His mother smiled and nodded at me, then a moment of silence settled over us.

I hoped I'd get the chance to know her better.

Once we were back outside, Sy and Linda set up the badminton net and started a game with Jay and Max.

I opted to sit out, since my ineptitude at any kind of sport was sure to embarrass me.

Jeff and I sat together on the patio. He was friendly and easy to talk to. We joked and laughed as he told me more about the job they'd been working on next door to my house. Turned out, the brothers had actually bought the house and were planning on flipping it. No wonder I hadn't seen my neighbors for some time.

Joel appeared in the doorway, stealing a glance at me and then Sy before stalking off into the house.

I drew a breath and threw caution to the wind when I asked Jeff in a hushed voice, "So, what's the deal with Sy and Joel?"

He let out a laugh that sounded like a deep grumble. "Sy and Joel usually avoid one another the way a prostitute avoids confession."

"It hasn't always been like that, though."

"No, not at all. We were all really close, until Sy got injured in Afghanistan." His eyes narrowed, and a friendly web of lines appeared at the corners.

"Yeah, he told me about his injuries from the attack. He told me you saved him."

Jeff rubbed his face with a large, callused hand that

scuffed across his goatee and shrugged. "Without question, and I'd do it again. I don't know how I ended up so lucky. Banged up a bit, but Sy…Sy was so broken. Even after his resuscitation."

I shook my head, still unable to imagine him in such an awful state. "So, the contract, that's what started the discord between the two?"

"Ah, you know about the contract," Jeff grumbled.

"Not much, just that he's only got one job left."

"Yeah, Sy refused to accept living in a wheelchair and contending with chronic pain. He'd rather have died. He found out about an experimental surgery that would fuse his spine, using stem cells or something. The surgery, along with a special rehab program, showed a lot of hope in others who'd…"

He paused, searching for the words, and then finally shook his head in what seemed like an attempt to erase the image of a broken Sy from his mind. "Well, anyway, the surgery and program were experimental, and not covered by any kind of insurance, and cost over a million…"

"*A million?*" I whispered.

"And between the business not doing so well, our dad passing the year before, and all of us scraping our money together just to be able to visit him as often as possible, there was just no way. Sy was getting VA disability, but even a lifetime of that wouldn't have been enough.

"Joel was with him the day he was approached by a rep from a private-contract military program. Sy was offered a job right from his rehab bed that would earn him cash, and he was more than willing to grab the opportunity to make money so he could have the surgery.

We warned Sy that a lot of these contracts were black-ops and that he shouldn't take it."

"Black ops? Like illegal operations?"

"Yeah, shady, barely legal at best. But we, meaning me, Max and Jay— told him we'd support whatever decision he made. Joel, on the other hand, wasn't having it. Joel told Sy that if he signed, he'd cut all ties with him. It spiraled out of control from there. Sy accused him of being insensitive to his suffering and thought Joel was trying to block his only chance at a normal life. Joel, on the other hand, said *Sy* was being selfish, and needed to be grateful he was alive instead of so bitter about his circumstances. Joel did everything in his power to get Sy transferred so he wouldn't accept the position, to no avail. Sy banned him from visiting, signed the contract, and they haven't spoken much since."

"That's a long time to hold a grudge," I said.

"Joel is still upset with him because he feels Sy is in over his head, and that these contracts never end how and when they're supposed to. And Sy is even angrier with Joel because if he'd listened to him, well, he'd probably still be in a wheelchair and in a lot of pain."

"Wow. I guess I can understand both sides, though." I shrugged.

"I do, too. Sy's lucky it worked out so well for him physically and financially. And Joel's heart was in the right place, but until Sy is done with his contract and off scot-free, there's no telling who is right or wrong."

Jeff looked over each shoulder before leaning in closer. "And, if I'm being honest, Sy has kind of gloated about the whole thing. The house, the boat, the car, sending extravagant gifts to his niece. Joel feels like it's a slap in the face, that Sy basically sold his soul just to prove him wrong."

Jeff leaned back in his seat and put his hands behind his head. He crossed a leg over his knee and stared at me.

"I can see why he chose to sign. It was his *life* on the line, his future." I looked toward the sky.

"Literally." Jeff fell silent for a long moment. "Don't get me wrong, he's done a lot of good things with the money, too. He regularly donates to the local boys' home for troubled kids." He leaned forward and rested his elbows on his knees.

"That's noble. I'm glad he's able to use his money to help other kids that might be going through what he did," I said.

"Yeah, but Joel doesn't see it that way. It's been years since he signed, and they're still as frigid with each other as they were before the ink even dried on the contract."

I looked over at Sy and smiled.

His strong arm swung the racket as he dove for the birdie, getting it just over the net and scoring the point, much to Jay's dismay.

A slew of profanities escaped from Jay, which made Sy and Linda laugh and high-five.

Sy looked over at me and gave me a wink and that crooked smirk.

"So, since I've been talking your ear off, what about you, Charlotte? What have you done to my brother that made him come here with the whole family for the first time in years?"

"That's a great question, Jeff—" I jokingly punched his shoulder. "—but he didn't even tell me we were coming until I was already on the boat…"

"…And unable to escape?" Jeff chuckled.

"Exactly!" I laughed back.

I gave him some details about *my* life, since he'd been so forthcoming with me. I told him about my past to imply that Sy and I had a lot in common in regards to near-death experiences, major injuries, loss of people we loved, and the military life.

Jeff nodded understandingly.

I couldn't read whether or not Sy had already told him about me. Jeff was a talker, but an even better listener. Maybe it was something about the common ground of the military and tragedy that seemed to make sense when it came to Sy and me and his family, something about the traumas that most people can't understand and fathom. But when I was talking to Jeff—and watching Sy— it just seemed to fit. I didn't feel like a poor thing, and I didn't look at Sy as a victim, either. His life, his family, and his past were messy, just like mine.

Chapter 6

We got back to Sy's dock, and I was deep in thought about the day. Sy helped me off the swaying boat. We stopped at the concrete stairs in his backyard.

He turned toward me. "I don't want you to go," he said quietly, his hand drifting to the back of my neck.

"I don't want to leave." I rested my forehead on his hard chest.

"Then stay," he whispered into my hair.

"Work…" I grumbled. The reality of the next day approaching hit harder than a home run. I looked up at him with a smile, planting another kiss on his lips before turning to head toward my car.

I had a lot to dissect about the eventful day.

Sy walked me to my car, then watched from the porch as I pulled away.

A pang of sadness hit my stomach as his image faded into the distance.

The sun was beginning to make its way to the horizon as I drove through the winding roads back to Newport. I was lost in thoughts of Sy and his family when it hit me. The witch, the harpy that had perched on my shoulder since waking from the accident, wasn't clawing at me, begging for attention. The grief I'd been holding onto for so long wasn't gnawing at my insides the way it normally did as I made my way home to an inevitably dark and empty house.

Is this what moving on feels like?

I thought about my family and friends, and all the years they spent gently reminding me that life would go on, that I was young, that I'd fall in love again.

Could this be it?

I idled at a red light on East Main, but something stopped me from turning down my street. Each familiar landmark tugged a fresh draw of emotions and memories—I drove past the diner Jared and I often ate breakfast at, the small boutique where I bought my wedding gown, the entrance to the base where he was stationed, and two miles later…

The intersection.

The light was green, and I glided through as if it wasn't the very place that stole Jared's last breath or swallowed copious amounts of our blood. Just another intersection, identical to a thousand others, with one very personal exception. This one was responsible for death and irreparable damage, changing the course of my life forever.

My mind contended with feelings of hope and love and memories of loss. I continued driving until I reached the ornate wrought-iron gates of Greenbay Cemetery. I parked just outside the gate—they locked it at dusk. Walking down the familiar stone path, I headed toward the northwest edge that faced the thick woods encircling the cemetery. I leaned down and picked a single violet that grew between the cracked concrete.

I trudged through the grass and stopped in front of the white marble stone engraved CARDOZA. I placed a quarter and the violet on top. Jared's name was followed by "*Devoted husband, Honored veteran, Beloved son.*" I dusted scraps of stray grass clippings and powdery dirt off the marble and sat in the grass, caressing the cold stone with my fingertips. Though I wanted to cry, it wasn't out of the deep grief and sadness that'd paralyzed me like before. It was out of nostalgia and perhaps a little guilt, though the vicious harpy-witch was silent.

Was moving on betraying his memory?

I wanted to tell him that I might move on, but that I'd never forget. I wanted to apologize for things both done and undone. I wanted to thank him for all the memories and the strength that I knew came from a force so much greater than just myself. I rested my forehead against the cold stone and closed my eyes for several long moments.

When I finally pulled back from the stone, the sky was getting dark. I sat numbly for several more minutes, ready to say a very meaningful good-bye.

My head snapped up when I heard the sounds of breaking twigs and leaves crunching against the ground. An oddly primitive alarm in the back of my mind froze me in place. I squinted into the darkening woods and strained to listen, but only a thick, unnatural silence surrounded me.

The birds had stopped singing, and the crickets were silent. Twilight had silenced the woods and all the creatures that dwelled within.

I brought my gaze back to the marble stone in front of me, but several minutes later I heard it again. This time the snapping and rustling increased in sound and speed, indicating a trajectory toward where I sat. I sprang to my feet, scanning the woods beyond the humped and angular shapes of the headstones—only to be met with aberrant stillness again. I scanned the brush, my senses all tingling with heightened awareness.

Then I saw it.

The shadow of a tall, dark figure stood in the wooded area, just out of clear reach of my vision. I stood in a catatonic stupor for several seconds, until my instincts took over, and I sprinted to the now-closed cemetery gate. The groundskeeper had closed the gates, so perhaps I wasn't completely alone, but that didn't relieve the pounding in my chest or the dread that was propelling me back to my car.

I reached the gates, but they were secured with a heavy chain and lock, which caused more panic as the only way out of the cemetery and back to the main road would be the path through the woods. The idea of walking through the woods never intimidated me before. I always felt that fear of such an area was only felt by people who hadn't already experienced the hell I'd been through. But this was different. Someone was in there, watching me, waiting for me. Dread and fear tugged at my chest, choking the air from my lungs.

I grabbed hold of the cold wrought-iron bars, not caring how ridiculous I looked, and jammed my foot onto the horizontal bar that spanned the middle portion of the gates. *A broken leg is better than being abducted in the woods* I reassured myself as I wiggled my legs and used all my upper-body strength to pull myself to the top of the large metal gate. I managed to get both legs over, despite my relentless shaking. I held tight to the pointy rails at the top, then allowed myself to drop to the sidewalk below. One of the very sharp ends of the top rails caught my forearm on the way down.

Cursing as I crumpled to the hard sidewalk below, I waited for the rush of pain. It came from a burning scrape on my right forearm that dripped cherry-red circles onto the cement.

I looked up through the gate to see the large shadowed figure standing at Jared's marble stone where I'd been sitting just moments ago. It looked up from the stone and stared right at me. I couldn't make out anything other than a black silhouette. I scrambled from my spot on the cold concrete and darted back to my car.

My hands shook as I hit the fob to unlock my door. I jammed the key into the ignition, and my tires squealed as I pulled away. A car horn honked, and I shrieked as I swerved to narrowly miss a car I hadn't noticed coming up behind me.

I tried to calm myself on the short ride back to my house by taking deep breaths, focusing on slowing the hammering heart in my chest. Intrusive thoughts demanded attention and offered a sanctuary from the terror I was feeling.

I huffed and gasped, losing control.

I spoke to myself out loud. "If I need to drive five miles south, toward home, that's eight-point-zero five kilometers, eight-thousand eight hundred yards, and I'm going—" I looked down at the speedometer. "—forty miles an hour, the time it will take me to reach my front door…" I slowed my breathing, sorting the equations in my head.

I converted the distance down to yards, feet, inches, and calculated the time in minutes, then seconds, that it was going to take to reach home. I factored in the variables of wind resistance and friction using estimations. By the time I pulled into my driveway, I was nearly composed.

As I walked into my house, I turned and scanned the neighborhood for anything suspicious before closing the front door and triple-checking the lock and deadbolt. I walked through the living room and into the kitchen, then down the hall to my bedroom, checking that each window was locked and secured before heading upstairs.

I looked around upstairs, weaving in and out of the packed boxes that held Jared's old clothes and possessions and the paintings I'd done while working through my grief those first few years. I checked that each window on either side of the upstairs layout was securely closed and locked, pushing up to ensure the lock had caught appropriately.

I pushed one of the dormered windows to ensure the lock was fully engaged and it swung open with ease. I gasped and went to close it, but when I looked down at the white sill, there in the dirt and debris that had collected over the years, sat the half-print of a large shoe. I stared at the print for a long time. Was it possible it was Jared's print from over four years ago? I recalled him going out on the roof through the upstairs windows to clean out the gutters each spring and fall, but *four years later?*

I dragged my finger through the dirt on the sill, rubbing my blackened fingertips together as I remembered his dark eyes as he would look back at me, roll them, and tell me to have more confidence in his ability to *not* fall off the roof, while laughing at my anxiety. I stopped the memory in its tracks by slamming the window shut and engaging the lock.

Only after ensuring that the house was completely locked down *and empty* did I allow myself to clean the now-dried blood that caked my arm.

My night was filled with the nightmares that used to plague me when I was in the throes of grief after the accident. I slept fitfully, waking every couple of hours. I tried to shake the familiar dreams that had returned with a vengeance, but the dreams came to me as clearly as they had back when I was in therapy, trying to recover physically and mentally.

In the dream, I was in the car with Jared, arguing about the rumors that had been swirling over his alleged affair while deployed. It was such a stupid fight. He was angry with me for having listened to Kayla, and I pressed him to answer my questions. Just after he looked over at me with his big chocolate-colored eyes surrounded by obnoxiously long black eyelashes, a sudden screech filled my ears, geometric shapes and colors flew by in slow motion, the shards of glass moving so slowly that I could see the rainbow prisms cast by the sunlight piercing through them. The color crimson, shaped into perfect spheres, suspended in the air around us. I smelled the burning rubber and diesel, heard the crushing of metal, shattering glass, and blaring horns. I felt my body being painfully extracted from the car and put onto a stretcher, followed by the very real memory soldered into my mind of the chaos in the emergency department as they attempted to stabilize me and stop the internal bleeding.

The dream would continue after the symphony of sounds and colors, to a memory of me in the car, but driving by myself this time, watching the road ahead with a feeling of horror and dread that I couldn't quite attach to one memory or another. It was as if I'd dreamed the whole accident in my mind and was actually on the road alone lost in thought, only plagued by the horror of an unknown tragedy that wouldn't clearly show itself to the strange feelings and memories that rushed over me.

This particular night, however, my dream offered clarity. A message. A few of those foreign memories became clear as the trauma bay disappeared and I appeared alone in the car, contending with a rush of conflicting memories. I was in the car, horrified about everything I could see in my mind's eye—the accident, the trauma bay, and in the new memories that were spilling in as I drove alone along the evergreen-lined road were vague visions of the soldier I had to save. The man I, for the several moments I was dead, felt compelled to warn. The man I was speeding to get to.

I couldn't see his face, but I could make out his uniform, his broad shoulders, a darkness that licked out from under the collar of his uniform. A single black feather visible at his neck disappeared around to his back. A tattoo.

It was six o'clock when I woke from the dream, covered in sweat. I decided to get ready for work to escape the unsettling dreams.

I locked the front door behind me, then I made my way to my car and smiled when I saw Sy sitting on the trunk, waiting for me with an iced coffee in hand. He hopped off the trunk, wearing his usual loose-fitting jeans and a white T-shirt. He reached out to pull me close, and his hands slid down my arms. He jerked my wrist up, inspecting the long scrape that trailed from my elbow to the underside of my forearm.

"What happened?" His brows pulled together as he slid his thumb over the length of the abrasion.

"Clumsy as usual," I lied.

I looked up at him while he studied the injury, then I looked at the skin visible where the collar of his shirt ended. I traced my finger over the black feather that licked out from under his shirt from the phoenix on his shoulder. "The phoenix symbolizes rebirth; is that why you chose it?"

"I got it before my accident, when I first enlisted. The phoenix is immune to conventional methods of killing."

"Just as fitting," I murmured. Before he could speak, I asked him, "Where did you go last night, after I left?" I sounded more suspicious than I intended.

"Watched some TV and went to bed. What did *you* do?"

"Same." I shrugged.

"While you're at work, do you mind if I get those shutters back up for you?" He looked over to my house, and back at me with a still-furrowed brow.

"Only if you have time."

He smiled. "I'll have time."

I rested my head on his chest, feeling safer than I had for the last twelve hours. I pulled back and tried to ease his worry with a soft kiss, then slid a finger along the visible portion of the tattoo near his collar again. "I have to go."

Sy handed me the iced coffee and opened the car door for me.

"Will I see you after work?" I asked after sliding into the driver's seat.

"I'll be here," he answered quietly.

****

Work was slower than I'd expected for the Tuesday after a holiday, giving way too much free time for Angela, Brian, and Nelson to notice my changed demeanor. Every time I tried to reel in my noticeable happiness, images of my weekend with Sy popped into my mind, making it impossible not to smile to myself like a fool. The incident in the cemetery and the rogue SUV seemed ridiculous to me now, clearly an artifact of being overtired and maybe overstimulated by the new events in my life.

I sat at the triage desk when it finally happened.

Angela and Brian wheeled two chairs over and stared at me with wild grins and wide eyes.

"So, are you going to tell us what happened this weekend that has you floating around this place, or am I going to have to get a medium in here to spill the dirt?" Angela was on to me.

"First of all, a medium speaks to the departed and will be of no help in finding out what I did this weekend." I laughed at her and Brian as they wheeled their chairs even closer to me.

"James reads tarot cards. Don't make me pull him in here to see what's going on with you," Brian teased.

"Tarot cards tell the future, Brian!" I kicked his chair, making it wheel away an inch or two.

"So, suddenly you're an expert on mediums and tarot-readers?" Angela asked. "You know we're not going to leave you alone now. You're hiding something!"

"Hiding something? I'm old and boring, remember? Housework and stuff."

I wasn't exactly dissuading their suspicions with my responses.

"Ya'll leave Charly alone!" Nelson called out from his seat by the entrance.

Angela and Brian glowered at him.

"Clearly, she's in *love*." Nelson drew out the word in his deep baritone, then smiled and raised his eyebrows.

"Oh, you too, Nelson?!" I hollered.

"James and I are having a fourth of July cookout," Brian said. "I know it's still a few weeks away, but wanted to make sure you penciled it into your schedule. Just a small get-together. Come by for a bit?"

"I'm going!" Angela looked over at me, waiting for my response.

"Sure, what time?"

"Two."

I paused before asking, "Can I bring a plus-one?"

Brian and Angela both screamed in unison, their chairs almost tipping as they bolted upright at my question.

"Is it Thor? Please say it's Thor!" Brian pleaded, unable to contain his excitement.

"Thor?" My eyebrows shot up.

"The guy who was in here to see you, Brian thinks he looks like the Greek god of thunder, apparently." Angela lowered her voice to mimic a man's deep grumble. "A *real* man." She quoted a line from the movie.

"Ah, yes." I laughed. "*Sy*."

I released a freeing breath when Angela started talking about the guy, Rex, that she was still seeing and the subject of me and Sy was dropped.

Driving home at the end of the day, my stomach was doing flip-flops at the anticipation of seeing Sy. I felt bad about our conversation that morning and the fact that I lied about my arm. I considered my options when it came to coming clean about my standoffish behavior and injury.

Sy was still working at the house next door and

looked deep in thought, which piqued my curiosity. I smiled at the freshly painted shutters now in place on my house, then went in to take a shower before he came over. I needed time to figure out what to say if I was going to come clean, and how to say it.

After showering, I dressed and walked into my living room— my hair still wrapped in a pink bath towel— and peeked out the front window to see if Sy was close to being finished.

"Looking for someone?"

I whirled around to see Sy sitting on my sofa with his arm resting along the back. The picture of leisure and comfort.

"You scared me!" I held a hand on my chest to keep my pounding heart from breaking through my ribcage.

"I figured you left it unlocked for me—" He leaned forward, resting his elbows on his knees. "—and I was going to lay into you for that. I told you to be careful. It's obvious you live alone."

"Oh? Well, I figured with four huge Marines next door, it was safe to leave it unlocked for you," I lied.

I thought I'd locked it. I squinted as I tried to recall coming into the house. I pulled the towel off my head and combed my fingers through my wet hair, feeling self-conscious.

Sy rose from the couch and took my wrist, slowly lifting my arm to look at my injury again. He wrapped his other arm around my waist and pulled me closer. "Leaving the door unlocked while you shower is reckless," he murmured. "I've had the pleasure of showering with you, and I won't allow any other the same luxury." He dipped his head, and the tip of his nose grazed my cheek.

Memories of showering with him came flooding back, and my skin heated with the vision. "I lied to you," I blurted.

His eyebrows shot up. "About locking the door?" he guessed.

"No, no. Not that. Well, that too, but…" My breath hitched.

"Charlotte, look at me."

I held his stare and my heart fell into a calmer rhythm. I still struggled for air.

"Take a moment. Breathe."

I drew a deep breath and pulled myself out of his arms. I paced the floor, counting my steps. Twenty-one, twenty-two, twenty-three. My breathing slowed.

I spun around and faced him. "I think someone has been watching me. There was this SUV outside my house a few times, once late at night, and someone was watching me in the cemetery…"

I started counting steps again. Thirty-seven, thirty-eight…

He looked away and out the bay window, deep in thought. "Yesterday?"

"Yes, after I left your house. I went to the cemetery, and someone was watching me. Heading toward me. I ran away; something bad was going to happen if I didn't run. I could feel it. The gate was locked, and I scraped my arm climbing it to escape."

I slowed my pacing, still counting. Forty-two, Forty-three…

"The counting, have you always done that?"

I stopped abruptly. "How did you know I was counting?" My face heated.

"I can tell. It's okay, don't be embarrassed." He

looked out the bay window again.

"Just another present bestowed upon me from the grim reaper." I sighed.

"You're perfect as you are."

"Anyway, I probably overreacted, I don't know. But that's how I got this." I lifted my arm to show off my injury again, referring to my sloppy escape attempt.

He turned back to me with unmistakable fury.

I backed away from him as he slowly inched toward me.

"*Why* didn't you tell me sooner?"

He spoke so quietly and calmly I wondered if I was only imagining his anger.

He moved toward me until my back rested against the wall.

My voice was small when I answered, "I don't know. I was embarrassed, I'm not even sure—"

"No, no, Charlotte..." He pinched the bridge of his nose and squeezed his eyes shut. "*Fuck*."

I tried to squeeze out of the position we were in, with my back against the wall and him towering over me less than an inch away, but he rested his forehead against mine. I didn't anticipate *this* response, but I knew better than to be afraid of him.

"Is there anything else I should know? Do you have any idea who might be watching you or have a reason to?" he asked with his eyes still closed.

I told him about the situation with Jordan who lived a few streets over. His history of drinking, physical interaction, and character assault on me was suspect, though he didn't strike me as the stalker type. Being actively enlisted and married didn't leave him with much time for extracurriculars like scaring the shit out of me at all hours of the day and night.

When he opened his eyes, the fury was replaced by impassivity.

Ah, that's how he copes.

Sy pulled his eyebrows in and sighed. "I can tell you with certainty it wasn't Jordan."

"How do you know?" I asked, though I knew the answer.

He rested his palms on the wall on either side of my head, ensnaring me between his large body and the wall. "I know, because the last time he messed with you, I beat the shit out of him. Unless he has a death wish, he won't bother you. Ever again."

He kept his gaze locked on me, assessing my response.

I stiffened and pushed his arm away roughly.

He turned to watch me as I stomped away from the wall.

I swung around and glared at him. "Why didn't you tell me about this when I asked what happened to your hand?"

"I didn't want to upset you. It was clear you were embarrassed and that asshole was trying to take advantage of you. I am very protective of the people I care about." His jaw ticked. "I will never hurt you, Charlotte. I will kill anyone who does. You've been through enough."

I shook my head. "I don't need you to protect me, I'm capable of handling myself."

He made his way back over to me in two long strides, stopping only when our bodies touched. "Make no mistake, I don't protect you because I think you're weak. I protect you because you're everything to me."

"Why? You could have anyone you want. Why choose the broken one?" My voice cracked.

"You're not broken. You and I"—he grasped my hips—"danced with death and lived to speak of it. It's okay that we returned to this world with more than we left it with."

"You have a way of making anything sound good." I rested my hands on his chest.

"No more of this self-deprecation." He put a knuckle under my chin to angle my face toward his.

I nodded, slid my hands up his arms, and locked them behind his neck, standing on my toes to press my lips to his.

I didn't want to feel the sudden rush of warmth his protectiveness gave me. It was the opposite of all I'd accomplished over the last few years alone. I was proud of my independence, my newfound strength. But there it was, exposed in all of its glory. Even if it was a little extreme. Okay, a lot extreme. I wasn't afraid of Sy, even though he gave Jordan the beating he deserved.

"You should stay with me," Sy said abruptly.

"I'm fine here, really. I've lived alone for a long time now. Maybe I'm just being paranoid. The SUV probably belongs to a friend of one of my neighbors, and the person in the cemetery was probably the groundskeeper or something."

"I hope you're right. But no offense, for you to notice, I think it's probably been going on for some time now."

"What makes you say that?" I was a little insulted.

"I've been working next door to you for a while now, Charlotte. Had you ever noticed me before we met at Thames?"

"I wasn't paying attention." I wilted in his arms. His point was made already.

"Exactly. When I saw you at Thames, I recognized you. I've seen you come and go since before we met. You're often in your own little world…"

I narrowed my eyes at him, unsure of what to say.

He smiled down at me. "It's actually endearing. You always look so lost in thought. I was trying to find a way to talk to you at Thames without coming off as creepy that I'd noticed you next door. Those white pajamas though—" He leaned in and kissed me. "—I like those."

I laughed in between his soft kisses, picturing all the times I'd gone to get the mail in my PJ's. I pictured the house next door over a month ago, trying to recall anything other than the loud saw that irritated me in the morning. Sy had seen me in my pajamas, doing yard work, coming and going to work, walking down to Jess's house. But he was right, I never noticed him. The workers had been like background noise—nameless, faceless voices and sounds. Then I began to worry. If he was right, someone had been watching me for a while.

"What are you thinking?"

"About whether or not you're right." I considered reconfiguring the suspects in my journal.

"About?"

"All of it. That someone likely is stalking me, that I don't pay attention to my surroundings…and that a few months ago *you* were the one watching me." I lowered my voice, "In my favorite pajamas, no less!"

"Those are the best."

He smiled and then lifted me off my feet as he kissed me, tossing me playfully onto the sofa. He climbed on top of me, cupping my face in his hands. "You're safe with me. I won't let anything happen to you." He gently bit my lower lip. "Nothing that you don't want to happen, of course."

My body trembled in response and I bowed closer to him, running my hands down his back and over his rough scar. Every part of him, scarred, muscled, tattooed—a complete masterpiece. I leaned in to kiss his neck and heard a low hum from his throat, both of us once again falling victim to the magnetic pull of our bodies when we were this close. We pulled at each other's clothes, leaving them in heaps on the shag rug while we made love on the sofa.

We ate together in the kitchen as the sun set.

Outside, the Donovan Brothers construction truck started up with a roar.

Sy walked to the window, peering at his brother in the truck. "I don't have my car today, Jeff picked me up this morning."

"I'm fine, really. I'll call you if I get paranoid."

He rubbed a hand over his face. "Are you sure you won't stay with me?"

"No, I have to get up early, and I have all my stuff here. It's fine. Really."

Sy reluctantly pulled out his phone to text Jeff to wait for him. "Make sure you call me if anything seems...off or suspicious, no matter how small or insignificant you think it may be, okay?"

I reassured him I was likely suffering from an overactive imagination.

His furrowed brow and stark silence gave away his frustration when I tried to downplay the incidents.

I walked him to the door and felt an overwhelming sense of loneliness as I watched him hop into the truck with Jeff and drive off into the black night.

The weeks flew by.

With Sy working next door, I got to see him every morning before work and every night afterward.

Sy became hyper-vigilant and took to looking out my windows often.

I was hoping that after the few uneventful weeks he'd relax, but just when I thought he might be, I'd catch him looking out my back windows and assessing the locks on my doors again.

On Friday night, I took Sy upstairs to satisfy his curiosity after I told him I used to paint often. I never considered myself any good, but it was therapeutic during some of my lowest points. My back was turned to him as I rummaged through a box, pulling a few small canvases out.

Sy sauntered over to a large canvas leaning against the back wall. He lifted the painting and stared at it for a long time in silence.

I walked up behind him, hugging the small canvases to my chest.

He held my largest painting. A weeping, twisted tree with a background of midnight blue, illuminated by a large white moon visible through branches that cast wiry shadows along the painted forest floor.

I was particularly broken when I painted it, recovering from the accident and grieving heavily. Instead of leaves, red and blue drops—symbolizing blood and tears—hung from each twisted branch, I explained to him. I used deep greens and browns on the forest floor that led to a background of more-normal-looking trees and wilderness silhouetted in the light of the large moon.

"This is unbelievable. I love this, something about it"—his fingers grazed the twisted bark of the tree—"reminds me of *my* scars."

"Keep it."

He looked at me, then back down at the canvas. "Are you sure? This must've taken a long time."

"I'm sure. I want you to have it."

He deserved a piece of my heart, because he was the one who made me realize it was actually still there, beating in my chest.

Later that night, he hung the painting over his bed. The colors matched his room handsomely, and the moonlight through the windows reflected off the shiny oil brushstrokes. In its new home, the painting no longer appeared to be born of sadness or grief. It appeared more like the rising phoenix—a symbol of strength, survival, and rebirth.

Sy quietly stared at the painting after hanging it.

I playfully jumped onto his back and giggled at his surprise. I regretted the action when he spun me wildly, and I clung to him piggyback, until we both collapsed onto the bed in a fit of dizziness and laughter.

Chapter 7

"The world will not be destroyed by those who do evil, but by those who watch them without doing anything." -Albert Einstein

The following Wednesday, I was exhausted and wanted to catch up on much-needed rest. Sy went home, and by nine, I was ready for bed. I went to my desk to grab my journal—light reading before hitting the hay—but it wasn't in the drawer I'd left it in. I opened and slammed each drawer of my desk, resolving to search for it in the morning. I pulled myself into bed, hugged the covers tightly around my body, and fell asleep within minutes.

I was awakened by my hair being gently pushed from my face. I kept my eyes closed and smiled, waiting to feel Sy wrap his arms around me.

But Sy hadn't stayed over.

My entire body went rigid, and my eyes snapped open. The room was engulfed in darkness. I moved slightly, and my foot hit something. Fear and uncertainty crippled me. The mattress was indented under the weight of something—someone— at the foot of my bed.

As my eyes adjusted to the darkness, I peered about wild-eyed, then focused on the silhouette of a man sitting on the edge of my bed.

I shot up from the bed and went straight for his

throat. I used both hands and wrapped my legs around him. I applied pressure, willing myself to strangle the stranger in my room.

The figure rose from the bed and grasped a handful of my hair. I let out a scream and adjusted my elbow to get his neck into a stronger chokehold, sliding my body onto his back.

In a quick movement, I was suddenly airborne, striking the wall behind my bed and rolling onto the floor with a painful thud. I scrambled up as fast as my shaking legs allowed, but he was already gone. I reached for the phone on the side of the bed, dialing *9-1* but hesitated before dialing the last digit for help.

Is this a dream? This can't be real. I'm losing it.

I hopped out of bed with my phone in hand. I stalked into the living room and then the kitchen, and not a door or window was open, not an item out of place. I checked the slider and bathroom, looking behind the shower curtain. I hit the 'end' button and dialed Sy instead, continuing my search of the house. I paced up and down the hall, checking and rechecking closets, under my bed and back into my living room.

I lifted a blade of the blinds and saw only darkness outside, no hint of a car or intruder. I was stunned out of my rumination when I heard Sy's panicked voice calling out my name from the phone that I had in my hand hanging down at my side. I slowly pulled the phone up to my ear.

"Please come."

"Charlotte, what happened? I'm staying on the phone with you until I get there."

"I think I'm fine, maybe a bad dream." I couldn't stop my voice from quivering as I spoke.

"Don't do that now. I'm tired of you dismissing everything. I'm on my way." His engine revved in the background. He was clearly speeding, but I wasn't going to protest.

It seemed impossibly soon, and Sy's headlights illuminated my living room as he came to a screeching halt in my driveway.

I went to let him in, and in typical Sy fashion, he seemed to just materialize behind the door, pushing it open as I was unlocking it.

He scanned my face, assessing that I was okay, then pushed past me to check the house. "What happened, Charlotte?" He vibrated with anger, possessiveness.

I struggled to answer and shook my head. I was counting again.

"Charlotte!" He swung around and grabbed my shoulders.

"I told you Sy! I was sleeping, I felt someone touch my face, and it took me a minute to realize it wasn't you. Someone was sitting on the edge of my bed. I thought I was dreaming but my foot…hit it. I didn't just see him, I felt him. I jumped on him, choked him."

"You *what*?"

Sy continued checking the rooms, the doors, the windows, while I followed him and spoke.

"I would've killed him, but he threw me into the wall. I didn't even think, I just…" a tear escaped and rolled down my cheek. "I checked everything. Nothing was unlocked or open, and no one was outside. I think I'm going crazy."

He stopped at the bottom of the staircase and pulled me close. "I'm here. Everything's going to be okay." He looked up the stairwell, then down at me. "You're not crazy, Charlotte. I need you to breathe. Stay here, okay?"

Sy reached around to the back of his waistband, pulling out a black pistol. It reminded me of the one Jared used to keep in the nightstand so many years ago.

He headed upstairs with the gun locked in hand.

I trembled as his quiet footsteps slowly walked the creaky floor upstairs, followed by the sound of boxes being pushed aside, doors opening and closing.

"It's clear," he called out.

I bounded up the stairs, and he checked each window individually. He went to check a dormered window, and as soon as he applied force, it swung up—disengaged from the faulty lock.

He bent down quietly. "Someone was here," he said as he stared at shoeprints on the dirty sill. Two more now accompanied the print I'd found the other day, the prints each facing a different direction. Someone had been coming and going.

Sy saw the defeat in my eyes and wrapped his arms around me tightly.

Cold metal pressed into my back when he hugged me, sending a shiver up my spine.

He cleared the chamber and put the gun into his waistband, then treaded down the stairs and straight into my room.

I followed behind him, watching as he swung the closet open and grabbed several bags, tossing them onto my unmade bed.

"Get your things. You're not staying here."

I began stuffing clothes into a duffel bag. In the bathroom, I grabbed an armful of toiletries that I dumped into another bag. I wasn't sure when I'd feel safe returning home, so I took everything I'd need for the rest of the week.

I returned to my bedroom. "I can't find my journal. I need it." I started pulling papers and notebooks from my desk and throwing them on the floor. I kicked the bottom drawer closed in frustration.

"What does it look like? I'll help you look."

"It's leather. Brown. Really worn, and it has a tie on the side to hold it closed." I used my hands to demonstrate the size of it.

"I've seen it before. Here, on your desk, right?" He tapped my desk.

"You've seen it?"

"Yeah, it's always around here. I've been in your room enough to notice," Sy said wryly.

I started dumping out the contents of my nightstand.

Sy looked in the bed, tossing the covers aside and under the bed, and then in the closet.

My shoulders slumped. "I'll look tomorrow. I just want to leave now." I sighed.

"Let's go." He grabbed my hand and took my bag.

****

In Sy's bed, the sound of the water rippling through the bay calmed me as I laid my head on his shoulder. The room was illuminated only by pale moonlight spilling through the window.

He rubbed my back soothingly.

I asked him if I should file a police report, and I was surprised by his response. He wasn't against it, but felt it would be a waste of time. He offered to install cameras and even suggested coming home with me without his car and staying up for several nights to catch the intruder.

He was determined to end this nightmare for me, but I was horrified that my sanctuary was becoming a place of danger. I was violated and afraid, unable to make sense of who could have been in my house, why they were there, and how they were getting in. Even if the upstairs window was faulty, how were they getting onto the roof?

I needed my journal. Without it, I felt naked, exposed, unprepared.

I made it through the last two days of work tired and worn. My co-workers noticed, but expressed their relief when they heard I was staying with Sy. They assumed I was tired from long nights with my new lover, and that assumption wouldn't have been *entirely* wrong.

Staying with Sy was amazing. I still couldn't get enough of him and felt exceptionally safe when I was with him. But I was angry that this happy new point in my life was being tainted by a potential stalker.

Friday, after work, was the first time I'd gone back to my house all week. Sy was finishing up work next door with Max, Jeff, and Jay, and I was planning to walk over to Jess's house while Sy ran a few errands.

I straightened up my house and looked around. It looked neat and harmless, all traces of that terrifying night vaporized in the daylight.

Once my clothes were washed, dried, and folded, I neatly packed them inside my duffel bag. When I lifted the bag off my bed, one pillow fell away and I noticed the brown edge of the journal tucked into the comforter. I was certain I'd checked the bed before we left that night, and so did Simon.

I reached down and grabbed the old book with relief. I stuffed it into the outer pocket of the bag, and put the bag in Sy's car before making my way down to Jess's house.

As soon as I walked in, she hopped over to me, hugging me tightly. "I haven't seen you in so long! Let me guess where you've been." She grinned.

"Yeah, I've been staying at his place." I sighed.

She looked at me with a pinched brow as we made our way to her sofa. "Is everything okay?"

I tried not to look at her face. I shrugged. My expression gave me away.

She leaned in. "Charlotte, what's going on?" Her voice was grave—she knew me too well.

I didn't intend on telling her everything, but once I started, I couldn't stop because with Steve being deployed, what if Jess was in danger, too? I told her about the SUV and the cemetery, the shoe prints, and the intruder in my house.

"Jordan!" She gasped. "He's the only one that makes sense. He's obsessed with you! And he knows the layout of your house."

"It's not him," I interrupted, my voice low.

She raised her eyebrows and straightened her back. "How do you know?"

"If I tell you, you cannot tell a soul. Promise." I pressed my lips together.

"Charlotte, you *know* I wouldn't." She drew in a breath waiting for me to explain.

I trusted Jess; she would keep our secret. I told her Sy was the one who'd attacked Jordan.

Jess sat silently for several minutes. She curled her legs up and hugged them, resting her cheek on her knees. "Charlotte...wouldn't that give Jordan even *more* of a reason to mess with you? Or maybe Kayla? What about someone upset that you moved on? A friend of Jared's, or..."

"Or?"

"Or his father? Or Sy, do you know him, like *really* know him? How do you know he's not the one?"

"No, no, no." I shook my head vehemently. "I haven't seen my *father-in-law*"—my lip curled involuntarily—"in years, and Sy isn't stalking me."

She cocked an eyebrow.

"I think this has been going on for a while, and I think I only noticed it because I've been paying more attention. I trust Sy, and he's certain it isn't Jordan. As for a friend of Jared's, you and Steve knew him as well as I did. He kept everyone at arm's length. I can't think of one person who would care that I moved on."

"But then *who* and more importantly, why?" She lifted her cheek off her knees and slid closer to me.

"I don't know, but I know I feel safe with Sy; he's already...*seeing* me, and he wouldn't need to stalk me to get near me."

I wouldn't admit it to her, but I'd already secretly researched him and his brothers, with a little help from Nelson at work. He'd given me a full, undocumented hour at the info hub, where I was able to look up their military files. Other than being nothing short of patriotic heroes who had completed multiple tours of duty, they were squeaky clean. I did, however, find out why Jay referred to Sy as *the silencer* that one time, though. Sy had been quite the sniper, a definite loss for the corps when he sustained his injury.

At the end of my hour, I finally stumbled across the government contract he'd signed, showing that he was still bound to a private contract outside of his enlistment. But none of what I'd learned brought me any closer to figuring out who was watching me, or more importantly, why.

"It's not always about that. Maybe it's a control thing, to get you to stay with him."

I shook my head. "Please, Jess. I'm telling you, trust me, it's not him."

"You really like this guy, huh?" She sighed.

"I do. More than I ever expected."

She was still uncertain if Sy had a role in what was going on. That was fair enough. I reassured her that I would bring my own car to his house that night and drive myself to the police station in the morning to file a report.

I walked back to my house, and Sy was sitting on the front porch.

His brothers and their construction truck were gone for the day.

I walked through the grass toward my front steps. "I hope I didn't keep you waiting long." I smiled.

"I've waited longer." Sy grinned and reached for my hand. He pulled me toward his car and stopped when I resisted.

"I was thinking about bringing my car to your place. I'm going to file a police report in the morning. I know you said it wouldn't help, but it'll make me feel better."

His eyes did that impassive thing again, and his shoulders hitched a little.

"I don't mind if you take your car, but I wanted to bring you somewhere. If you drive yourself, it'll ruin the surprise. I'll take you to the station tomorrow to file the report and afterwards we can come straight here to get your car."

I looked at him warily. "Where are we going?"

He smiled and wrapped his arm around my waist. "I told you, it's a surprise. You've had a hellish week. Let me do this, please."

I relented and followed him to his car. I looked over at him, and he gave a wide smile and wink. He opened the door, and I slid into the passenger seat.

My stomach knotted. I wasn't a huge fan of surprises, and had no idea where we could be headed. I closed my eyes and hoped it wouldn't be anywhere public—my nerves were wound to the max.

Sy drove out of Newport, passing through Middletown and Portsmouth and over the Sakonnet River Bridge. We took an exit off the highway and drove down a long serpentine road by the water, and then turned down a dirt road that led deep into the woods.

"Not a fan of the forest?" He laughed when he saw me staring nervously at the narrow road ahead, my knuckles white as I gripped the seat.

"You've seen my reaction to wasps. I'm no entomologist, that's for sure."

"I'll keep you safe." He chuckled.

Branches clacked along the windshield as we made our way deeper into the darkening forest. When the car came to a stop, I looked over at him, confused. Nothing but dirt road lay ahead, and either side of the car was surrounded by thorny brush.

"Slide over here, there's more room to get out on my side." Sy opened his door and held his hand out to help pull me through the driver's-side door.

"Where are we going?"

"It's a *surprise*." He enunciated the word slowly.

We held hands and walked down the dirt road for several yards, then turned onto a small foot path that led even deeper into the thick forest. I held tightly onto him, releasing my grip only once Sy announced we were almost there.

We walked into a clearing, and I gasped.

There, standing out among the rest of the tall pines and maples, stood an enormous weeping willow.

I immediately noticed the thick, twisted trunk and its large roots that snaked through the ground keeping the immediate area around the tree clear. My painting had come to life.

I gaped at Sy, speechless.

"It gets better, follow me." He forged ahead of me, disappearing around the other side of the tree.

I made my way around the large trunk, still in awe of the serene old tree.

Sy had his hands in his pockets as he stared up at the tree. He turned to me with a smile, then pulled some weeping branches out of the way, revealing a row of old, moss-covered two-by-fours nailed up the bark.

He motioned for me to go up. "Ladies first."

I carefully climbed up the tree. As I neared the area where the trunk cleaved into thick branches, I pulled myself up through an opening in a piece of plywood and sat on a blanket laid out on the floor within.

Sy made his way inside right after me.

I closed my eyes and took a deep breath. I opened them to Sy watching me, and a smile broke across my face.

We were in an old treehouse, built of thick wood weathered by the years, completely secluded from the forest. Rows of small white lights were strung across the ceiling, and a wooden box sat in the corner.

Sy sat on the blanket beside me and opened a bottle of wine he pulled from the box, filling a glass for each of us.

"This is beautiful, what is this place?"

My words failed me at exactly how exquisite I found this secret house in the forest. It was romantic, but deeper than that. It spoke to a part of me that I'd long considered dead: To the artist, the lover, the introverted dreamer within me. My breath caught in my throat.

"I wanted to show you a place that healed me growing up. This place is what turned my cousins into my brothers. When my mother dropped me and Jay off at my Aunt Marta's and never came back for us, we eventually built this place with our bare hands. It was our sanctuary right up until our teen years. If one of us needed the other, this is where we'd meet. If these walls could talk…" He let out a short laugh. "Then I saw your painting, and it answered something I'd been struggling with."

"What's that?"

"After my divorce, I had hook-ups but I never *dated* anyone. I had no desire. Then I met you, and any typical date—dinner, movies, bars— didn't seem right. It didn't seem *you.* You're not comfortable in crowded places. So, I was struggling with how I could take you on the proper date you deserve, and here we are." He raised his glass to mine.

He put his glass down and lifted me off the blanket and into his arms, holding one of my hands to his chest. We swayed slowly together, dancing to the sounds of the forest—the buzzing of the summer cicadas in the nearby trees, the singing birds perched high above the forest, the rustling leaves.

I rested my head on his chest and he put his chin on my head.

"I want you to be mine," he whispered.

"I've been yours from the moment I first saw you."

He drew a deep breath. "I wish I could tell you why that's not so."

I pulled away slightly and furrowed my brow. "You're going to have to explain that."

He shook his head. "I saw you first—" He smiled. "—and got caught in your web."

I narrowed my eyes at him, then I laughed.

I rested my head back on his chest and breathed in his warm scent. His embrace was home to me, a lighthouse that beckoned me out of my darkness. Perhaps I'd never understand what caused us to connect so immediately. Maybe there weren't clear-cut answers to the mysteries of love after loss. But of one thing I was certain: I was in love with him.

"I love you, Charlotte," he said in perfect timing with my thoughts.

I pulled away again and stared at every angle of his face—his sky-blue eyes, the scar through his eyebrow that I found endearing, the angle of his sharp jaw, his perfect nose and delicious lips. I lifted my hand to touch his face. I gently ran my fingers over his lips, then traced his jaw, up to his scarred eyebrow, trying to figure out if he was real. I couldn't have dreamt this man up. I wasn't looking for love, and I wasn't looking for him, yet here he stood as the answer to a question I never even asked.

I was broken from my wordless trance when my phone buzzed loudly from where it sat on the wooden floor. I bent and looked at the text from Jess:

Went for a run, your car is home but his isn't. You promised!

He raised his eyebrows as he read the text on my screen. I swiped the message away and opened the camera on my phone, angling it toward Sy and me.

"Smile," I instructed him.

I snapped my first-ever photo of us and sent it to her. I didn't analyze the photo too closely, but the happiness in my eyes would tell a story that needed no words. I dropped my phone back onto the blanket.

Sy pulled me in tightly. "Now, where were we?" He brought his lips back to mine.

****

Saturday morning, I had Sy take me to my car, and even though he'd offered to come with me to file a police report, I declined, figuring I'd spare him the inevitable long wait to speak with a deputy.

Sy wanted to cut the grass and install a camera system at my house while I spent the day stuck at the station.

The station entrance was the typical white-tiled, plexiglassed vestibule with worn charcoal leather chairs.

I waited for twenty minutes before Deputy Sanders ushered me to his desk to take the report.

He pulled out a ballpoint clicker pen and obnoxiously clicked it open and closed several times before placing the tip to a small notepad. After taking down my full name, address and phone number, he nodded to indicate he was ready for my statement.

I told him everything from the SUV, to the person in the cemetery, to the figure I'd seen in my bedroom.

When I finished, he looked up at me expectantly, but I confirmed that I'd given him all the information.

He didn't hide his annoyance as he dropped his pen haphazardly on the desk and leaned back, lacing his hands behind his head. He condescendingly mentioned the information I'd provided was circumstantial, and that

I should've called the night there was an intruder in my house. Without a license plate number or a description of an individual, there wasn't much the police could do.

I felt foolish. I should've listened to Sy when he told me the police wouldn't help, but at least now there was a record of me reporting the incidents, and I could tell Jess I followed through on my promise.

When I pulled onto my street, Sy was on the front porch wiring my new camera doorbell in place. I parked the car and joined him on the front porch.

"How'd it go? he asked without looking up.

"You were right. They can't do anything without more information."

He shrugged. "Maybe this will help." He motioned to the camera.

I nodded.

He took me for a walk around the yard, showing me where the cameras had been concealed in the eaves of the house, two in the back and two in the front, not including the doorbell cam.

"A little much?" I asked playfully, bumping my shoulder with his.

"Not nearly enough," he chided back.

"None in the house though, right?"

"Just the hidden one over the bed." He winked and laughed.

I elbowed him.

He looked at me thoughtfully. "I was thinking we should stay here tonight."

I raised my eyebrows. "Because of the camera over the bed?"

"Ha! If I'd known that was your thing…" He grabbed me by the waist and growled into my neck.

"What's that?" I nodded at the coil of wires in his hand.

"Old wires I found through the attic and eaves. Did you have a hard-wired system before?"

"No, I don't think so."

"Maybe the previous owners, then. I didn't find cameras, just the old wiring for it."

I nodded, but unease prickled at my neck.

****

I must've fallen asleep around one or so, and when I awakened to Sy's panicked voice around two, I knew something was wrong. Before I could get my bearings, he was peppering me with questions. I'd had one of my nightmares and had been talking in my sleep.

I reluctantly told him about the recurring dreams. I never had the dreams when I stayed at Sy's, so perhaps my mental guard was down when staying at my house, allowing my dreams to wreak havoc? I tried to reassure him my nightmares were just a byproduct of my past, but he didn't seem comforted.

Sy told me he understood; he used to have nightmares from the PTSD he suffered after the attack in Afghanistan, but his expression held more concern for my dreams than necessary.

"How did you make them stop?" I asked.

"They just faded away with time. Sometimes I'll get one or two a year, but nothing like it used to be. I'm more in control of them now; I know when I'm dreaming. I guess you could say it's a gift." He laughed. "I can lucid dream."

"Then why do you seem so concerned about mine?" I was stunned by his reaction to my nightmare, it made me wildly self-conscious.

"The content. Is that exactly how the accident happened, the way you see it in your dream?"

"Pretty much." I wondered if I should go all in and tell him that I knew *everything* that happened.

Well, almost everything, I was wrong about one very important fact initially. Jared didn't survive. We sat in silence for a long time. I was uncomfortable, so I decided to finally ask what he was thinking.

"About your accident. I know this probably isn't the best time…but one day, could you tell me everything you remember?"

"I told you everything I remember. What is this about, Sy?" I propped myself up on my elbows to face him.

"The end of the dream. When you realized you were alone in the car, Jared wasn't there. And you said that you were in a state of shock, dealing with an influx of foreign memories."

"Yeah, that has always baffled me. I dwelled on that scrap of a memory for far too long. I even told the neuro doc about it. But I was told it was probably a mental protective mechanism of sorts. That my brain was taking me away from the trauma and creating a safe place for me until…"

"Until you were stabilized," Sy offered.

"Yes. Resuscitated."

"So, what memories came rushing in?"

"I don't know. I felt like I was trying to fight the memories from coming in. It was like a primal panic, I was afraid if I allowed the memories in, it'd erase my real memories. I know, stupid." I twisted my fingers together and stared at them.

"No, not stupid at all. You're too hard on yourself."

Sy gently brushed my hair from my shoulder.

"It's weird, though. After I met you, a few of those memories showed up in my dreams. And I'm sure it's just artifact, but—" I stopped abruptly.

Should I admit he'd made an appearance in my dreams?

"Please, tell me," he pressed.

"There I was, alone in the car after all the chaos in the trauma bay. And while I fought the new memories coming in, I was racing to see a soldier. All these years, I couldn't identify who this man was that I was in a panic to get to. But last night I noticed something that may have identified him."

"What was it?"

"A tattoo, or part of one. Identical to yours." I ran my finger along the black feather peeking out of his shirt collar.

Sy drew in a sharp breath, but said nothing.

"I felt like I had to go warn you about something. But dreams can be strange like that, I suppose."

"Wow."

"Wow?"

"Yeah, the human brain, the human spirit is incredible. Like we've been linked in some capacity before. The way I feel about you is disproportionate to how long I've known you. Maybe we knew each other in a past life." Sy shrugged.

"Quantum entanglement." I yawned. "I'm tired, but since you're so interested in my dreams, here's something that'll make you wish you never asked."

I reached over the side of the bed and felt around clumsily. I pulled the duffel out from under the bed and grabbed my journal. I lay on my back and ran my fingers

145

across the worn leather.

"You found it?"

"Yeah. It was on my bed the whole time. This is the most thorough documentation of the accident, and after you flip through it for, say, a minute, you'll realize why I question my own sanity."

Sy reached over and took the old book. His brows pulled together as he untied the outer leather straps.

I yawned and let my eyes close.

Now he'll really see I'm crazy. Oh well. Call a spade a spade.

"Get some rest, love. I'll be here." He kissed my forehead.

I nestled into the crook of his arm, falling into a peaceful slumber within minutes.

I buried my face in the pillow to escape the sun shining through the slats of the blinds. I heard a page turn and quickly lifted my head. "Sy! Have you slept at all?"

He sat upright, reading the last few pages of the journal. "What can I say? Compelling stuff right here." He closed the book and smiled.

"Shouldn't you be running away screaming right now?"

"Not a chance. You're gifted. Very gifted." He looked down at the worn cover. His complexion was pale, and his brows pulled in tightly.

He definitely thinks I'm nuts! He looks downright sick over it!

"Let me make you some coffee, then I need to go see Jeff," Sy said.

He hopped off the bed and headed into the kitchen.

I draped my arm over my face.

Maybe I made a huge mistake.

Chapter 8

Work was busy, with the usual summer injuries and rashes, which made the days fly by.

Sy and I were enjoying evenings together, and between his security system and my newly installed one, he was comfortable leaving so he could visit his brothers and I could run errands or spend time with Angela and Jess.

All in all, things were perfect, and the morning of the fourth of July was no different.

The day started in Sy's bedroom, and I opened my eyes to the sun rising above the bay, casting its warm glow across the bed. Sy was already awake, with his head resting on his elbow watching me. I rolled toward him, and he reached over and grabbed the back of my knee, shifting my leg over his hip and leaning in for a kiss.

"It's a big day."

"Is it?" I closed my eyes. Every day was a big day now. Days filled with so much happiness and hope and sex.

"I get to meet your friends." He smiled.

I scanned his face. "Nervous?"

He pulled me on top of him. "I'm never nervous." He grasped my hips, holding me in place.

I leaned down and kissed his nose. "Au contraire, you were nervous when I went through a paranoid phase due to my imaginary stalker."

He turned serious. "It wasn't a phase." He rolled over again so now he was on top of me, then leaned down and softly kissed my eyelids, then my lips. He gently slid his lips from my jaw to my neck.

He nipped soft kisses down to my collarbone, and I shivered at the sensation. His weight was heavy but not suffocating, and he pressed himself against me while I allowed everything uniquely him—his scent, his hands, his lips—to consume me. I closed my eyes, allowing the feel of him to resonate through my body and soul.

My eyes snapped open at the sound of his doorbell.

He groaned and rolled off me.

"Maybe Jeff?" I considered out loud.

"He wouldn't come this early on a Saturday, if he knew what was good for him." He draped his tattooed arm over his eyes and hesitated.

The doorbell rang again.

I playfully pulled the sheet over my head to hide.

"Oh, no you don't!"

Sy went digging to find me beneath the covers but I evaded him, wriggling out of his grasp and deeper into the sea of sheets and comforters, laughing at his failed attempts. I squealed with delight as he continued his search for me beneath the blankets, letting out a loud scream when he finally grabbed ahold of my thigh and slid me out from my hiding place.

He stood beside the bed and leaned down, scooping me up and tossing me over his shoulder.

He laughed, and I cried out in protest as the doorbell rang again.

"*Let's* see who it is!" he boomed as he walked down the stairs with me draped over his shoulder.

I was wriggling and chuckling in remonstration.

He went straight to the front door, with my body still draped over his big shoulder like a ragdoll. Sy hid most of me behind the door as he opened it and angled his body toward the narrow opening.

My hair hung all around my face, blocking my view.

A man's voice asked for Simon Donovan, and Sy confirmed his identity. His arm moved, presumably signing something, and the door shut.

I squirmed again, trying to get a view of what had been delivered. "Put me down!"

He slapped my ass and I squealed.

He tossed a large manilla envelope onto the coffee table and snickered as he bounded up the stairs, finally tossing me back down on the bed, this time hopping right on top of me to finish where we'd left off.

Later that morning, I took a shower and pondered what to wear to the cookout. After putting together my iced coffee, I took a long, dramatic sip and looked over at him on the couch. Something was different. His posture was too still, too guarded, and it caused my heart to skip a beat.

"You okay? What got delivered?" I took another sip and studied him.

"Nothing, just stupid paperwork from the VA." He reached over and stuffed paperwork back inside the manilla envelope. He folded the top closed and looked up at me. His eyes lit up. "Wow. You look breathtaking." His body remained stiff as he clutched the envelope, his knuckles turning white.

"Thank you, as do you." I walked toward him.

He stood and put the envelope into a drawer before grabbing my hand.

"Nothing important?" I nodded at the drawer he'd

just shut.

"No." He shook his head. He kissed my forehead, grabbed his keys off the side table, and threw them up in the air and caught them. "Shall we?"

"You're nervous." I laughed.

"Am not. How scary can your friends possibly be?"

"You have *no* idea—" I chuckled. "—but don't be surprised if they call you Thor."

I winked before turning and heading to the front door. Today was a big day, and I was going to enjoy it and ensure he enjoyed it, too. All the people I loved, except for my parents who were separated from us only by sheer distance, would be together on the fourth of July.

"Thor?" He called after me as I made my way to the car.

We arrived at Brian and James's around two.

I introduced Sy to Brian and James; Angela and her boyfriend, Rex; Beth; and Nelson and his wife, Shonda. I looked around and saw Jess just coming into the backyard from the corner. She held a huge bowl of pasta salad. I ran to her, grabbed the bowl, and leaned in for a tight hug. I was surprised when she pulled away so quickly.

"Is he here?" She looked over my shoulder. "Oh my God, I see him. Oh, *wow*."

I laughed. "Yeah, he's obnoxiously hot."

"Yeah, he is. Hot damn." Jess beamed.

Brian and James took Sy for a walk around the property, showing off the updates and renovations they'd done on their new home, and asking Sy's opinion on projects they hadn't started yet.

Shonda helped pour sangrias for everyone while we

chatted.

My heart was so full, my breath caught in my throat. I was no longer the outsider, the one everyone felt bad for.

"Does he ever stop ogling you?" Beth chuckled as she scooped a heap of pasta salad onto her plate.

I looked up and caught Sy's eyes from across the yard. James and Brian were still in deep conversation with him about something renovation-related, and he smiled at me before turning back to them. My heart skipped a half-beat, and I looked over at Beth, speechless.

Shaking my head, I laughed and made plates of food for Sy and me.

Brian and James had outdone themselves—they had trays of shrimp, steaks, and grilled vegetables, a large bowl of salad and fresh fruit, a huge clam boil still simmering on the large built-in grill, and several large cakes and pies sitting on top of a long ice tray.

Brian, James, and Sy finished their tour of the yard and joined the rest of us at the table.

"You guys should really consider catering for a living." I waved my hand out to the spread of food. "This is impressive."

Everyone agreed and James beamed. "I told you, Brian! It's my calling!"

James's dream was to be a party-and-event coordinator, and the couple were saving to invest in making his dream a reality.

Sy was engaging and pleasant. He'd undoubtedly already won my friends over.

We talked and joked, Nelson's velvet laughs bellowing louder than the rest. Together with my favorite people, we ate and conversed, laughing at the fun banter as we spoke of our lives.

Shonda and Nelson were considering renewing their vows and wanted to hire James to coordinate the affair.

Jess gave us an update on Steve's deployment status and said she was looking forward to him coming home in a month.

Beth was eyeing a nurse-management position, and we encouraged her to apply for it.

Angela and Rex appeared much closer than I'd realized, their relationship evolving into something much deeper than a one-night stand.

I squinted across the table at Jess, who was turning an alarming shade of green. I hopped up from my seat and took her by the arm.

"Help me inside for a minute." I pulled her into the house through the French doors.

She shot me a thankful look.

As soon as she was out of view, she darted down the hallway and into the bathroom with me following closely behind.

I held her hair back, and she heaved and vomited.

When she was done, she rinsed her mouth and looked at me bashfully. "I guess this is a good sign, right?" She fluffed her hair in the mirror and sighed.

"The higher your hCG levels, the sicker you'll feel."

They had gone through hell trying to get pregnant, so her illness was a good sign. I bit back a smile.

"When's your ultrasound? Maybe it's twins," I jested.

"In a week. I *hope* it's twins! Two for the price of one!"

She giggled and went to the fridge to fetch a bottle

of water. She hadn't announced her pregnancy to anyone, not even Steve, so I grabbed more plates from the cupboard, and she brought more utensils out for the desserts.

Her secret was safe with me, and when we re-joined the others, no one noticed anything out of sorts, except for Sy, who was watching me closely.

I shifted on my feet when I noticed his stare, uneasy again as I had been that morning.

Beth teased that Sy kept ogling me, but she was right, today he couldn't seem to keep his eyes off me.

It sent a shiver up my spine, and the hairs on my neck prickled in response to his atypical alertness.

He knew something and he wasn't telling me.

Sy *looked* happy and relaxed to an unkeen observer, but the mask he wore wasn't fooling me. He was looking at me as if it might be the last time, a look of love and longing. The same look he gave me the day I'd tended to his injured arm.

By nightfall, we had a perfect view of the fireworks from Brian's backyard, and we all sat by the fire pit watching the fizzle and pop of the colorful explosions overhead.

Sy drove us back to his place, and fireworks were still lighting up the sky, shot up in all directions from the shore across the bay.

"This goes on all night. You sure you want to stay here?" He looked over at me watching the sky from his bedroom window.

"I don't mind, the view is incredible."

He pulled me into bed with him and hugged me so tight I gasped. He loosened his grip and rested his head on my chest.

I ran my fingers through his short hair.

"The night we met. At Thames, you remember?" Sy asked.

"Of course."

"The guy fighting with Jeff. Was he familiar to you?"

"No, not at all. Why?"

"Jeff approached him because we'd been seeing him everywhere. When we were working, and then at the bar. Drove through your neighborhood with out-of-state plates a few times. Seemed shady."

"What's going on?" I held my breath and waited for his response, but he never answered, which only validated my concern.

We sat in silence, interrupted only by occasional crackles and booms from the people across the shore setting off their bootleg fireworks. After each whistle and crack, the bedroom lit up in flashing hues of green and pink.

After a long time, Sy finally responded to my question. "The delivery today was orders for a contract job. My last one. I don't think you were being followed. I was."

"But the cemetery, my bedroom? Why didn't you tell me this before?"

"Until I got my orders, I had no idea. Maybe they weren't after you at all. Just looking for me. You should be safe now."

"Why didn't you tell me this morning?"

He was quiet again, holding onto me while I caressed his hair.

My pulse quickened and my stomach roiled with nerves.

I can do this. Jared used to get deployed all the time.

"Do they always follow you before sending out orders?" I asked.

His eyes closed.

I waited for him to speak, but he didn't.

"How long will you be gone?" I pressed. I didn't want to hear the answer, but I needed to prepare myself. When Sy didn't answer I pulled him off me and sat up to face him.

He didn't look at me. He stared out the window with his head on the pillow, and folded his arms across his chest. His face grew cold and impassive as more blue-and-green lights illuminated the room, detonated in the sky outside.

"Sy!" I demanded.

He finally answered, "I'm not coming back."

I hopped out of bed and angled myself at the foot of the bed so he couldn't avoid my face. I wrung my hands and counted the seconds in between the crack of fireworks. More discreet than steps.

"What do you mean? Why?"

Eight, nine, ten, eleven….

Another boom lit up the sky, this one illuminating the room yellow.

Sy sat up and looked at me, his eyes still cold and distant. "My contract."

He laid back down, then adjusted his gaze to look past me and out the window.

Another crackle and boom shook through my chest, and the room illuminated pink.

Fourteen seconds.

"That's it? That's all you'll tell me?"

"The less you know, the safer you'll be."

My heart thundered in my chest, and the blood rushing in my ears rivaled the sound of the fireworks. "Bullshit! You're being an asshole and calling it heroism. I don't need you to protect me, or to save me. I need to know the truth!"

He sat up and swung his legs over the side of the bed. He braced his hands on the mattress, his knuckles white. "You want the truth, Charlotte? Every moment I've spent with you was selfish, dangerous! I could've inadvertently gotten you killed. And the worst part? I knew, *knew* I shouldn't fall in love with you here. But I did, and now I have to break your heart. There was no other way it could've ended, you know."

He dropped his face into his hands.

"Oh really? You knew that, did you? Well, thanks for letting me know, now that you've already sunk your claws into me." My chest heaved with tight breaths. I stomped to the closet and grabbed my duffel bag. I began stuffing my clothes and belongings carelessly inside.

I pulled the bag over my shoulder and hesitated. "Talk to me, Sy. We can figure this out."

"I'm sorry, Charlotte—" He shook his head. "—I can't."

I trucked down the stairs. I looked down to get my keys in hand and froze when I saw Sy standing in front of the door with his arms crossed. We stared at each other. When he didn't speak, I pushed past him and he moved aside, allowing me to open the front door.

I hesitated, waiting to feel him grab my arm and stop me, but as I stepped over the threshold, nothing and no one held me back. I couldn't speak now anyway over the enormous lump in my throat, and I looked back one last time to see Sy still staring at me.

"I love you so much more than you know." He reached out and touched my face. "My undoing."

I crossed my arms. "*I'm* your undoing? Your ruin? No, Simon. You're doing that to yourself."

He looked down. "For you."

"You once promised you'd never hurt me."

He nodded. "And that I'd kill anyone who did."

I waited for him to explain himself, but he didn't. Cryptic as usual.

How could he not explain anything, allow me to leave, and on my way out the door tell me he loved me? That I was his undoing? His chaos? What was the point of that? He'd tell me nothing, and disappear with the morning light. Despite the lump in my throat, I managed to choke out three final words to him.

"Fuck you, Simon."

I threw my duffel bags into the passenger seat and slammed my car door shut. The tears overflowed as I backed out of the driveway faster than I should have, squealing tires as I drove down Bayview Avenue for the last time.

And I didn't look back.

Chapter 9

"Life can only be understood backwards; but it must be lived forwards." –Soren Kierkegaard

To make matters worse, I had the week off, so I had nothing to distract me from the pain that gnawed at my heart relentlessly. The cruel harpy of guilt and grief didn't revel in my wallowing, she was surprisingly quiet. Maybe I'd broken her, too.

It was Sunday morning, and I'd only left my bed to use the washroom and then immediately threw myself back into bed. I couldn't sleep, and I considered calling Brian and relinquishing my vacation time for the week. I ultimately decided against it because I wasn't ready to tell anyone what had happened. How could I? I didn't even know what'd happened.

I was angry at myself. I knew better than to allow myself to be put into a situation that would bring back the pain I'd spent so many years recovering from. I'd allowed my obsession with the concept of entanglement to cloud reality, and it gutted me.

I spent the entire next day in bed, sleeping on and off, leaving only for a trip to the bathroom and for a glass of water. I didn't eat or watch TV, I just let my body absorb the waves of pain as they rolled over me, relieved only when I'd doze off for an hour or two. I checked my phone multiple times, my stomach hollowing out each time I saw no missed calls or messages. I opened my gallery and stared at the one photo I'd taken of me and Sy.

Then, I deleted it.

It was like someone hugged me too hard, causing the thread left behind by the loss of Jared to pull on the invisible scar across my chest, opening it up into a gaping wound again. Fresh grief spouted from my chest, a wound that would never heal if it kept getting re-opened like this.

Then the nightmares started. I didn't scream when I woke from them, I didn't react at all. I accepted my reality, relaxing into old habits. *I'm not scared, I've been here before.* I'd remind myself: *you can't break the broken. I've watched this accident—Jared's final moments, racing down an evergreen-lined road to see a tattooed soldier while dead, the trauma room chaos—for years in my dreams. Perhaps I'll watch it for eternity, a continuous game of death and seek that would never be satisfied. Just a loop of trauma of every type—emotional, physical, spiritual—pervading my sleep and tormenting my mind, and the meaning, never revealed.* And despite knowing I should get out of bed, give my mind a break from the nightmares, I'd once again roll over and will myself to escape my intrusive thoughts and fresh pain through sleep.

It wasn't until Tuesday night that my body began to physically reject spending any additional time in bed. By this point my body was sore and stiff and my head dizzy. I took a shower and pulled myself together physically. I'd had almost 72 hours to wallow, and though the pain hadn't subsided, I was determined not to fall victim to it. One foot in front of the other, I'd move on. Just as I'd always had to do. Whether I liked it or not, whether I kicked or screamed or cried, I couldn't change what now *was.* No one could.

I did laundry and unpacked the duffel bags I'd left thrown on the floor. I pulled the old leather journal from the front pocket and ran my hands across the cover.

Finally, the harpy spoke. *You should never have survived. You should never have thought you could figure out the meaning of your survival through equations and research and denial. Delusions of grandeur, to think you were resuscitated a savant. You were brought back broken, a cruel gift imparted from Death himself.*

I stopped the self-flagellation long enough to realize what I had to do. I had to admit there was no magic, no supernatural meaning, no bigger picture, no making sense of what happened when I died and came back, and when Jared died and didn't. There was nothing to figure out, no code to crack.

I walked over to the slider and slipped out into the darkness, then brought the journal up to my nose, smelling the familiar scent of paper and ink and leather. I tossed it into the fire pit, and used a match to ignite the edge of the police report that hung out from where it bookmarked a page. I watched despondently as the journal went up in flames. I put the netted cover over the burning pyre and slipped quietly back into the house.

I cleaned up the house and made a sandwich. I plugged my phone into the charger and turned on the TV, letting the news drone in the background as I stared out the bay window and into the dark street, eyes locked on nothing in particular.

I finally forced myself to focus on something,

anything, and so I looked at the row of cherry blossoms, now devoid of their bright-pink blooms and filled out with thick, dark green leaves. My gaze wandered to the corner of my driveway that led to my neighbor's house, and there, parked beyond the line of trees, was the black SUV again. My breath fogged the windowpane when I leaned my face toward the glass for a better view.

Devoid of fear, I strolled to my front door and headed down the walkway barefoot, ready to solve the mystery. Was it going to be the scraggly-bearded man from Thames Place in the vehicle? Hadn't he gotten the memo that Sy got his orders? The fact that he was looking for Sy here told me he was no Bond. Was he looking for retribution for the busted lip Sy gave him? Or would I find Jordan waiting for me now that Sy wasn't here to attack him?

I walked straight down my driveway and directly toward the SUV.

To my disappointment, the vehicle roared to life and backed away, disappearing behind my neighbor's large arborvitae bushes. I upped my pace, half-jogging to the end of my driveway, just in time to see the SUV pull a U-turn in the middle of the road and speed away.

I stomped my foot and winced in pain. The next time I came across this SUV, I'd have to be a lot more covert in my approach if I wanted answers. I sauntered back inside, staring out the dark window again with my living room illuminated only by the flickering lights coming from the TV.

Wednesday morning, I headed to my mailbox in my pj's.

Jeff approached me. He nodded a smile-less hello, a clear indication he knew what had happened. "You okay,

Charlotte?" A worried line appeared across his forehead.

"Never better," I replied wryly.

"Do you know where he is?"

"No. He got orders, said he's going on his last job and not coming back."

Jeff rubbed a huge hand across his goatee thoughtfully. "I'm sorry, Charlotte. He doesn't have a choice, you know."

"Yeah, I heard." I swallowed hard. "You knew this would happen, didn't you?"

"I tried to get him to stay away from you, but he got too attached. He didn't want to hurt you."

"And let me guess, you can't tell me why he's not coming back either?"

He looked down and shook his head.

I nodded and gave a half wave as I turned to head back up the walkway.

"Take care of yourself," he called after me.

"Thanks, Jeff."

"If you want to talk…"

His voice faded as I walked into my house and closed the door without looking back.

On Wednesday night, I pulled myself out of bed and texted Jess. I'd forgotten she was in Jamestown visiting her parents. I played it off that I'd reached out because I was in the mood to swim. She gave me permission to use her inground pool while she was away, and though I'd used it as an excuse to justify my text to her, I decided it wasn't a bad idea.

I strode down the dark, empty street to her great blue colonial.

The air hung warm and humid, and fireflies twinkled in the dark like stars.

I reached Jess's yard and headed toward the back. I punched in the passcode, then entered the pool area through the large wrought-iron gates. The motion sensor on the gate triggered the lights on inside the pool, illuminating the water a deep cerulean hue. I threw my backpack on a lounge chair, shimmied out of my shorts, and lifted my shirt over my head.

I jumped into the deep end without hesitation. My body sank to the ten-foot depth. I opened my eyes, and the surface of the water above me sparkled like glass. Tiny bubbles created by my jump danced around my body. I stayed under until my chest burned, lungs hungry for air, and I pushed off of the bottom. *The law of action and reaction,* I thought, as the movement allowed my body to counteract the force of the water and my head to break through the surface.

I stretched my body—sore and stiff from grief and too much sleep—and each time I swam a lap in the dark silence, with only the sound of the water rushing into my ears, my body released the tension that'd been wound around it like a rubber band.

An hour later, I exited the pool, quickly toweling off and, with my towel wrapped around me, I shimmied out of my suit and pulled my sweat-shorts and a white tank-top back on. I pulled my sneakers on and took my hoodie out of my backpack. I zipped my hoodie and stuffed my towel and bathing suit back into my backpack, slinging it over my shoulder as I left the pool area.

I shut the gates, and the lights automatically turned off. I numbly walked through the grass toward the road that intersected my street and could see into some of the houses, illuminated by lights or flickering TVs. I saw a family watching TV in one house, and in another, a couple sat at the dining room table together. In a third house, two teenagers raced by the bay window. I shifted my focus to watching the rocky asphalt disappear beneath my feet instead.

I rounded the corner back onto my street and slowed my pace when I saw the SUV parked at the foot of my driveway again.

This was my chance.

My car was parked outside my house, so whoever was in that damn SUV undoubtedly thought I was inside, not walking the streets late at night.

A rush of adrenaline propelled me across the street. I walked behind the houses that led to mine. I pulled my hood over my head and put the other strap of my backpack over my shoulder. My heart pounded. I needed answers.

When I reached my neighbor's house, I crossed the front yard and stayed hidden in the line of arborvitae bushes. I spotted the license plate on the SUV, a rental, and pulled out my phone. I pushed aside some of the branches and stuck my phone out, taking a photo of the rear of the vehicle. I stayed in place, waiting to see if I'd given away my position.

Confident I was safely hidden, I pushed the bushes aside and made my way through them until I was almost to the driver's side door. The smell of cigarette smoke wafted through the heavy night air, and the hairs on my neck stood on end.

I stepped up to the window and peered in. The interior was illuminated by the in-dash navigation. The SUV was running, but empty. I heard movement behind me and before shock could paralyze me, I whirled around.

"Hello, Charly." He sneered.

His voice was deep and gritty, familiar and foreign at the same time. My estranged father-in-law, Mitch.

He tossed the remnants of his cigarette onto the rocky edge of the street and leered at me as smoke flowed from his nose like a dragon ready to breathe fire and burn me to dust.

"What are *you* doing here?" I fumed.

As far as I was concerned, this man was dead to me. He'd buried Jared before I was discharged from the hospital, and I saw him only once after I'd gone home, at a memorial service for Jared.

Then, he'd disappeared.

No calls, no check-ins. His phone number was disconnected. My parents sought him on base, and he avoided them.

Information that I needed—birth certificate, military documents—were missing. I never knew where Jared had put them. Mysteriously, the insurance policies paid out anyway, signed off by Mitch, and were mailed to my house. All without him ever making contact.

I was cut off, as if I'd never been married to Jared at all.

"We need to talk." He twisted his heavy boot over the cigarette butt on the ground and took another step toward me.

"A little late for that." I backed away. "I have nothing to say to you."

He gripped my elbow.

I pulled back on my arm and cried out.

He tightened his grip and shoved me toward the driver's side of the SUV. "Charly, don't be difficult. Get the fuck in the car. We need to talk."

Mitch was a general in the Army and looked every bit the part. He was built like a grizzly bear and had a deeply lined face that showed just how many years he spent yelling at his subordinates.

My arm ached in his tight grasp, and any attempt to free myself was futile. He was twice my age, but after his twenty-some years in the military, I stood no chance against his strength. "Get your hands off me!" I shouted, roughly attempting to shake off his grip.

He ignored me and opened the door, forcefully pushing me through to the passenger's side without letting up his grip on my arm.

I grabbed the passenger handle in an attempt to dash out of the vehicle, but he pulled away so quickly gravel hit the underside of the SUV, making a sound like hail.

We drove for a few miles, and I stared at him in silence, watching the streetlights cast shadows that danced across his face. He looked like an older version of Jared, with dark eyes, copper skin and black hair, but Mitch had a touch of silver streaking through his hair, something Jared didn't live long enough to get. He had deep creases that trailed down his cheeks like cracked leather through his dark skin.

"Where are we going, Mitch?" My voice sounded annoyed and bored. I had no time for his dramatic nonsense now.

"Charly, how've you been?" he mocked.

"Wonderful, Mitch. Yourself?" Two could play this game.

"Heard you got a new boyfriend?" His tone changed slightly, inquiring.

"No." Goosebumps rose on my arms. I rubbed them.

He let out a short laugh, and looked over at me with

his eyebrows raised. "Sure, you do."

"No, I don't. Where are we going and what do you want?" I contemplated clawing his eyes out and taking over the wheel if he kept up his charade.

He sighed dramatically. "I have some important information for you," he hedged.

My stomach knotted. I thought about Sy—did Mitch know where he was?

We pulled into a motel right off of the highway and he turned off the engine. "I need you to stay calm and clear your head. I know I haven't been father-in-law of the year."

"That's an understatement."

He ignored me and continued, "Hell, I wish Jared had married anyone but *you*. But you were the one he chose, and I have to respect that. And I'm his father and you can't change that. So, come in, let's talk, and I'll take you right back home."

I looked at the motel. The parking lot had several parked cars, and the lobby was lit up with a bored-looking front-desk host reading a magazine behind the desk. I wasn't alone. If he tried to murder me, people would hear. I felt around in the side pocket of the door, and grasped the long, hard plastic of a pen. I slipped it into my pocket, ready to use it as a weapon to his eye if I had to.

Mitch unlocked the doors, and we both exited the SUV.

I followed him to his room and took a seat at the round table inside. It was a typical motel room, with paisley bedspreads and maroon curtains.

Mitch poured himself a coffee from the room's coffeemaker. He took a sip and sat at the table across from me. He narrowed his eyes and put a fisted hand on the table. "I know the last few years have been…hard. Can you imagine how I felt, as a father, seeing my son after he was extracted from the car? They had to cut the roof off to get to him, you know. You were in bad shape, but nowhere near as mangled as him."

I recoiled and fought the image threatening to come into my mind. I still hadn't worked out how he died. My last memories of him showed a moderate head injury, something that shouldn't have killed him. I refused to allow my mind to envision how death consumed someone as strong as Jared, preferring the scenario in my dreams to the grotesque reality of what really must've happened.

Mitch continued, "While you were in surgery, I was watching them work on Jared. I told them not to stop CPR, since I knew he was strong and would pull through. I made some calls to get him airlifted to Boston. People can survive unthinkable things, Charly, but you can't give up on them."

"Eventually, you have to," I whispered.

"No! That's the problem with people like you!" He slammed his fist on the table. "You're *weak*, you don't sacrifice and fight *hard enough*!"

"I fought like hell!"

He ignored me, continuing, "I got him to Boston, the doctors there said there was no hope. He was intubated, transfused, and his core body temp cooled to preserve what was left of his brain cells. I waited and waited, and finally, I gave you the closure you needed. I buried him and let you mourn and grieve and move on."

I listened to a side of the story I'd never heard before. I never knew he ended up in Boston. Mitch had told me he died on impact. "Why did you lie to me, then disappear? I loved Jared, and I wouldn't have given up on him! Losing Jared was one of the worst moments of my life!"

I swallowed hard, remembering Jared with his soft brown eyes and huge white-toothed smile.

"You needed to heal, and telling you gory details wouldn't have helped," he said.

"Bullshit, Mitch. I deserved the truth. I deserved better from you!"

"And, that brings us to why we're here." Mitch nodded slowly.

A deep, hollow chill ran down my arms and settled into my stomach. "Mitch, there's something else you don't know. I was told after—"

"You were pregnant. I know." He shrugged.

"You knew?" I wrapped my arms around my torso, trying to chase away the painful chill.

I hadn't even told Jess that I lost a baby I wasn't even aware I was carrying.

And Mitch blew it off like nothing.

"Despite what you think, I did check on you. You were out of it so you wouldn't remember. You were only a few weeks along. Jared always wanted a son."

Mitch looked away before continuing, "You say you wouldn't have given up? VA docs said he wouldn't make it, and then the Boston doctors said he wouldn't regain brain function. But *I didn't stop there*, Charly. I had him transferred to Maryland to the most elite military hospital in the country that was more than willing to care for him, a veteran who'd served our country selflessly."

My gaze snapped to his. I tried the math in my head. The timeline made no sense. Transfers took time, stabilization of the patient, travel arrangements. I tried to recall dates, the accident, my hospital discharge…

"There's no way…" I whispered, checking my math again.

"I told you, Charly, I need you to listen and keep an open mind." He nodded slowly, satisfied when he saw my panic.

My mind reeled, and I scrambled with numbers: weeks, days, hours. My gaze darted around the table, then to Mitch, and back to my clenched hands. I ran the numbers again, and still they made no sense. The dates didn't align. I pulled the pen from my pocket; it quivered in my unsteady hand. "That paper…"

Mitch snickered and slid the notepad toward me.

I tried to jot down the dates, but the trembling made my handwriting illegible. Frustrated, I slapped the notepad to the floor and tapped my foot.

"Perhaps I could get you a cup of rice to count." Mitch was enjoying the show.

"Fuck you, Mitch!" I snapped upright, the hard chair toppling over behind me.

Something dark appeared in my periphery. I held the edges of the table, knuckles white, and hung my head while gasping for air.

"You are so fragile, Charlotte. *Weak*." Mitch stood.

I slowly turned my head and saw the tall figure standing there, still and motionless. He looked at me with dark eyes and an expressionless face. My heart began drumming so rapidly my vision blurred, and black closed in on my field of vision. Just before losing consciousness, one word escaped my lips as I stared at the figure standing in the room with us…

"Jared…"

Chapter 10

When I regained consciousness, I was lying on the paisley bedspread in the motel room. I studied Jared, and my stomach turned with nausea. He looked different, older by a few years, sure. But more shocking was the scar that trailed from his hairline to his jaw, slightly pulling on the corner of his left eye and lip. The ashen scar juxtaposed against his bronze skin, yet it didn't steal any of his physical allure. I gaped into his dark brown eyes for a long time without saying a word.

This can't be happening, this isn't real. It's a dream. Or I've died. Maybe I drowned in Jess's pool.

My eyes flickered at the click of a lighter, breaking me from my trance.

Mitch lit one of his smokes and went outside.

"Hey, Charly." Jared's voice was smooth and soft, almost a whisper.

He stared at me with his intense eyes.

I tried to sit up, but quickly put my head back on the pillow when the room started spinning again. I rolled my face into the pillow. "Why? How?" I groaned.

He put his hand on my back and my body recoiled away from it. For so many years I longed to feel his touch, now it petrified me.

Dead man's hands.

"It's me, Charly, look at me." Jared coaxed.

"No." I kept my face stuffed into the pillow. "Why,

Jared, why?" I sobbed.

"I wasn't supposed to survive. It took almost two years for me to learn how to eat with a damn spoon. My father figured he'd spare you that."

The mattress released as he stood abruptly.

I rolled over to face him. A small part of me should have wanted to fall into him, embrace him, pretend it had all been a bad dream. But I was used to bad dreams, and this was surely a nightmare. I'd been betrayed, abandoned, left for dead. All the guilt that weighed on me vanished; the witch, the heartless harpy of survivor's guilt disappeared, burned to unrecognizable ashes and carried away in the wind.

She was replaced by fury.

I swiped at the tears that streamed endlessly from my eyes.

"I wanted to call you, once I started to recover. But my father already had a fake death certificate drawn up, a burial, a fucking *memorial service*. He honestly didn't think I'd make it, but he knew if I did, he could get me a new identity so that I could still serve…"

Typical Mitch, always about *serving.* The reason he hadn't wanted me and Jared to get married was because he planned on having his son take the path he did, unmarried and earning up the ranks without a ball and chain holding him back.

I sat up and hugged my knees, pushing my body as far from Jared as I could. My back ached from the hard headboard pressing into my spine. "You had an opportunity to start over and you took it," I accused.

"I did, and I'm sorry." Jared pressed his lips together and furrowed his brow. "I was mourning too, Charly. Knowing you lost our baby and knowing I couldn't just come back to you. My father could get court-martialed for this. He put his whole career on the line when he falsified a death certificate. No one thought I'd recover, not even when I was in Maryland. They held me as a courtesy to my father, kept me on life support longer than—" Jared sighed and looked away. "—longer than they probably should have. But I woke up, against all odds…"

"And he got you a new identity, just like that?" It wasn't a question I expected him to answer. New identities, fake deaths—all small feats for someone as powerful as Mitch.

"He had the death certificate done so he could keep me at the hospital under the radar. It was considered unethical to keep me in limbo like that, with minimal chances of recovery, yet, here I am. And he did it for you, so you could move on without having to hover over me confined to a bed and being kept alive artificially."

"I grieved every day and every night, even in my sleep! How could you let me carry this alone *for four years*?"

I was hyperventilating, unable to draw a strong breath. The anger and pain and confusion hijacked my frontal lobe. I found nothing to count. Nothing to grasp onto for support. My mind began a horrific, slow collapse. I clutched the bedspread and hung my head.

"My father made sure you never went without. The house, the cars, the insurance policies…"

"Do you expect me to thank you? Why are you here now, Jared? Why not just stay John Doe living in God-knows-where? Why did you come back?"

My breathing was audible as I gasped for air, and my heart beat so quickly my lips tingled with numbness.

My vision began tunneling out again.

Jared lifted me under the shoulders, and my feet dragged across the carpet as he hauled me to the bathroom and dropped me into the tub.

"Don't touch me," I whispered in between gasps.

I sat up quickly, and he pressed his hand firmly behind my neck.

"You're having a panic attack. Put your head between your knees. If you can't get yourself under control, I'm going to have to turn on the shower."

I kept my head between my bent knees and took long, slow breaths. Just as I began regaining control, I shrieked.

He'd turned the ice-cold water on overhead.

"Stop! I'm fine!"

He turned the water off and looked down at me in the tub.

I lifted my soaked sweatshirt over my head and tossed it aside.

Jared cocked his head to the side and smiled.

Remembering I was braless, I quickly crossed my arms over my white tank top, my ample chest visible through the wet top. I scowled at him.

"To answer your question, I'm here now because you put yourself in danger." He was sharp and condescending.

"Oh? How so?" I gritted my teeth.

"Well, the first guy you decided to date after me is one of the most dangerous people you could've possibly taken up with. He's a murderer, Charly, involved with a black-op private military contract that we've been trying to bust for a few years."

I stared at him wide-eyed. I needed him to tell me

more, to tell me everything he knew about Sy. I tried to provoke him. "He didn't seem murderous to me, Jared."

He let out a short laugh. "Of course *you* didn't notice anything. How is it, you suppose, he has all that money? What do you think *Simon the Silencer Donovan* does as a side job?"

Jared paced outside the bathroom slowly, clenching and unclenching his fists.

Sy was a sniper in the Marines. I suspected his contract job was as a hitman, but figured it was for higher-up adversaries. Now I questioned who he was hired to kill off this time. I suppressed a shiver and lifted myself out of the tub.

Jared stopped and held the doorjamb, hands braced on either side. "Charly, we have a history. I know I can't fix the past, but now that I've risked everything, maybe we could change the future. I know you're hurt and angry, but I need you to consider this, I came back to protect you."

"Protect me? The damage is done. There is nothing left to protect, Jared."

"I never stopped, for one minute, loving you, Charly."

I stalked toward him and shoved him.

He lost his grip on the doorjamb and stumbled back. He glared at me, but said nothing.

"You don't get to say things like that after what you did," I hissed.

He reached for my shoulder, and I leaned away from him. I walked back to the main room and sat on the edge of the bed, staring off into space. What decisions in my life had brought me here?

"I can't force you to believe me. But here's our

offer: come to Virginia with us. My father and I can keep you safe. Your choice."

"So, if I'd never met Sy, you wouldn't have come back for me?"

"Charly, I've been trying to come back for you every day since I learned how to say your name again. You just made a dumb enough decision that gave me an excuse to risk it all."

Mitch returned to the room, and Jared stopped speaking.

His father sat back at the round table, and I could hear the tip of his pen scrawling a note onto a piece of paper.

"If you try to call anyone, or do anything stupid, we'll disappear again, and people will think you're crazy. No one knows he's alive except you and me," Mitch said.

I looked over at Jared. "I want to go home."

"You have a lot to think about. I'm only here until tomorrow, and I need you to decide by then. If you choose to come with me to Virginia, to start over, you can have anything you want. You won't even have to work anymore. If you choose to stay here, you'll never see me again, and I won't be able to protect you from that maniac."

"What's your name now?" I asked.

"You'll know everything you need to know once we're in Virginia. I can't stay here. If someone sees me, recognizes me…"

"And what about my friends? My parents? What would I tell them?"

"You're moving to Virginia with your boyfriend." He looked at me pointedly.

I blanched. He wanted me to give up everything in my life, leave everyone behind to be with him and his new identity? Then I realized I'd done this for him once before. It was why I lived in Rhode Island, because I'd married him.

"I want to go home, now."

Mitch rose from his seat. "Let's go, Charly, I'll take you home."

I didn't speak while Mitch drove, his face a stoic mask. Salty tears silently rolled down my cheeks, I wiped them away with the back of my hands. When we pulled into my driveway, he handed me a piece of paper.

"This is the number you call when you make your decision. It's a throwaway phone, and after tomorrow, we're gone. There will be no way to contact us."

I nodded and took the paper, then I gripped the door handle.

"And Charly, don't try anything senseless. We're always watching. And I don't just mean Jared and I."

"You've just got everyone in your back pocket, don't you?" I snapped.

"People are so very easily bought, aren't they?" His smile dripped with arrogance.

I exited the SUV. I struggled to get my key into the front lock with shaking hands. Once inside, I tried to turn on the living room light and let out a groan when I realized the power was out. I dropped my backpack on the hardwood with a loud thud and walked to my bedroom, feeling my way down the hall. I flopped onto my bed in the dark.

A crushing weight was suddenly on top of me, and my mouth was covered by a large hand. I couldn't squirm or struggle. Between the weight on top of me and the hand covering my mouth, the air was being crushed from my lungs. Then, hot breath fanned near my ear and a calm, familiar voice spoke.

"Please, I need you to trust me, don't say a word," Sy whispered.

I grabbed onto his forearms and nodded.

He slowly released his hand from my mouth and ran his fingers gently down my cheek. He brought his finger to his lips to indicate staying silent.

Sy pulled me from the bed and walked quickly down the hallway toward the living room.

The dark outline of the gun tucked into his waistband caught my eyes as they began adjusting to the darkness around us.

He grabbed my backpack and handed it to me, pointing at it to indicate I needed to pack.

I unzipped it and let my wet towel and bathing suit spill onto the floor. I didn't need to look to know he was hovering, in his characteristic silent way, following my every move as I walked back to my bedroom and stuffed whatever clothes I could feel inside the dark drawers of my bureau. I moved to the bathroom where I threw my bag of toiletries into the backpack.

I walked back into the living room, feeling my way around by putting my hands in front of me in the darkness, until his hand grasped mine again.

He pulled me outside through the back slider and quietly shut it behind us. The crickets hummed harmoniously around us, and he didn't look at me or say a word as we crept through the backyard and into the woods beyond.

I should've been more afraid than I was. Was this how I was going to die? Or did he come back for me?

Stupid, stupid, stupid, I chided the naïve voice in my head crooning to follow him, that he wasn't here to cause me harm.

We stepped over the thick briars, and my eye was drawn to the gun in his waistband, well within my reach. Running on pure adrenaline-fueled instinct, I overrode my fear and grabbed the pistol from him. The gun in my shaking hands didn't give me the feeling of power or relief I thought it would. But I was either being led to my death or to the answers I so desperately needed, so when he looked at me with frustration, I kept the gun pointed directly at him, determined to get answers and not a bullet to the skull. "Don't move," I ordered.

He let out an impatient sigh and, in a motion so swift I almost couldn't recall how it happened, the gun was back in his possession. I froze in place when I realized how stupid a move that had been.

He pulled back on the slide of the gun, piercing the quiet around us with the quick sound of metal across metal. He looked up from the gun, and in another quick motion turned it so he was holding the barrel. He waved the handle of the gun toward me. "Now it's loaded. Here, take it, if it makes you feel better," he said in a low voice.

I grabbed the gun, confused but slightly reassured that he didn't intend on blowing my brains out. Not yet, at least.

"I'm not the bad guy, Charlotte." He shook his head. "Now, where's your phone?"

I pulled it out of my pocket with my free hand, and before I could hand it over, he grabbed it and launched it toward my backyard. I looked at him with wide eyes, waiting for him to speak, but he grabbed my hand and kept pulling me through the trees.

His face was somber, blue eyes focused on getting us through the trees to the other side.

I stumbled when my foot got caught on the wiry briars, but Sy caught me before I could fall out onto the street.

He pulled keys from his pocket, and we walked along the edge of the road to a classic Firebird parked in the grass just off the shoulder.

I climbed into the passenger seat, and Sy pulled away so quickly I gripped the edge of my seat.

"Do you have anything electronic? A smartwatch, anything?"

He spoke quietly, and I struggled to hear him over the rev of the engine as he increased his speed.

"No." I looked over at him nervously, and then watched the needle on the speedometer reach eighty-five.

Sy looked over at me. "I know you have a lot of questions, and I'm going to do my best to answer them. You were being watched, but by now, I'm sure you already know that."

"How did you know?"

"I was still getting your camera notifications. I saw you the other night, trying to approach the SUV, and then you did it again tonight, only this time you succeeded." He shook his head. "Charlotte, why would you do that?"

"I wanted answers. I was tired of feeling like I was going crazy."

"What I did a few days ago…I was protecting you," he said. "I thought if it was me they wanted, you'd be safe if I left."

I shook my head. There was no where I was safe. Not now, anyway.

He took a deep breath in. "But even after getting my orders, checking in and confirming I was going and not seeing you anymore, it didn't make sense that you were still being watched. Jeff and I were right. Jay and Joel were wrong. The stalking wasn't about me and my orders, especially after we realized you had no idea about General Cardoza and Jared."

"What the hell did you just say?" My hand involuntarily tightened around the gun. I was about to beat him savagely, maybe even pistol-whip him. That was a thing, right? The only thing that stopped me was the knowledge that Sy had put one in the chamber. I didn't want to blow my own brains out if the gun misfired.

"You *knew* Jared was alive this whole time?" I shouted.

"I just found out tonight. For a while we thought it was Adam Cardoza, his brother. We didn't know your level of involvement in this initially, which is why I didn't say anything to you."

"Level of involvement?! You can't be serious!" I let out an angry wail. "And Jared didn't have any brothers!"

"Well, faking a death is a pretty intense feat, and we didn't know who was involved, so we covered all our bases. Turns out, he *did* have a brother, a few years younger than him. The contract I got into—the Quantym program—has gotten more corrupt, starting about four years ago."

Four years ago, after Jared supposedly died.

"They're trying to turn it from a research program into a for-profit endeavor. Like big pharma, lots of money to be made. General Mitchell Cardoza is the liaison between Quantym and the Army, giving them access to the records and equipment they need. And his right-hand man is—"

"Sergeant Jared *fucking* Cardoza," I said quietly.

"Joel did some digging for us. Jared's half-brother, Adam, went missing a few years back, and that's the identity Jared assumed. The accident changed the way he looks just enough that most assume he just resembles his deceased brother. And, being the general's surviving son, for all intents and purposes, it's perfectly kosher to everyone that they work together."

"Where is the real Adam?"

"Good question. He was a transient, hooked on drugs. Easy enough to pay him off or make him disappear, I suppose."

"Jared never mentioned having a brother."

"Jared never mentioned a lot of things, Charlotte. I'm sorry."

"So now that he's Adam, and back in action with Mitch, they want to take over Quantym?"

"General Cardoza has a lot of connections on the inside. We assume when he thought Jared was going to die, he involved himself with the program to ensure…he was okay on the other side. But when Jared survived, the stars aligned for them, and the opportunity to take over the most powerful program on Earth was right in their lap."

"You've completely lost me, Sy. None of this makes sense, what do you mean *on the other side*?"

"On the Periphery."

"Glad *that's* all cleared up!" I rolled my eyes.

"You're not going to believe me, but I'm going to try my best to explain. You and I have talked a lot about theories that intrigue us. What if I told you that I knew for certain some of them weren't theories but proven facts?"

I crossed my arms defiantly. I'd seen enough of the unbelievable for one night.

"What if I told you that we didn't get just one chance, that there are actually more chances for us to live out our lives if they get cut short?"

I looked over at him.

"It's real, Charlotte. The multiverse exists. All the different choices, decisions…"

I shook my head and dropped my face into my hands. I didn't believe him. "What's *your* motive in all of this, and what do Mitch and Jared want from me*?"* I wailed.

"What did they tell you they wanted from you?"

"To protect me from *you,*" I answered.

Sy punched the steering wheel. "Don't believe them, Charlotte! Don't believe them!"

I crossed my arms.

"Look at me, please. You really want to know the motive?" he asked.

"Yes, I want to know the motive! Yours and theirs!"

He glanced at me. *"You're* the motive, Charlotte. You're in danger. I have to get you out of here."

"Me? What the hell do I have to do with any of this?"

"You have an ability that will be useful to them."

"You can't be serious." I shook my head.

Sy's silently watched the road ahead of him, his eyes hardening.

"Where are we going?" Panic started tingling the back of my neck.

Before he could answer, the car was bouncing over

the familiar dirt road, swerving to avoid the boulders and the branches clacking against the windshield as we made our way deep into the forest.

"Joel and the guys have a trailer set up out here. It's where they've been surveying Quantym from a distance."

"Are you a hit man?" I asked pointedly.

Sy looked at me and let out a tight laugh. "I was a sniper in the Marines, and I did sign on to eliminate some targets, but not *for* Quantym, for international security. I told you, I'm not the bad guy, Charlotte."

"Let me guess, Jared is?"

"And his father, yes."

"Then tell me, Sy, what *do* you do in the program? Why is this life or death, why can't you just get out?"

"There is no way out for me. This program"—he shook his head—"is beyond anything you'll easily believe. I knew after a few years, I'd likely be giving up my life. People disappear all the time when their job is done, and the classified intel they have, erased."

"You signed on knowing that?"

"I didn't want to die in a long-term care facility, draining my family of their time and money. So, I signed and I got what I wanted—to live a few more years without limits, and to set my family up financially."

"So that's it, then? You're just going to let them kill you?"

"I was selfish, I let my desire to be with you override what I knew could only end in pain. For that, I'm sorry. But know that everything I did and am about to do is because I love you, Charlotte."

"You weren't with me," I muttered. "You were investigating me."

"Initially, yes—" He let out a deep grumble. "—but it's more complicated than that."

"Ha! And here I thought you really cared." I shook my head in disgust.

"It wasn't just the investigation, don't you see? We're connected, Charlotte. I've cared about you since before we even met here! And the last few days without you, they were torture!" His grip tightened on the steering wheel.

I gasped and looked over at him. "*Here*?"

The car tires started grinding as they drove over gravel.

We stopped in front of a large trailer overgrown with ivy. Roof antennae rivaled the height of the trees.

Sy killed the ignition and looked over at me.

I stared at the trailer in front of us, my mind reeling with the implications of his last statement.

"Come in with me, and maybe Joel can explain it better…"

"Joel?"

"Desperate times." He shrugged.

"I want to hear it from you first. What is your job at Quantym? What do they pay you to do?" I spoke slowly, deliberately.

"I was resuscitated and found to have an…ability." He barked out a laugh. "I can jump to the Periphery. I can retain my memories when I go on to the other side."

"Come again?" I was starting to consider the very real possibility that the word salad he just spewed indicated he'd had a stroke, likely within the last hour or so. I considered getting him medical help but decided to let him continue first.

"I always knew I had a pretty good aptitude for

holding onto consciousness. I'm a lucid dreamer. I can remember every detail of the day of the 'copter crash, despite the blood loss. When I woke from the coma, I told the neuro doc what I saw while I was supposedly dead, and then later comatose. What I saw on the other side."

"What did you see?" I was confounded. We'd both talked of our near-death experiences *but he never told me about what he saw on the other side.*

"My life continued where it'd left off. I fell into a parallel life. We were still in the helicopter; the crash didn't happen… I was the same age, looked the same, minus the scar. The crash never occurred *there* but I could *see* it vividly, *remember it* because it happened *here*. It was like a light switch flicked, and instead of being locked inside my body while my heart stopped here, I was just continuing on there…me and Jeff, Michaels, and Thompson—our comrade and the pilot who got killed—still alive and flying back to base." He drew a deep breath.

"Because I could see the crash in my mind, I assumed it was a premonition. I started freaking out, telling the pilot to land, telling Jeff and the guys we were about to be ambushed. They didn't know what was happening to me, and they didn't believe me. I ended up jumping from the helicopter as we were descending, intent on taking out the terrorists before they shot down our men. I got hurt and broke my back, but not the same way I did *here*. Difference is, *there*, there weren't terrorists waiting, *there* I was taken into surgery immediately. Recovered much quicker.

"I tried to figure out what was going on, but as the days went by, my memories of this life were fading, being replaced by the memories of…well, I guess you could say the other life I fell into. I liken it to the concept of reincarnation, except not starting over from birth, starting over at the same age, living alongside the same people who are also living out their alternate realities."

I looked at him, perplexed.

"Shortly after telling this revelation to the doctor," Sy continued, "I was visited by the reps from Quantym who heard I had the ability to jump and remember. So, to answer your question, I get paid to jump into the alterna-life, the parallel, known as the Periphery, gather or plant information, sometimes eliminating assigned targets, and then I come back here. They call people with my ability *jumpers*."

"Joel didn't want you to sign, but now he's helping you?"

"Yeah, Joel briefed me on how clandestine these contracts could be way back when. I wasn't in a place where I could hear what he was trying to tell me initially. I was ready to sign, until my commanding officer came to visit me. He had a better proposal. I'd still need to sign, but I'd actually be working as an undercover agent for the government to eliminate some really lethal jumpers and to collect enough intelligence to bring the whole program down. I never told Joel, until recently, that I wasn't actually signed into Quantym per se."

"And you *eliminate* some people who jump over?"

"Only the worst of the worst, the ones who're jumping to evade justice." Sy looked down and put his hand in mine, interlacing our fingers. "I'm sorry I didn't tell you sooner."

I let out a huff as I slowly digested the information. "It's impossible," I whispered unconvincingly. It sounded ludicrous, but it made perfect sense. More than one chance to live, to choose, to be judged on.

The multiverse was real.

"How do you get to the other side and back without dying?"

"They make the body uninhabitable for consciousness. They stop my heart, then resuscitate me into a deep coma. The cooling protocol preserves my brain while I'm on the other side and maintains bradycardia. They basically trick my brain into thinking I'm dead, allowing my consciousness to relocate to my alternate—parallel—life. Kind of like what happened when I was in the real coma after the crash."

I squeezed my eyes shut, recalling the few moments I was dead and what I'd seen—the evergreen-lined road. Racing to see *Simon*.

Sy leaned in, and trailed his thumb along my cheek while staring deep into my eyes. "Remember when you said you wished there was a window you could peer through to see the outcome had you made different decisions?"

I nodded and smiled at the memory of that perfect night and the morning that followed.

"This program lets you peek through that window."

Chapter 11

"The universe is under no obligation to make sense to you." –Neil deGrasse Tyson

I followed Sy into the trailer, and it was like I'd fallen into an alternate universe.

Jay, wearing a headset, was seated at a computer with three huge monitors.

Max stood behind Jay, watching him clack away at the keyboard at lightning speed.

Satellite images of a large base appeared on the screen to the left, and the military ID photos of Mitch and Jared appeared on the screens to the right. On the center monitor, the screen was split into several small squares streaming the live feed of the cameras at my house.

Joel motioned for us to sit at the long wooden table in the center of the room.

I took a seat between Joel and Jeff.

Sy and a gray-haired gentleman sat across from us.

Joel nodded in my direction, then in the direction of the older gentleman. "This is Dr. Gustav. He's been researching the science behind the program for over twenty years. He can answer a lot of your questions."

I looked across the table at Dr. Gustav, a familiar face with bushy gray eyebrows and a thick mustache to match. He was the neurologist who managed my case after the accident.

"Ms. Cardoza." He greeted me with a thick accent.

My blood turned to ice. "I know you." I looked at him accusingly. "And please, call me Charlotte."

"Glad to see you look well."

"I'll be better when you explain what the hell is going on."

Dr. Gustav sighed and removed his glasses, cleaning the lenses with a handkerchief. "My colleagues and I are not the first group of physicians to study near-death experiences and the potential alterna, or, parallel, life. We should've anticipated that it'd be abused by those who wanted to profit off it, but initially we were just eager to prove its existence." He put his glasses back on and looked straight at me.

"How could you possibly prove an abstract concept like that?" I grumbled.

"We were able to finally prove the theory hypothesized by some of the greatest minds in history through multiple rounds of blind jumps. We had multiple jumpers collect information from the other side. When they all came back with the same story and same observations, the evidence was undeniable. We did this many times, over many years. Each time, the information they returned with was the same, proving the existence of a parallel life. A place, now known as the Periphery, that was tangible, discoverable, *inhabited*."

I was rendered speechless. People jumping to the other side and coming back with the same information, proving that there was *another side, another place to exist after clinical death.*

Dr. Gustav continued, "You can imagine our dismay when we learned that this knowledge was being used to build the Organized Research Association at Quantym, known as ORA. I didn't like the direction Quantym was heading in. I didn't want to allow any more jumper recruits until I could investigate the allegations of unethical research further."

"It got too big for you," I guessed.

"Yes, and no. I stand by the research we worked tirelessly to compile over so many years. But the program has taken on a life of its own, and it's gotten too big, too profitable, too powerful, to be of any benefit now."

Joel rested his elbows on the table. "The ultimate paradox. Big pharma makes money to keep you alive *here*, and Quantym makes money finding out if you'd rather die and live *there*."

"This is bad, really bad. The implications of this…" I looked away.

"We were blinded by our drive to prove the theory, not realizing how many people in power would work to abuse this knowledge for profit," Dr. Gustav said defensively.

Sy finally spoke. "Profiting isn't the worst part. The Periphery is the perfect getaway, an escape, a second chance for corrupt politicians or elitist criminals who unleash hell *here*, and escape to *there*. They're turning our world into a social and science experiment, then jumping over to escape it."

My head drooped. "And that's why you have to chase people across the universe to eliminate them?"

"It's more than that, Charlotte. What Sy did, well *does*, worked for a time, but now it's like trying to patch a dam with duct tape. All hell is about to break loose if we don't bring the whole thing down." Jeff puffed out a breath and shook his head.

"All hell has already broken loose, if the past few years are any indication of what this does to society," Jay interjected.

My mind raced, recalling major events, humanitarian and political, that'd plagued society increasingly over the past several years. I started counting the heavy beats of my heart. "Do you have a plan?"

Sy looked at me through his lashes. "The plan hasn't changed. I report to my post in twenty-four hours. Complete this last mission, and before they can unplug me, I take out the servers on the other side. Eliminate all traces of the protocols, the database of jumpers."

"And while he does that, I'll be wiping the servers here. Took me months to crack into their server, but I'm in like Flynn." Jay leaned back proudly in his chair and folded his hands behind his head.

My head snapped up. "Unplug you?"

The room fell silent. Jeff and Sy locked eyes. Max and Jay looked down. Dr. Gustav rubbed a hand across his face.

"They'll call it an accident, like the others, that his body just couldn't handle the protocol." Jeff shook his head. "Amazing how they always seem to lose jumpers on their last mission."

"You can't go, Sy! We can report it, tell someone higher up the chain of command. Joel, you must know who we can report this to?"

"There're very few on our side in this, Charlotte." Joel shrugged. "Money talks, and our desire to preserve humanity isn't quite as lucrative. I have a small team, and Sy's commanding officer has a squad of troops we can trust, who will help us the day Sy is supposed to be unplugged."

"You can't just let him die!" I hugged my chest.

Jay swiveled around in his seat to face us. "We're not agreeing to let him die, Charl. He's our brother. Most all of the jumpers that will be sedated and intubated that day are innocents. We're going to do our best to get everyone out alive. But because we're going in all at once, it's a numbers game, a race against time to get to everyone before—"

Joel shook his head and interrupted Jay. "We're *hoping* we can get to him in time when we raid the facility. But there are no guarantees. He's going to be under deep sedation and intubated. Dr. Gustav is going to be scanning the medical data to ensure Jay and Max wiped the servers of everything of significance on this side."

"You don't have to go, Sy…" I reached out and brushed my fingers over the top of his hand.

"Yes, I do. This is what I signed up for. It's a short-term solution to a bigger problem, but a solution nonetheless."

"Why you? You're willing to give your life to save the world?" I asked.

"Why not me? I was a sniper, so I have a lot of blood on my hands." He shrugged.

"You're looking for redemption? You've done your part, and you nearly gave your life in the process."

"Not redemption. Purpose."

Dr. Gustav spoke, and I turned to face him.

"We aren't the first in history to do what we're about to do. Since ancient Egyptian times, knowledge of the Periphery has been acquired and subsequently destroyed once humans realized how perilous it could be. The burning of the scrolls in the library of Alexandria is hypothesized to be one of the many times in history we humans have attempted to erase any trace of the discovery of peripheral lives. It is the *only* way." He bowed his head.

"I can jump, so send me! I told you what I saw when I died, and you told me it was a hallucination from medications and trauma. Why didn't you tell me?" I fisted my hands.

"Charlotte, I have to do this." Sy reached for my hand.

Dr. Gustav spoke. "Charlotte, you have to understand, not everyone who has a near-death experience is a jumper. It's an anomaly, a fluke. Being a jumper makes you a target. That's why we're here today. You discounted your experience—with my help, admittedly—but you wrote of it in vast detail, didn't you?"

"My journal? That's the motive for Jared coming back around? My journal documents what I saw, for a flicker during death. How can he be so certain that I can actually do what Sy does?"

Sy shifted uncomfortably in his seat and then stood. He paced nervously and rubbed his hand over his short hair.

Jay and Max both turned to face me.

Every eye in the room was on me when Dr. Gustav clarified.

"You can jump. And your gift—" Dr. Gustav cleared his throat. "—your understanding of mathematics and physics. That's another phenomenon known as *acquirement.* You brought back a piece of your other self. Apparently, on the Periphery, you understand physics, and it's an important part of you."

I remembered Sy's face after reading my journal. It was at that moment he'd figured it all out. The motive, the mission. The stalker wasn't focused on *him,* they were after *me.*

Joel leaned in again. "After General Cardoza and his son began directing the ORA program at Quantym, they decided to revamp the whole system to maximize profits. Their goal is to eliminate all the current jumpers and start over with their own. Jumpers who will work for free."

"Who would do that?" I asked.

"Jumpers are rare, and they're sought over the whole Earth. Survivors of death who retain their memory when on the other side. But they're expensive, and that cuts into the profit Quantym turns. So, they're obtaining their jumpers on the black market. They're being trafficked, forced to undergo the missions for free," Joel answered.

"This is the reason we think General Cardoza came back for you. He was with you in the hospital when you spoke of your visions. He disappeared and built the program into the monster that it is today, with his son. They watched you, looked for the signs, and probably read your journal and learned of your value." Joel crossed his large arms over his chest and stared at me.

"Charlotte, I have to go. Everyone I love is at risk if I don't. But I won't go until we have a plan to keep you safe. That's why you're here." Sy looked over at Jeff.

"Linda and I have a vacation home in Maine." Jeff spoke gently, as if he knew his suggestion was going to be met with my stiff rebuttal. "She'll go with you. You can take as much time as you need there until the dust settles."

I shook my head. *No way. Not happening. I'm not running. I don't run. I* won't *run.*

"Jared and Mitch have been tailing you for a while. What do you think is going to happen if you stick around?" Jeff asked.

I shrugged. A plan was sewing itself together in my brain, I just needed a few minutes to gather my thoughts into coherent sentences. To make them listen, no, *hear* what I had to say.

I held my hand up and stared at the knotty grains of the wood table. "Wait. I have an idea." I looked up, and the room went silent.

"Hear me out. What if you had someone on the inside? Not just Sy or Joel's team or you guys with the fancy equipment?" I nodded at Max and Jay.

Jay smirked.

I continued. "What if you had someone close to the Cardozas, who could potentially gain access to the base, to Quantym? Someone who knew her way, very well, I might add, around an ICU and the sedation, cooling, and extubation protocols…"

"No." Sy shook his head vehemently.

I ignored him. "Someone who could ensure Sy woke up safely *before* the shit hit the fan."

"I'm deploying to Virginia; I'll be on the same base as you and the Cardozas…" Joel considered my proposal.

"And Jared will be preoccupied, with you there," Jay said.

"A diversion and someone close to the Cardozas." Jeff hummed.

"No!" Sy's temples pulsed, and his jaw tightened. His hands balled into fists, and the veins in his arms protruded.

"It's our only weakness, Sy, and you know it! We don't know their next move until they've uploaded files, protocols. We can't account for last-minute decisions. With her there, we'll know their plans, be able to anticipate their next move. *Save* you and the others!" Joel bellowed.

"We won't let anything happen to her." Jeff looked at Sy, waiting for a response.

The room fell silent. We all stared at Sy.

"When I get to Virginia, I have to sit in an isolation tank learning the information they want me to bring to and retrieve from the Periphery, in addition to the location of the servers that Max and Jay are hacking into and including in the coding. I can't do it, I won't be able to focus if—"

"If what, Sy? If I'm involved?" I asked incredulously.

"No, if I think you're in danger," he growled.

"You asked me to trust you less than an hour ago, despite breaking into my house and abducting me with a gun stuffed into your jeans. Maybe you could return the favor now, and trust *me?*"

"I trust *you*. I don't trust the Cardozas."

I waved my hand across the table, motioning to everyone gathered around. "I'm not afraid of them," I lied. "I've known them longer than all of you."

"She'll know how to stop the anesthesia and paralytics once you're under, and the rest of the team can focus on waking the others. We'll be cutting it close, but if she can wake you up before we infiltrate—" Dr. Gustav took a shuddering breath. "—and before they can unplug you, it's another soldier fighting for the cause."

Gustav supported my plan. I nodded at him gratefully.

"NO!"

Sy sprang out of his chair, and I jumped in response.

"She has to play along with Cardoza," Joel started. "If she goes with him, you know she'll be safe for a short time, and they'll think you're making good on your contract. It's the only way to stop them from coming for her. Charlotte's plan is safer for *both* of you."

Sy kicked his metal chair across the room, making us all recoil from the deafening clang.

"No! This isn't what we agreed on! I wanted you to help *her*, not *me*!" He stormed outside into the rain.

I exchanged a long, meaningful look with Joel. "You'll be in Virginia, on the same base?"

"Yes." Joel scrawled his number on a paper and handed it to me. "Don't call me unless it's an emergency. I will find you and contact you once you're in Virginia."

I stuffed the paper into my pocket and nodded at Joel.

"Quantym operates below the hospital on base. You won't have access without Jared, or his badge." Dr. Gustav stood, walked over to me, and took my hand. "If there were ever a reason to risk your life again, this is it. Don't trust the Cardozas…tell them nothing."

I glanced around the room at Jay, Max, Jeff, and Dr. Gustav.

They each nodded in response to my unspoken words.

Dr. Gustav gave my hand a squeeze.

I squared my shoulders, and then headed out the door to say goodbye to Sy.

The metal door of the trailer slammed behind me.

Sy's back was turned when I got to him, and he was staring into the black forest, raindrops darkening circles where they fell upon his broad back.

I touched his arm.

He swung around and crushed me against his chest. He leaned down and put his face into my hair. "There're other ways," he grumbled. "The motive… is just a theory. If you can jump, you did it for a minute, at best."

"Nothing about my accident or nightmares or savant syndrome made sense until now. I jumped, and you know it. I *remember.*"

"I shouldn't have brought you here." Sy spoke into my hair again. "If things go wrong, they'll think nothing of killing all of us, Charlotte. If I just finish my contract, like I signed up for, I'm the only one who will be eliminated."

"Do you really think Mitch and Jared will just let me walk away now that I know Jared's not dead?" I rested my hands on his chest.

"I'll have Joel get you into a protection program…" He pulled in a deep breath.

"Okay, yeah"—I nodded in reluctant agreement—"that's what Joel said in there." I tipped my head toward the trailer. "He gave me his number. I'll reach out to him when I'm ready to leave the state. I have to make arrangements, pull together a believable story for my family and friends."

"Do it right away, Charlotte. I'll have my brothers watch your place to keep you safe. Don't tell a soul where you're going. The Cardozas won't easily give up trying to find you."

Joel came out and stalked over to his brother.

I backed away.

He shoved Sy. *"I told you not to sign up for this shit!"*

The statement hung in the air like an ominous raincloud.

Sy swung and landed a punch across Joel's jaw.

Joel staggered, quickly steadied himself, and then they stared at each other for a long minute.

"If I don't come back, you will look out for her?" Sy's chest heaved with rough breaths.

Joel spit blood onto the ground and wiped his face. "You have my word." He stomped back inside.

Chapter 12

The wet ground perfumed the air around us with the earthy smell of the forest. I stood staring at Sy, who still had Joel's blood spattered across his knuckles.

Sy wrung his hand. "Come with me." He unlocked the doors, and we sat in the car to escape the rain.

In the distance, thunder rumbled.

"I came for you tonight to keep you safe." He looked out the window deep in thought before turning back to me.

"And if we hadn't met? You'd still be going on this mission, and Jared would've still come back for me. I'd be in more danger *without* you."

"Maybe, maybe not. Where's your bag?"

I reached into the back and pulled out my overstuffed backpack, sad at the realization that I'd no longer need it tonight.

Sy reached into his glove compartment and pulled out a small black case that held a pistol. He went over how to load and unload it, where the safety was, how to handle and store it. His shoulders loosened when he learned I'd been to the shooting range before.

I wasn't a fan, but guns weren't foreign to me. Jared had taught me a thing or two years back. I didn't tell Sy that, but I was sure he assumed as much.

Sy unzipped my bag and put the gun case at the bottom.

Once he was satisfied that I had some small token to keep me safe, he reached out for me, and I fell into his arms.

I kept my head buried into his shoulder as I thought about *my* strange ability. My sudden obsession and ability to understand physics that I brought back with me from the Periphery. A quirky souvenir. I brought back the ability to comprehend a difficult science, and I couldn't help but wonder what I was doing on *the other side* that gave me such knowledge.

"Sy, when you go to the other side, you said you inherit memories of that life while you're there, while retaining the memories of this life, right?"

Sy looked at me uneasily. "Yeah, I have to focus hard on not letting the new memories overtake me. I hold on tightly to the memories of this life…"

"What is your life like over there, on the Periphery? I mean, are you married or still in the service?"

"I'm still in the service." He sighed and furrowed his brow. "I fight the urge to think, to remember. I'm afraid if I do, it'll erase the memories I've carried over with me. Sometimes, when I cross over, after they've put me under, I wake up in a bed, in a house I've never seen before, and I'm alone. Once, I crossed over, and I was driving on a base in Virginia. The only time my life seemed completely parallel was the first time, after the accident, when I was still in the helicopter with the guys, with no crash."

"But you must know *something* about your other life?" I couldn't comprehend waking up in a completely different life and deviating from whatever you were doing to complete a mission from *this* life.

"Charlotte, I go over, I go straight to the place or

person they want me to, and I get or give the information they want. It's mostly research and observation, finding out where someone lives, what their job is, what social status and financial status they have, whether a certain scandal or massive event has happened there. Sometimes I have to plant information, and other times, I have to take out a certain target."

He was avoiding my question. He was giving me so much information, and dodging the very part I asked about. "Sy—" I persisted.

"When I come back, when they wake me, it's surreal. There are cameras and audio recording, doctors and nurses and the client watching me wake from this coma from behind a mirrored wall. Waking up isn't pretty, it's painful mentally and physically. They get the information from me quickly because just as my memories of this life fade while I'm there, they fade even faster once I return. Kind of like a dream that you can recall in the morning, but by evening, if you try to retell it, you only remember bits and pieces."

"Have you seen me on the other side?"

An emotion I couldn't place flickered across his face for an instant.

"Yeah."

A rush of electricity surged through me. *The kinetic familiarity. The entanglement.*

"I've seen you and the Cardozas…" He trailed off.

"I'm married to Jared over there?" I blinked rapidly, the words sitting on my chest like concrete.

"Yeah, but you and I talk a lot on base. We have a special connection. I'm in love with you there, too, but you have no idea. At least, I think you don't. I almost died the first time I saw you here, getting your mail in those pajamas." He laughed and dropped his head back. "I couldn't believe it was really you. It was as if someone from a dream materialized before me."

"You were investigating me."

"I *was*. But seeing you *here*, meeting you *here*…was surreal. I love you here, too, you know, and at least here I can tell you that." He leaned forward and kissed my forehead.

Sy knew me *before he met me*—as little sense as that makes—and loved me in both lives. In my parallel life? I still chose Jared. My eyes burned with unshed tears.

Sy softened when he spotted my tears. "Don't cry, Charlotte. It's almost like we're destined to make the same mistakes over and over. I'm getting ready to join Quantym on the Periphery." He clutched the steering wheel and rested his forehead on it.

He was right. We were repeating the same damn mistakes. Maybe this is also why we should never, ever, know about the Periphery. It was devastating.

I nodded. "The human variable. We choose self-destruction every time, don't we?"

He shrugged. "Maybe it's not always a choice. Others' choices impact us, too. Jared—"

I shook my head and held up my hand. "Don't." I thought about how Jared and I had met, and the evolution of our relationship. He chose me, chased me, courted me. I'd never felt more desired at the time, more wanted. It was superfluous, exactly what young love was made of. But, I chose him back. I'd married him, loved him, even.

"We all make mistakes. I'm divorced. Went through a tumultuous adolescence, made some shitty choices, signed this contract. But I don't regret a damn thing. Every choice I've made was necessary, to find you."

"So, did I only interest you here because you'd met me *there?*"

Sy stopped me by putting his finger over my lips. "No. I didn't seek you out over here because of the Periphery. I thought I'd see what you knew about Jared, or Adam, Cardoza and leave you be. But I couldn't. Charlotte, no matter what life we're in, no matter what our circumstances, I'll always find you and love you. Always."

Quantum entanglement, I was on to something, wasn't I? I knew him there before I knew him here. Two particles, once bonded, even if separated by vast distances still react to one another in synchronicity once entangled.

I nodded and reached for him, slamming my lips to his. I pulled back just enough to speak against his lips. "I want to yell at myself on the Periphery, to leave him for you, to tell you to run from them and from Quantym."

He traced the outline of my lips with his finger. "Leave the mistakes for over there, Charlotte. Here is all that matters."

"So, is this the worst part, knowing about the mistakes you're making in your other life?"

"There's nothing I can do about my choices over there, as long as I don't live there permanently. The worst part is when they bring me back, and I have to unload all this information while my body is in a state of shock—they're screaming and yelling for info while I'm still struggling to breathe just minutes after I'm taken off the vent."

I blanched at what I was hearing. I'd extubated patients in the ICU, seen how painful their throat was and how delirious they were from the medications. I couldn't envision being woken from a state like that and being screamed at for critical information before it dissipated back into my mind.

"How do they know you're telling the truth?"

"That's what makes this so dangerous. They'd never trust just *one* jumper. Their life depends on the information I'm giving. They send several of us, which is why I can't just simply go over there and eliminate targets and return. I have to actually carry out whatever Quantym gives me for a mission, and then sneak off to do my duty for the government, too. Same with this jump. I can't just destroy the servers. I have a mission to complete for Quantym as well. I'll have to make the time to sneak off, undetected by the other jumpers, to get rid of the servers."

Now it made sense that in the trailer Joel mentioned me waking Sy before anyone else could. To make sure he could tell us if the servers were gone, before they could realize that he might not have all the information he went over to get or give. I was terrified now, horrified that Sy really could end up getting killed over this. I wouldn't let it happen.

"I'm going to do everything I can to come back, Charlotte."

"I'll be waiting for you, Sy." I blinked back the burning tears that begged to escape.

Dawn was breaking, and the clementine sky was visible through the canopy of trees in the forest.

Sy turned on the car and looked over at me. "I want you to be happy, and safe. And to go on and *live* no matter what happens to me."

"I didn't even realize I survived until I met you."

He placed his hand on my chest, feeling my beating

heart. "One day you'll realize just how important you are. This, here—" He motioned to his hand over my heart. "—is beating for a reason. You're everything to me, but the universe also needs you, and one day you'll find out why. The universe doesn't work the way it does by accident."

I nodded and closed my eyes.

Sy pulled away and drove down the dirt road, ready to take me home.

"You really would have gone to Virginia with Jared?" He looked straight ahead at the road as he spoke.

"Do you think I still have feelings for Jared?" I thought about his outburst of anger earlier, the shot across Joel's jaw, all after hearing my suggestion.

He shrugged. "A little jealous, maybe."

"Don't be. Jared's sins go deeper than abandoning me in my darkest hour. Much deeper. "

Sy stopped at the thin strip of woods I had to trek through to get home. He kissed me forcefully, a kiss that felt like goodbye.

I pulled back and stared at him for a few moments, trying to commit every angle of his face to memory. Just in case.

The sun was just breaking over the horizon.

My heart shattered when I shut the door behind me and he watched me walk away, disappearing into the woods.

It didn't take long to find my phone in the wet grass before I headed inside through the slider Sy had left unlocked. I pulled myself into bed and fell into a light, restless sleep after having been awake for nearly twenty-four hours. Nightmares caused me to relive the memory of why this was all happening in the first place.

I woke around ten and showered. I sat on my bed, phone in hand, trying to work up the courage to make the call. I looked down at the crumpled paper, and dialed the numbers written there.

He answered, and I froze.

"Charly? Is that you?"

"It's me."

"What did you decide?" His soft, smooth voice held a smile.

"Come home, Jared. Just come home."

"I'll be there in a couple hours, doll. I'm coming home."

Chapter 13

"See now the power of truth; the same experiment which at first glance seemed to show one thing, when more carefully examined, assures us of the contrary." – *Galileo Galilei*

It was exactly 11:57 a.m.

I opened the door before Jared even had a chance to knock.

He was wearing a white baseball cap, pulled down to conceal most of his face, jeans, and a black T-shirt. He smiled his brilliant-white smile, and the left side of his smile pulled askew from the scar that slashed down the side of his face.

I noticed my favorite dimple of his, just one that he had on his right cheek, when he smiled that big. I'd always adored it because it gave him a look of innocence he didn't deserve.

He pushed the door shut behind him and removed his hat. His skin was golden brown, and his dark hair was shorter than he'd kept it in years past.

I wasn't prepared for how seeing him walk through our front door would affect me.

He was here again, against all odds and laws and limits of the things that could and couldn't happen in life. The impossible, now possible.

And at that moment, none of it mattered. I'd needed

this moment for so many years, and now I was watching it happen right before my eyes. I took in the reality of it, allowing myself to see what the world would look like, what it would feel like, if the accident never happened. And I wasn't surprised when my insides felt hollow. My world only spun correctly on its axis *after* the accident.

I backed away as he approached me.

"You look like you've seen a ghost. Oh, right."

Jared circled me like prey.

"This can't be real," I whispered and hung my head. My hair fell over the side of my face.

He reached out and twirled a lock of my hair between his fingers. "But I'm like Casper."

Instinctively, I pulled away.

Jared's face darkened at my response. He snaked his arms tightly around my waist and slowly slid the tip of his nose across my jaw. "My wife," he whispered into my ear.

My neck prickled, and a shiver slithered down my spine.

"It's okay, Charly, I'm here now. I'm sorry I wasn't here sooner."

"Me too." I tried to swallow the lump in my throat.

"Atta girl. We'll get through this. I'll make it up to you," he purred.

He released me and I stumbled, grabbing the dining table for support. I tapped my finger inconspicuously on the table top.

One, two, three…I counted each finger-tap, and my shoulders loosened.

His hand grasped mine, squeezing my fingers uncomfortably tight. "No need for that, Charly—" He smiled. "—I know a way to fix you, you know."

I counted the barely audible ticks of the clock. Seven, eight, nine… "Fix me?"

"This—" He tapped my finger, then discreetly tapped his temple. "—I know someone on base in Virginia. A doctor. He can help."

"That sounds…good." I nodded.

"I'm starving. Is there anything to eat around here?"

Oh, good. Something to do with my hands. "Have a seat—" I motioned to the table. "—I'll make you something."

I slowly pulled out the ingredients for a late breakfast. Bread, eggs, bacon. I heated the pan, scrambled the eggs, and toasted the bread. I put together two iced coffees, and Jared watched me closely the whole time.

While I worked, Jared spoke of his life over the last four years. He had a talent for flipping any situation in his favor, and his version of events over the last four years was no different.

By the time he was finished telling me how, at many points, he wished he'd died rather than face the rehab and recovery he did, I almost felt sympathy for him.

Jared was well aware of my feelings about Mitch, and he played a victim to Mitch's inhumane approach to saving him.

He'd always done this—understood why I hated Mitch, but instead of cutting ties with him, acted as if he didn't have a choice against the power and fury of his father. I often wondered, even before today, if this was actually true—that Jared didn't have the fortitude to stand up to him or, if it was his way, as usual, of flipping the situation into him being the victim instead of villain.

We finished breakfast, and I cleared the table,

thankful I no longer had to face him. I started scrubbing the dishes.

Jared sauntered up behind me, and I froze.

He reached around and turned off the faucet.

I wrung the suds from my hands into the sink. My heartbeat thumped in my throat.

"Stop avoiding me, Charly. If you're upset, say so. Let's talk about it."

I gave him what he wanted, fed his need for emotional vampirism.

I spun to face him. "You started over without me *by choice*. You didn't have to listen to Mitch, but you did. I didn't have a choice. I *had* to start over without you."

"I'm so sorry." He closed the small gap between us and cupped my face. "Come with me to Virginia, Charly. Give me a few weeks to show you what life could be like again, I'll make it up to you, I swear. All of this is part of a bigger plan for us, I just need you to trust me." His lips brushed against mine.

I pulled away, ducked out of his grasp, and grabbed my phone, scrolling through my contacts. "I have to call Brian to arrange a leave of absence from work. I'll go, Jared, but I can't make you any promises. I need time, space, and I need you to be patient with me." I looked down at the phone as I spoke.

Jared was confident. "You're going to love Virginia. The house I got for us is incredible."

I met his eyes and put the phone to my ear. "Hi, Brian. It's Charlotte. I'm going to need to arrange an LOA to go see my parents in Florida for a family emergency…"

After a thousand questions and genuine concern, the call ended. I called Angela and Jess, repeating the same story.

"You're making the right choice." Jared crossed his arms and followed me to my room to pack. He pulled the old suitcases out from under the bed, and opened the closet to grab the duffel bags. The way he navigated the house, my room, made me feel like he'd never been gone at all.

I slowly began loading clothes and shoes into the first open suitcase. "I still have some of your things upstairs—" I looked up from the suitcase at him. "—If you want to pack anything." I shrugged.

He cocked an eyebrow and slowly walked over to me. "I have everything I need." His eyes gleamed as he looked down at me.

I quickly looked down at the suitcase and swallowed hard. I was doing this for a greater good, more than just my life or Sy's, or my deep hatred for Mitch, or anger at Jared. I was doing this because, as Gustav said, we *shouldn't* know about the Periphery, and the Quantym program shouldn't exist. Maybe, just maybe, I could play a small role in righting some wrongs. Maybe I could find *my* purpose in this chaotic mess.

That night, Jared crawled onto his side of the bed.

I held my breath as he slid closer, pulling me into his strong arms. I wanted to pull away; a voice in my head screamed at me to move, to recoil, to get out of his grip. But against all the silent screams ricocheting inside of me, I turned toward him, and rested my forehead against his hard chest. "Can you tell me your new name now?"

"Adam Cardoza."

"Adam, huh?" I mumbled, tapping his chest with my finger. "I guess I should start calling you that."

"Only in public. I'm still Jared, Charly. It's just a name."

"Just a name," I repeated before pretending to fall asleep.

After picking up Mitch from the hotel and returning the rental SUV, we rushed through the bustling airport toward our gate. I was taken aback when Jared handed me an anxiety pill for the flight. I grabbed the pill and stuffed it into my jeans pocket.

What he didn't know was, after the accident, counting, calculating distance and time, and solving equations calmed me better than any pill could.

I didn't need to be sedated.

I lugged my overstuffed carry-on, and Jared checked the bags for us.

The blonde agent was enamored with him. She laughed loudly, flipped her hair, and when he murmured something to her, she even reached out and touched the collar of his service uniform.

He didn't rebuke her blatant flirting. When he noticed my annoyance, he grabbed me by the waist and planted a kiss on my cheek well within her sight. "Kill 'em with kindness. You do want our bags to get there, right?" He narrowed his eyes at me.

I nodded.

"And, since you packed my old gun without telling me, we could've gotten in a world of shit for that. Thankfully"—he motioned to his uniform—"I told her it was an oversight."

Shit, shit, shit. "It's in a locked case. I thought—"

"You didn't *think*, Charly." He cocked an eyebrow. "Next time, you'll tell me, understood?"

"Yes. I'm sorry." I sucked in a breath.

Jared grabbed my hand, leading the way toward the gate.

Mitch hadn't said a word. He stared at me like a vulture, watching my every move.

I avoided him as much as I could.

Navigating through the crowded airport was exceptionally easy with Jared and Mitch leading our small pack. Jared and Mitch walked with ramrod straight backs and palpable confidence.

People seemed to unconsciously separate and make way for them, sensing their air of authority.

Our flight was on time, and soon we were seated in first class, and then in the air.

When the flight attendant came around, I ordered a rum and cola. My past had literally come back to haunt me, and if that didn't call for a drink, then I don't know what would.

"Charly!" Jared jokingly put his hand to his chest in shock at my drink request. "I guess I'll join the lush, make that two." He flashed his dazzling smile at the stewardess.

"So, you drink now?" He elbowed me and raised his eyebrows.

"No, but now seems like a good time to start."

"I like this new vibe you got going on—" He motioned vaguely around me. "—not always so serious."

I elbowed him back and laughed.

It was hard not to get caught up in Jared. He was an absolute whirlwind of confident energy. Add to that his intelligence as well as his ability to conceal his emotions, and he was the man people looked to when a situation needed a leader, a hero, a wrangler. And he could certainly control a situation.

Everywhere we went, there was always someone who knew him, and liked him enough to wander over and keep us in conversation for far longer than necessary. People wanted Jared on their side, in their corner. He commanded attention, and people not only listened to him, but loved him for it.

I used to tell him he was wasting his time in the military, he'd have made a fantastic politician.

I toyed with the straw in my drink while reading on my phone. The lines of words began to squiggle and blur. I put my phone down and leaned forward.

"You okay?" Jared asked.

"I'm fine, but I think she made it…too…strong." My words slurred.

Jared shrugged and turned back to his laptop. "Sleep it off."

I reached for my drink and missed. I was seeing double. I stared at the half-full cup; a powdery residue clung to the edge, and I swiped it with my finger. Then I looked up and saw Mitch watching me.

Mitch smiled. "You forgot to take your pill."

My lids were heavy. I tried to stand, bumping into the open tray in front of me. My drink spilled, and my phone clacked to the floor.

A few passengers looked over at me, and Jared pulled my arm down roughly. "I said, sleep it off," he growled.

And that's the last thing I remember before we landed in Virginia.

After disembarking and getting our luggage, we headed outside.

Jared had his Jeep parked in the long-term lot.

The air was hot and thick with humidity, and my

legs and head were still heavy from the drugged drink. I made my way through the scores of people bustling in and out of the airport in silence. I tossed my carry-on into the trunk of Jared's jeep, and then I climbed into the back.

I looked out the window, taking in through heavy eyes the views Virginia had to offer. Mitch said we were going to have at least an hour ride before we got to base, so I was trying to pay attention to Richmond as we drove through, the sights turning into a cascade of green foliage and lawns and far too much red brick.

We turned off the main road, and I immediately recognized the evergreen-lined road ahead. The road I drove on while I was dead, searching for Simon.

I shut my eyes and nodded off. I vaguely dreamt of a stop we'd made, and being led from the back seat into the passenger seat by Jared. I thought I heard him ask what dose I'd been given. And then, heavy darkness consumed me again.

"Welcome to Caroline County!" Jared's voice made me jump.

I struggled to get my bearings. We were parked in the driveway of a stunning house. Mitch wasn't in the car, so perhaps the stop hadn't been a dream.

The regal house was mostly brick, with white, ornate accents in the peaks above the garage and front door. It looked to be a two-story colonial, but its size and multiple peaks and gables made me unsure of my assessment.

"Wait until you see inside," Jared said with assurance.

"It's beautiful," I said mechanically.

"You okay to walk? I can carry you over the

217

threshold," he teased.

I opened the car door. "Maybe next time don't let Mitch drug me," I snapped. My knees wobbled, but I quickly steadied myself before he could notice.

"He meant no harm." Jared chuckled while exiting the vehicle.

My mind sharpened as I shook off the lingering effects of the drugged drink. I needed to learn as much as I could about this temporary new life. It felt like waking from a dream, only to find I was living in a nightmare.

Jared led me inside, then headed back outside to get the bags. He returned with the luggage and shut the front door behind us, the sound echoing through the large house.

I stood in the foyer, overwhelmed by my dead husband standing behind me, the large house before me, and the impossible tasks that lay ahead.

Jared's arms wrapped around me from behind, shattering my thoughts into pieces as he squeezed me uncomfortably tight. I tried to focus on everything at once, my eyes still trying to adjust to the light.

Tall windows cast sunlight across every floorboard and flat surface.

He released me and grabbed the suitcases.

I pulled my bags over my shoulder and followed him deeper into the house.

He took me through the downstairs layout.

The living room was furnished with a large black sectional sofa in the living room, a wall-mounted TV, and a brick fireplace that looked like it had never been used. The kitchen was just as magnificent, with gray cabinets and gleaming black-granite counters.

Upstairs held four bedrooms. One had been turned into a workout room, complete with weights, a treadmill, and a scary looking bench-press system. Another was an office with several overstuffed bookshelves and a large desk stacked with books, papers, and folders. A huge framed world map hung on one of the walls with at least a hundred pushpins stuck randomly into states and continents. The desk sat in front of a large window revealing a backyard peppered with Bradford pear trees and longleaf pines.

Jared led me to the master bedroom, where he removed his service jacket and hung it in the closet.

I heard sequential beeps as he opened the safe with his back to me.

He turned and motioned to my bag. "My gun."

I pulled the case from the backpack and handed it over.

He opened the case and removed the magazine, placing it in the safe.

I spotted several weapons and badges inside before he closed it again.

He handed me the case with the unloaded pistol. "You can have this one. Maybe I'll take you to the range again one day."

I put the gun case into the backpack with trembling hands. It was useless now that Jared had locked up the ammo. "This is a lot of room for one person."

"It was never just for me, Charly. I always knew I'd come back for you."

He turned and led me to the final room. He opened the door, and slowly walked to the center of the empty room. He slid his hands into his pockets. "This room can be our nursery."

I balked.

He sauntered over to me and put his hands on my shoulders. "We can make another," he whispered.

I was struck speechless. When I thought I'd lost my husband, I had memories of what had been—the good and the bad—to carry me through the pain. But finding out I'd lost a pregnancy forced me to lose something that hadn't even had a chance to begin, and it was beyond unfair. I'd cried so many tears over my dreams for the life that never had a chance to manifest.

I stared at Jared's face for a long time, searching for his intent, but I couldn't find it.

He smiled wide, and his dimple appeared again. He walked slowly to the window and slid his hands back into his pockets.

I started to describe my recovery, in gruesome detail, my words echoing in the empty room. I told him about how Mitch had delivered the news that my husband died, and told him of the day the doctor revealed I'd been pregnant. I told him what it was like to be confined to a hospital bed injured, widowed, and alone, staring at the wall after being told there was a baby who was no longer in the safe confines of my womb but sleeping in eternal peace instead.

I told him of the physical pain, the emotional pain, the searing heartache at all my life was, could've been, and had become. I told him of the four years of pretending I was recovering, healing. I told him what it was like to live numbly, putting one foot in front of the other just so others would think I was okay.

He silently stared out the window with his tongue pushed into his cheek.

My words cut into him, as I hoped they would. I

hoped hurting him would help me feel better, throw water on the flames of anger that burned inside of me, but it didn't.

He didn't turn around to look at me, and when he spoke, he described what it was like being kept alive by machines. He described, in painful detail, the physical and mental ramifications of finally waking up from the coma he'd been in for the better part of a year.

He turned and met my gaze. "Being married to you was all I had. It's all I *have*. Mitch stole everything else from me. You know how I pushed myself to walk again? What kept me going through my rehabilitation?"

"What?"

"You. I'd picture your face, and what it felt like to hold you." He took a long breath, then turned to stare out the window again. "I knew I'd come back for you, no matter what Mitch said, but I needed to be able to walk, so I could hold you, take care of you, first."

My head buzzed with conflicting feelings of sadness and anger and sympathy, but ultimately the anger won over all the rest. "You didn't have a choice when you were nearly dead, but you had a choice when you recovered. Why did you let him take complete control? It's *your* life, not his."

I walked over to him while I spoke, and I looked down to see I was unconsciously reaching for his arm.

He turned and looked down at me. He grabbed my outstretched arm. "Would *you* know where to start and how to undo a death certificate?"

I shook my head.

"Would *you* know who to turn to who isn't on his payroll? How would I get an I.D.? A job? A fucking credit card?"

I tried backing away, but his grip on my arm tightened.

He brought his face closer to mine.

I looked down so I didn't stare at his disfiguring scar.

"And don't get me started on the physical effects I had to contend with. Muscle wasting, cognitive deficits. Physical therapy," he growled.

"I know it must've been hard," I conceded.

"So, you tell me, Charly, would you have fought to pull yourself from the grave he put you in, or relented and chosen the easier, more logical option?" He gritted his teeth.

"Easier to become Adam, I'm sure," I whispered.

His free hand pulled my chin up so I would meet his eyes. "Easy? Ha! You know, I had to enlist as Adam and go through boot camp again. I had to pretend my body wasn't in excruciating pain just to pass the PT test."

"I'm sorry, Jared."

"You got to grieve, and recover, and move on, on *your* terms. So, forgive me if I have a hard time believing you had it worse than me." He released his grip on my arm.

Tears spilled down my cheeks.

"House is yours, Charly. I need to get some air. Help yourself to whatever you need; the fridge is stocked."

I stood frozen, tears overflowing, as he stomped down the stairs and out the front door. I heard his jeep door slam and the engine roar to life. The sound faded into the distance. Was I poking the bear with my words? I quickly pushed the thought away. I was disgusted with myself for feeling awful for what I'd just done, for the look on Jared's face that I'd put there with my words.

I was used to guilt and shame, but what he wouldn't get, was my sympathy.

Chapter 14

I spent the better part of an hour replaying what I'd said to Jared and his response. To distract myself, I made my way into the kitchen and started pulling out food to prepare for dinner. Despite keeping my hands busy, my mind kept wandering back to our conversation in the empty bedroom upstairs. I was debating whether I was out of line, or whether it was high time he heard what I'd been through. I couldn't decide which was right— either I was a horrible person or he was.

Or maybe we both were.

Finding my way around the kitchen was relatively easy. While frying the chicken, I boiled water for the potatoes and another pot for sweet corn. I turned the oven on and seasoned the asparagus, and put it in to roast. I found an open bottle of wine in the fridge and poured myself a glass, hoping it'd help ease the conflicting thoughts in my head. I set the table and made my way to the washroom to clean up before Jared returned.

After washing my hands, I stared at my reflection for a long time.

Maybe I am a horrible person. What if Jared is genuine about all of this? What if we were wrong about his intentions? Was I about to break the broken, do to him what had been done to me?

My purpose in Virginia was for the greater good. That should right any wrongs that were about to happen,

I reassured myself. I smoothed my dark hair, now wavy from the humidity, even with the central air. I leaned toward the mirror and stared at myself with contempt. Remembering my long nights recovering in the hospital brought me to the brink of insanity, a brink where if I inched just a millimeter closer would send me falling into a bottomless void, so I hid it deep within, safe from the world as my womb had been for the baby before the fateful accident.

I was tormented by waves of guilt when I thought about my future, which undoubtedly would include me being with Sy if everything went according to plan.

Where does that leave Jared? If he's actually innocent in all of this, a pawn to his father's bidding, does he deserve to have his life ripped apart at the seams again?

The reflection in the mirror staring back at me was that of a pale, withered stranger whose very character I, at the moment, questioned.

When Jared returned, I was sitting at the dining table with dinner arranged in front of me. I was two glasses of wine deep when I heard the front door shut. I took slow, calculated breaths, reminding myself not to get swept up in any more conversations about the past.

"Hi, Charly." He kissed my head and sat across from me slowly. "I'm sorry about before. Everything you said...I'd already had a chance to picture in my mind a thousand times, but hearing you describe it..." He trailed off.

"I'm sorry, too." I stared at him, wondering what emotion I was *supposed* to feel. What emotion he wanted to elicit from me. I took another sip of wine, then rested the glass on the table. I twisted it in a circle by pinching the stem, and adjusted my gaze to stare at it. I counted each complete rotation of the glass.

"I'm sorry, Charly. I'll say it from now until forever, I'm sorry." He put his hand over mine to stop my mindless glass-twirling.

"Who told you I was seeing Simon?" I asked without looking up.

"We saw it ourselves. Simon was about to get orders, and we were tracking him because the program he's in is affiliated with the program we oversee."

"You and Mitch?"

"Yes. And Simon is part of an illicit branch at Quantym, known as ORA. It's a black-op, top-secret-clearance operation doing psy-op experiments. People like Simon are used to experiment with the sedation protocol. They're testing the ability to alter consciousness and memories through the process. We suspect it's being developed as a coercion tactic for POWs and detainees, like a biological interrogation weapon."

"But you don't know for sure?"

"I can't talk about it, Charly, but this is huge, and we're about to blow the whole thing wide open."

"And that's how you talked Mitch into coming back for me?"

"Yes and no. We were in Rhode Island tailing Simon anyway, and I begged him to let me see you, even if just once. He staked out your house, wanted to ensure you weren't with *him*, so I could see you."

He tensed, anger flashing in his eyes for an instant. "The first chance I had, I went to you."

"That night, in my bedroom. It was you."

"Yes. Nice chokehold, Charly. Didn't think you had

it in you." He snickered.

"You scared me."

He smiled and began putting food onto his plate. "Then we gathered more evidence. It turns out, Simon's brother, Joel, has been poking his nose in places it doesn't belong. They're both up to no good."

I suppressed a shiver. Jared and Mitch knew more than Sy and his brothers realized.

"Simon has a record number of kills in Afghanistan. Absolutely brutal." Jared shook his head. "A little less than half his kills were civilians. He's got rage in him, Charly. That's why he got this contract job. They knew someone like him would be more than willing to participate in a program that makes waterboarding look like a firm handshake in comparison."

"But again, this is all hearsay?"

Jared slammed his fist on the table.

I jumped at the unexpected motion.

"I told you! It's classified. But since you want to know so bad—" His nostrils flared and he sneered. "—they've got detainees they're using the protocol on. Like science experiments. Simon kills them once they're done with them. He's a monster, Charly, and *that* is how I talked Mitch into taking you back with us. Some things are worse than death, you know, and I wasn't going to sit around and see if you were going to be his next victim!"

I started twirling my glass again.

"So, what do you and Mitch do over there?"

His shoulders relaxed, and he looked up, triumphant. "Charly, you'd love it." He took a bite of chicken. "The program at Quantym is incredible, and the doctors and scientists we've got are the best in the world."

My gaze shot up to meet his.

He continued, "They're about to cure, yes, *cure,* not simply treat, mental illness. I've never seen anything like it. They collaborated with the Army for security—which is part of what I do—and resources, which is what Mitch does. The facility is highly guarded because the treatments require patients to be sedated to the point where they're barely alive. In that state, the doctors can reach the deep subconscious." He flashed his brilliant smile at me.

"Barely alive?" I raised my eyebrows. "They must employ nurses, no?"

"Yeah, no chance, though. The clearance you'd need would require you to enlist."

"Oh."

"But imagine, PTSD, anxiety, depression, and—" He reached across the table and brushed my hand with his fingertips. "—obsessive-compulsive disorder, all about to be things of the past. I told you I knew how to fix you, Charly. This is it."

I flinched. "Are you close to shutting down the ORA side of the program?" I ignored his statement.

"We're in the process." His eyes darkened, and he cocked his head to the side, examining me. "Do you miss him?"

"I barely knew him, Jared." I brought the glass to my lips and finished the rest of the wine in one gulp.

He watched me closely, narrowing his eyes at me when I held his stare. "Aren't you going to eat?" He picked his fork back up and took another bite of chicken.

After dinner, we cleaned the kitchen together. It was an odd dance, he and I, orbiting each other in the kitchen. It almost started to feel normal, and that scared the hell out of me.

Later, Jared showered and hopped into bed to watch TV.

I retreated to the office to read and avoid being with him. I unpacked my books, deciding to re-read my favorite, when I became distracted by the bookcase in Jared's office.

I slowly padded over to the rows of books, dozens of which were about near-death experiences and the multiverse. I didn't have to read the book jackets, I knew the works of Parnia, Gribbon, Holdsworth, and Greene, and it was all the flimsy evidence I had at the moment, tethering me to Sy and his brother's version of what Quantym really was.

I settled into the soft sage-green armchair with my book but didn't open it. I looked around the room at the cherry-wood bookshelves, the gray-and-green area rug, the matching sage-and-cream curtains. *Who decorated the house for Jared?* He was barely able to fry an egg, let alone hang curtains, and the home seemed to have a woman's touch. *Had he lived alone for the last four years, or had he had a companion?*

Before I could form an opinion on that thought, I opened my book, scanning the familiar pages without absorbing the actual content. Within minutes, my lids were heavy from the long day we'd had, and I fell asleep with the book laid across my chest.

The next morning, I woke up to the sound of Jared in the kitchen making coffee. I planned on a full day of gathering information, and I looked forward to having the house to myself to do so. I went downstairs to the kitchen when I heard him call my name.

"Why aren't you ready yet?" He looked me over.

"Ready?"

"You're coming with me today."

"I'm tired, I wanted to stay—"

"Get ready, Charly." Jared turned his back to me and slid his arms into his uniform.

I showered and dressed quickly, my heart racing the whole time.

We climbed into his jeep, and he navigated the winding roads on base with ease.

I could see the hospital in the distance, closer to the house than I originally thought.

"Now, Charly, you remember what I told you, our story?"

I nodded.

"Who are you?"

"Charly, your brother's widow," I answered dutifully.

"And what happened when I was deployed to Rhode Island recently?" He raised an eyebrow.

"We reconnected, fell in love, and got engaged."

"Good girl." He watched the road ahead.

We sat in a prolonged silence, the air between us charged like a lightning bolt waiting to be released.

He leaned his body toward me and smiled, keeping his eyes on the road. "You know, for centuries it was customary to marry your brother's widow and take care of her."

I nodded. "A levirate marriage."

He stole a glance at me. "We have to get married again, in the eyes of the law, with me as Adam Cardoza."

"Oh." I bit my lip.

"I know, I know. Patience. We have all the time in the world." He smiled and his dimple popped.

He parked in a reserved spot in the hospital lot, then reached over and squeezed my hand.

I squeezed back. We exited the jeep and headed inside.

We stepped into the elevator, and when the doors rolled shut, he pressed his badge against a black scanner pad. A darkened button illuminated, an option that hadn't been there before. The lower level.

The doors opened to a bustling, wide-open space, with a waiting area, a reception desk, and a large glass office straight ahead.

Jared introduced me to his troops, and no one seemed surprised by my attendance. Mitch must've prepped them with our story.

Everyone treated Jared and me with exceptional kindness and respect.

After the rounds of introductions, Jared walked me into the large glass office.

Mitch looked up from his desk and smiled mockingly. "Welcome to Quantym, Charly."

Jared walked over to his father's desk and leaned forward. He squinted at the papers in Mitch's hand.

Mitch nodded. "I had copies sent to your office. He's here, and we've moved his jump ahead of schedule. You'll be pleased."

"I'll be happier when it's unplugged," Jared responded.

"Patience. That can't happen for at least another week," Mitch snapped.

A primal alarm sounded in my head, and for a second, the room spun.

Jared turned back to me and pulled me close.

Mitch looked down, engrossed in the papers before

him.

"You're going to stay with Mitch today."

"What?" My eyes widened, and I grabbed onto Jared's forearms desperately. There was only one person I distrusted more than Jared. Feared and loathed, in fact. Mitch. *And he was going to leave me alone with the man for hours?*

"Where I'm going requires top-secret clearance, so you can't come."

"I'll go home then," I whispered.

"No, Charly, you're here with me today. Have a seat," Mitch ordered.

Jared walked me over to the leather-and-mahogany chair facing Mitch's desk, then leaned down and kissed me, once, twice, and then roughly pulled me in closer for a third kiss.

"That's enough," Mitch barked.

I nearly fell backwards when Jared released me, and my face reddened. I wasn't going to survive this. Any of this.

Jared put a heavy hand on my shoulder, and I stumbled into the mahogany chair.

"See you later, wifey." Jared tapped the door jamb and laughed quietly as he left the office.

Mitch looked up from his desk and tossed his pen on top of the papers. "What shall I do with you today?" He looked around the office. "Ah! Here. I've got some things for you to deliver on this floor. The office numbers are on each folder."

He handed me a large stack of manilla folders.

I stood and took them to my chest.

"The doors to go outside don't unlock without a badge, so don't do anything stupid. Everyone here knows your face now, and everyone here works for me." He glanced up at the camera by his office door.

I nodded. "I didn't plan on going anywhere."

He cocked his head. "We'll see about that." His gaze returned to his papers.

I was dismissed.

I spent the day doing menial errands for Mitch. It was degrading. The only consolation was the friendly face I met at the water cooler. I'd poured a cup of water, and a woman with cropped black hair approached.

She filled a cup and stared at me while she took a sip.

"Must be a boring day for you, waiting for Adam," she noted.

I smiled. "I can't possibly recall a day longer than today."

She laughed and offered her hand. "I'm Diogo. Becca Diogo."

I shook her hand. "I'm Charlotte, it's nice to meet you."

"I'm sure I'll see you around. I work over there, if you need anything." She tipped her head toward the door. She was a guard at the entrance.

Toward the end of the day, Mitch had run out of errands for me.

The unfulfilled child in me took great pleasure in annoying him. I knocked over some of his things, and I asked too many questions.

He sighed and rubbed his temples. The office walls were glass, so he certainly couldn't yell at his daughter-in-law with so many of his troops around.

Jared came for me at the end of his shift. We went home, and the night ended similar to the way the night before had. Dinner, TV, reading, and bed.

The next day I was babysat by Mitch again. And the day after that, too. Panic rose in me. I wasn't going to be able to help anyone, not if I was never left alone to make a call, obtain a badge, or try to crack the code to the safe in Jared's closet.

I was in Mitch's office for the third day in a row when I started noticing the curious glances from his subordinates. I'd finished my menial tasks and sat in the chair facing his desk with my chin resting in my hand. I stared at him, but he didn't look up.

Someone stood in the doorway behind me.

Mitch finally looked up. "Enter, soldier," he barked.

Becca Diogo entered the office and saluted the general. "Sir, may I be dismissed for an hour?"

"Where you headed, Soldier?"

"Ground House, sir."

Mitch looked at me and back to her. "Take Charly with you."

"Sir, yes sir!"

"And soldier, have her bring me back one."

"Yes, sir." She saluted him.

He dismissed her.

I flew from my seat and approached her with a smile. I didn't care where we were going, as long as it wasn't inside of Quantym.

Becca used her badge to open the elevator, and it ascended to the ground level.

"What's the Ground House?"

"You're not from around here, are you?" She eyed me skeptically.

"I'm from Rhode Island."

"I can tell."

"You can?" I turned to her.

"Your New England accent—" She smiled. "—and not knowing the Ground House has the best coffee in the south."

We walked from the hospital to The Ground House, and the fresh air was the first taste of freedom I'd had since arriving in Virginia.

Becca and I talked about Virginia, and she told me about a few local food shops to check out.

I held my iced coffee in one hand, and Mitch's hot coffee in the other hand. I looked down. "Ugh, how degrading," I grumbled.

"I have to get him coffee all the time, that's how I knew his order." Becca shrugged.

My shoulders slumped. "Sorry, I didn't mean it like that."

"Don't apologize. I understand. You're not his employee." She looked at me questioningly.

"No, I'm not. But you can't tell him that." I laughed.

Becca laughed with me.

"You won't tell anyone if I spit in it, right?"

"He is my superior, Charly."

I immediately regretted my words.

"If you're going to do it, at least let me know when to turn around." She elbowed me, and we laughed.

"In that case, turn around, soldier!" I barked.

The day finally ended, and I took great joy in watching Mitch drink that hot cup of coffee.

****

Another long day passed in Mitch's office. Becca Diogo wasn't at work, so I was not only bored, but lonely, too.

After dinner, Jared's phone rang.

I listened to the one-sided conversation while I washed the dishes.

"What do you mean, losing it?" Jared spat into the phone.

There was a long silence.

"I don't care what it saw over there, if it wasn't related to the mission. No."

I turned off the faucet to hear better.

"Well, that's what it gets for deviating from the mission. You find out things you don't want to learn. Feel things you don't want to feel."

Another long silence ensued while the other person spoke.

He sighed heavily. "I'll have to go unplug it, then. General Cardoza isn't available tonight. Buy me an hour, soldier." He hung up the phone.

I turned the faucet back on and scrubbed the same dish, over and over, my hands trembling. *Someone was getting unplugged.* Eliminated. Erased. And Jared was going to be the one to do it. Worst of all, there was nothing I could do to stop it.

It can't be Sy, it hasn't been a week, I thought, recalling Mitch's words to Jared a few days ago.

Jared walked into the kitchen, sliding his arms back into his uniform. He hurried over to me and kissed my forehead. "I have to run into work for a few hours." He studied me for a moment. "Will you be okay alone, or do you want to come?"

"Please, let me stay here. I'd love to go for a run, see the neighborhood before the sun sets. I've been stuck inside for days," I bleated.

"Don't go too far, Charly," he warned.

"I won't!" I said quickly. "Just a run, maybe a stop

at the Ground House…"

He raised his eyebrows.

"Mitch let Becca Diogo take me the other day," I clarified.

His brows lowered. "Just be home before I get back," he ordered.

"I will."

And with that, I ran upstairs to put my running clothes on.

While Jared was at work, I entered the master-bedroom closet. I punched in a combination on the safe's keypad. A high-pitched buzz and red light indicated I was wrong. Again, and again. I exhausted myself trying to crack the code with every combination of numbers I could come up with that held any significance. Birthdays, enlistment dates, anniversaries. I stomped out of the bedroom, unsuccessful, and headed down the stairs.

I put my earbuds in and stuck my phone into my pocket, and I went out the front door to the open street ahead. I jogged to the hospital first, and counted every step along the way. I made it to the hospital entrance in exactly twenty-five minutes, taking note of landmarks and alternate entrances to the campus. I stopped at the hospital entrance and scrolled through my playlist, choosing an upbeat song. I jogged off the hospital grounds, headed for the Ground House.

Even as the sun headed toward the horizon, the thick air remained humid and hot. The aroma of freshly-laid mulch gave the air a deep earthy smell.

I jogged at a comfortable speed, fourteen paces a minute. I was startled when a large group of women jogged past me, I didn't hear their approach with my music playing. They bounced by gracefully, all blonde ponytails and bouncing curls and colorful leggings. Military wives, no doubt.

I ordered my coffee at the Ground House, and waited for it inside.

"I told you, best coffee in the south." Becca turned from the counter and faced me. She was wearing her civilian clothes. A large tribal tattoo hugged her forearm.

"Thank you for teaching me." I bowed to her.

"Next, I'll introduce you to our very own ham biscuits," she drawled.

"Now *that* sounds southern!"

We laughed.

The group of female joggers walked in, talking and laughing loudly.

Becca's name was called by the barista, and she gathered her order. "It was nice seeing you, will you be in tomorrow?" she turned and asked me.

The group of women stared at me and whispered amongst themselves.

Becca turned to glare at them, and they quieted.

"I think so," I said, unsure.

"Well, hopefully tomorrow then," she said in her southern accent.

I smiled as she turned and left.

The barista called my name, and I took my coffee.

The women stared at me and whispered again.

I left the Ground House and headed home.

I was showered and in bed by the time Jared came home.

He crawled into bed beside me, and as I pretended to sleep, he pulled me against him with hands that were covered in death.

Chapter 15

"It is not the strongest of the species that survives, nor the most intelligent that survives. It is the one that is the most adaptable to change." -Charles Darwin

I woke before Jared and put on my running clothes. I decided to test the limits of my freedom. I stood over Jared and watched him sleep for several minutes.

He had one arm behind his head, the other draped across his stomach.

He was shirtless, so I reached down and traced my finger over a tattoo above his heart. Roman numerals.

His hand flew up and grasped mine.

I jumped.

He quickly loosened his grip when he focused on my face.

"What does it mean?" I asked, touching his tattoo again.

"It's the date I died, and the date I came back." He rolled over and looked at his watch. "It's not time to get ready yet. Get back in bed," he grumbled.

"I'm going to go for a run," I whispered as his eyes slid shut.

He mumbled something unintelligible, and I loosely interpreted that as acknowledgement. I darted down the stairs before he could stop me.

I found an alternate way to the hospital on foot. This

route, only twenty minutes. From there, I headed to the Ground House and drank my coffee inside, grateful for the air-conditioned reprieve.

The sun was rising as I jogged, and coming toward me as I turned down a street was the same gaggle of ogling women.

They bounced past, suspiciously quiet.

I stared straight ahead, counting my paces and taking in the flowerbeds bursting with color that lined each home and barrack meticulously landscaped to perfection.

The neighborhood was waking from its slumber, and people jogged along both sides of the street.

A tap on the shoulder startled me, and I spun around.

A statuesque blonde greeted me with a smile so big it revealed her top and bottom teeth. "Fancy seeing you around again. I'm Claire. Over there, that's Ashley, Jen, and Liz." She motioned to the small group wearing colorful leggings behind her, and they each gave a small smile and half-wave in my direction.

"Nice to meet you. I'm Charlotte."

She wasted no time digging in. "Adam mentioned reuniting with his brother's widow, but my, you've already moved in! Welcome to the neighborhood!" she squealed, her tone fake and condescending.

"I've known Adam for a long, long time." I started to put my earbud back in when she started talking again.

"Well, it was devastating for Heather." She shook her head. "*She* thinks he was probably seeing you the whole time, but you don't look like the affair type."

She put one hand on her slender hip and looked me up and down.

I scowled and stepped forward two paces.

She backed up a step.

"Claire?" I leaned in. "Tell Heather she has terrible taste in curtains."

The women gasped in unison.

I put my earbud back in and began jogging down the street. I put my music on as loud as it would blare into my ears. I needed to get my anger under control. I ran faster and faster, allowing the sweltering ground to disappear beneath my feet until I could barely take a deep breath of the humid air.

I ran until my legs burned and my chest felt tight, the lush lawns and houses rushing past me in a haze. I was trying to stave off the anger that was boring its way through my sternum, the anger that made me want to blow the whole operation and go and tell Jared everything I thought of him and his lies.

A force slammed into me so hard that I was airborne before I hit the ground. I felt the warmth of blood before I felt the pain in the elbow that broke my fall.

"Oh, shit! I'm sorry, ma'am!"

A brown-eyed stranger extended his hand to me. He was wearing desert camo pants and a brown military-issued tee.

I grasped his hand, and where our hands met, something was passed to me. He pulled me from the ground, and I slid the hidden flip-phone into my pocket.

"Are you all right?"

I wiped the gravel from my elbow, and from my backside, then I bent and gathered my ear buds. I nodded. "I'm good."

"You need anything, ma'am?"

"A magazine for a 9mm?"

"It'll be at the bottom of your trash bin on the curb

tomorrow. You take care now, ma'am." He jogged away, the sound of his boots fading into the distance.

A thrill ran through my body. Sy's brothers were looking out for me. I wasn't as alone as I felt.

When I walked in the door, I could smell breakfast cooking.

Jared was standing over the stove frying eggs. He was shirtless, slender but muscular, and wore just his camo uniform trousers. He looked up at me and smiled. "You look like you had a good run."

I plopped down at the table, still breathless and sweating. "I don't know if I'll ever get used to this heat."

"You will."

I peered into the frying pan.

His cooking skills hadn't improved. The bacon was already blackened and burnt, and the eggs were turning brown, but at least I could take a shower while he cooked. I lifted myself off the chair and turned toward the stairs.

"Charly, wait."

I stopped and turned to him slowly. I said a silent prayer that he wouldn't see the new phone in my pocket.

"Come here." He hooked his finger and motioned for me to step closer.

I took two steps forward.

He put the spatula down and stalked over to where I stood, pulling me toward the sink.

My heart pounded. One, two, three, four, five...I counted each vicious beat pulsing through my veins.

If he found the phone, he would kill me, simple as that.

He turned on the faucet and ran water over my arm. Pink swirled down the drain as he cared for my wound.

"What happened?"

"I fell, and there were witnesses." I closed my eyes, and my face reddened.

He chuckled and shook his head. "Still clumsy."

He dried my arm, then pulled me up against him.

The phone in my pocket sat heavy in between our bodies. I glanced at my regular phone on the dining table.

"I've been patient, Charly, but you can't walk around here like this"—he trailed a finger over my tank top—"and expect me not to touch you."

"Jared, stop. I need a shower."

"Let me come with you," he pleaded and pressed himself closer to me.

I shook my head. "You're going to be late. Not now," I whispered, looking down. I tried backing away. The hard countertop bit into my lower back.

There was a stretch of silence as he stared at me with his hand resting on my ribcage.

I knew he could feel the wild pounding of my heart beneath his hand when he inhaled sharply.

He suppressed a smile. "Then go get ready." He pushed me away gently, and returned to his breakfast.

Before heading into the bathroom, I ran into the office upstairs and tucked the phone inside the hidden compartment of my backpack near the gun case. I zipped the pack closed and hurried into the shower.

When I came back downstairs Jared was waiting for me. I grabbed a strip of horrifically burnt bacon, and nibbled on it as we headed out the door to his work.

It was another endless day. Mitch had me deliver mail, organize a file cabinet, and wipe down a few vacant desks. At noon, he still hadn't returned from his meeting.

I sat in the chair in his office, close enough so I could

use the edge of his desk. With my chin propped in my hand, I sketched an intricate mandala flower. I was just putting the finishing touches on it when Becca dropped by.

"You look like you could use some company. May I interest you in a meeting by the water cooler?" She stood wide footed outside the office door.

I smiled at her. "I'll meet you there in five." I added a final touch to my drawing, a quote by Hellen Keller:

Walking with a friend in the dark is better than walking alone in the light.

I met Becca at the water cooler.

"Geeze, what'd you do to your arm?" she asked.

"It looks worse than it feels, just a scrape. I wiped out running this morning." I filled my cup, then downed it. My stomach grumbled.

"Have you eaten yet?" she asked.

"No, I don't know where Mitch is; he should've been back by now."

"Oh, Charly, he's not coming back today. He's in the ORA wing for the next few days."

"Great." I chucked my empty cup into the trash with a thud.

"I can find you something, Medeiros always has a stash." She rubbed her hands together contemplatively.

I followed her to a desk in the corner.

"Tough times, he must be running low. Sorry."

She handed me a fun sized chocolate bar.

I took it gratefully. "No, this is fine, just enough to keep my blood sugar from plummeting."

"Is he going to make you do this every day?" she asked in a low voice.

"I don't know the answer to that." I paused

thoughtfully. "I hate this. Back home, I'm a nurse, I'm not used to all this idle time. I'm usually doing ten things at once. Here, I feel like I'm going to tear my hair out."

"A nurse, whoa, that's a tough job. So why are you hanging out here all the time, then? Why don't you apply upstairs at the VA hospital?"

I shrugged.

"He won't let you," she guessed.

"Becca, do me a favor?"

"Sure, sure. What do you need?"

"Don't ask too many questions."

I handed her the drawing I did in Mitch's office.

She looked at it for a long moment. "If you ever need to talk, I keep secrets."

"Thanks Becca. But what I could really use right now, is some juicy gossip to distract me."

A wide smile broke across her face, and as she walked me back to Mitch's office, she filled my ear with hot, hot gossip about her comrades around us.

"I can't go in." She stopped outside of the office door.

"It's ok. The day is half over, and I don't want you to get in trouble."

She nodded.

"One last thing, though," I started.

She turned on her heel to face me.

"Who were those women that were staring at me in the Ground House the other day?"

"Claire and her clique? Hemlock in heels is what they are. Claire is married to an officer; she thinks she shits gold."

"She said something about Heather."

"Of course she did. They broke up months ago, and

you've known Adam for years. Don't even worry about that. Not everyone is that judgmental."

I looked down at my feet.

"They're just a gaggle of army wives that take not working *very* seriously. Don't give them a second thought."

I nodded.

"Will I see you Monday?" she asked. "Oh, right, no questions."

I smiled at her. "Have a good weekend, Becca."

She smiled and turned to walk back to her post.

Chapter 16

Saturday morning, I awakened before sunrise. I pulled the trash bins up the driveway and back into the garage. Sure enough, a magazine for Sy's gun was at the bottom of the bin.

I flew up the stairs, dashed into the home office, and shut the door. I dug my backpack from its hiding place in the closet, stowed the magazine with the pistol, and then pulled out the flip-phone. I powered it on. One contact listed. Joel.

I searched the internet for Adam Cardoza, clicking on links that showed his history. I found one grainy photo online, and his resemblance to Jared was extraordinary. I found his date of birth on an old arrest record, and the numbers tattooed on Jared's chest finally made sense.

It was the date on Jared's death certificate, followed by Adam's birthdate. I configured the numbers in my head. I'd have to try it as a combination on the safe when Jared left.

But he didn't leave.

We ate breakfast together, and he sat at the table afterward, looking over paperwork. At noon, I made us lunch and cleaned the kitchen out of boredom.

"I have something for you." Jared didn't look up from his paperwork.

"Oh?"

He straightened the papers, closed the folder, and stood. He grasped my hand and led me to the bedroom upstairs, where a large silver box sat on the middle of the bed.

"I hope it fits." He smiled and slid his hands into his pockets.

I opened the box and lifted the scarlet gown by the spaghetti straps. I ran my fingers over the soft silk.

"Well, try it on. Need to make sure it fits; it's the Military Gala tonight."

I tried to hold the gown in front of me as I shimmied my shorts down.

Jared watched my every move as he leaned his back against the wall with his arms crossed in front of his chest. "Stop hiding. I'm your husband, Charly." He pushed away from the wall and headed toward me.

I removed my top and stepped into the dress.

He strolled up behind me, and his hands rested on my hips for a moment before he zipped up the gown slowly.

My body wanted to move away from his touch, but I remained still and composed. I heard a low hum from his throat when his hand lingered on my back.

Jared spun me around and stared at me for a long moment, then pulled me up against him.

He kissed my neck while grumbling something about the dress, but I was too far away in thought to even respond.

The last time I'd worn heels was at Thames Place, the night I met Sy. Sadness burned my stomach.

The dress was too snug, but I didn't complain. I was relieved we'd have an event to attend because it was easier to keep physical distance from him in public.

When evening came, I reluctantly started to get ready. My hair wouldn't behave in the unremitting humidity and heat, so I swept it up into a messy bun. I'd been avoiding my reflection lately, though I wasn't quite sure if my repugnance was due to my actual appearance, or the guilt and pain that were often found hidden in the shadows on my pale face. I was happy to paint over the past trauma with makeup and gloss, but I let out a sigh when I realized that no matter how much or little makeup I donned, I'd still be able to see something in myself that was hard to face. I put away my makeup bag and slid into the silk scarlet dress.

Red was too flashy, and the thigh-high slit in this gown only emphasized that fact. I'd always preferred blacks and grays in an attempt to blend into the background. Seeing my reflection was somewhat shocking when I glanced in the full-length mirror behind the door. I moved my body to the left and to the right, almost to prove that it was me.

My skin looked alabaster, almost inhumanely so, juxtaposed with the screaming red silk that draped over my décolletage and hugged my waist. Jared used to tease me about my unusually fair skin and call me his porcelain doll. In this dress, I felt like one.

Jared's reaction when he saw me flit downstairs was flattering but vexing, and I flushed when he stared at me in awe.

"You look absolutely delicious."

I shook my head. "It's a good thing I've been going running. I don't have a centimeter to spare." I pulled at the dress where it hugged my waist tightly.

"You're blushing a lovely shade of red to match that dress." He sauntered over to me.

"We're going to be late, Jared."

"I don't care," he mumbled into my neck. He dragged his lips from my neck to my shoulder. "I've missed every part of you."

I pulled back, and he held his elbow out for me. I held on to him as he led us to the jeep.

Walking into the gala felt like walking straight into our pre-accident life.

The soldiers wore their Class A's, adorned with their ribbons, awards, and ranks. Candles flickered in the candelabras at round tables, and soft music filled the hall.

The room was so vast I could barely see to the other end.

Jared showed me where our seats were and started introducing me to scores of couples and soldiers and officers whose names I forgot as soon as they were told to me. I smiled politely, and people flocked to Jared.

He was authoritative and charismatic.

I tried to look away when I saw Claire, but she caught my eyes before I could divert them to the closest bar. I excused myself from Jared and the small group he was talking to and went to grab a drink.

As I ordered, I felt Claire's presence approach me from behind, and sure enough, just as I took the first large sip of liquid courage, there she was, flanked by Jen and Ashley, if I remembered their names correctly. I spun to face her.

"Nice dress…" Claire was again condescending.

"Thank you, Claire. Good seeing you again."

"I wish I could say the same. You don't belong here, you know. The gala is for military *families,* not mistresses."

She turned up her nose and ordered a drink in her

nasally voice.

I pressed my lips together, and anger welled in my chest. I stepped uncomfortably close to Claire, causing her to lean back a half-step. I kept my voice worryingly quiet and calm as I addressed her. "Claire, I need you to listen closely."

She leaned forward.

"I don't, and I cannot stress this enough, give a *shit* what you think. Now, kindly go fuck yourself." I lifted the drink to my lips and took another a long sip.

"Well, at least I'm not a homewrecker!" She stormed off with her wine, and her two friends followed.

A few soldiers at the bar snickered, and one covertly gave me a thumbs-up.

After dinner, drinks, and mingling, Jared led me toward the dance floor despite my resistance. He tightened his elbow around my grasp when I tried to divert us back to the table.

"Just let me lead, Charly. It'll be easier than you think."

The dual meaning to his words hung in the air. With one hand on my waist, he clasped my hand, and we swayed to the soft tune. I kept a fair inch between our bodies. I wasn't a fan of being so close to him, but was grateful he could stabilize me. I still didn't trust myself in heels.

"I hear you really pissed off one of the officers' wives." He laughed softly and brought his head down to meet my eyes. "You are so different now. I'm really digging this Charly two-point-oh."

"Word travels fast, doesn't it?"

Jared lifted me and swung me around.

I clung to him with a small gasp, but only out of fear

of falling. My scarlet dress fluttered at my feet when he put me down gently.

He smiled and locked his arm around my waist, no distance between our bodies now. He beamed. "Are you surprised? You're well aware of the way gossip flies in these circles."

"Some things never change." I inhaled his familiar cologne. I closed my eyes and allowed my head to override my heart for a few moments, and pondered something Jared had said on our first day in Virginia.

Would you have fought to get your life back, or just accepted the easier, more logical option?

It was his explanation for why he never came back to me, why he became Adam, and allowed Jared to die at Mitch's direction.

I thought about how much that idea applied to my current situation. If I decided not to infiltrate Quantym to wake Sy, what would become of me?

Of him?

Would you fight for your life back, or just accept the easier, more logical option?

I tried to envision staying with Jared, forgetting about the Periphery and Sy and his brothers, but pain seared through me at the attempt. I longed for Sy, and hollowness echoed in my bones in his absence, even as Jared held me. I didn't desire a future riddled with the insecurities of my past: Jared controlling me, bending reality to conform to his idea of life, or his convincing me that I *needed* him. Jared exploiting and taking advantage of not only me, but those around him. Jared and his loyalty to his evil father, his temper, and his stopping at nothing to get what he wanted.

Pretending the last four years didn't happen isn't

possible. It's not easier, and it's not logical, I decided definitively. My heart wasn't here with Jared, buried in the rubble of memories, broken promises, and lies. And sadly, with newfound awareness, I realized that perhaps it never was. In the past, I'd fallen in love with who he pretended to be, not who he truly was. At his core, he wasn't an honorable man. A darkness resided in him, a darkness I was too scared to acknowledge and breathe life into. Until now.

"Claire told me about Heather," I said abruptly.

He chuckled. "I knew you seemed off. If you'd asked me, I would have told you."

"Told me what?"

"That I told her I couldn't be with her, despite her infatuation."

I studied his dark eyes for a long moment.

He leaned down and whispered, "She wasn't you, doll. You've always been in possession of my heart. I couldn't give her what I don't have."

Jared took his hand from my waist, twirled me under his arm, and pulled me in again. He grasped the back of my neck, sliding his fingers into my hair, and pressed his lips to mine.

I tried to pull away, but his grasp on the back of my neck tightened. When our kiss broke, I stared at his chest, my breath coming wildly and my heart pounding painfully against my ribcage.

We danced in silence, and my knees trembled.

Sy was somewhere inside Quantym now, lying in a sensory deprivation tank, being inundated with information that he needed to complete his mission of taking down Quantym. He was less than a mile from where I stood, and while all my actions were to try to help Sy, I couldn't help but feel I was dripping with betrayal.

So easy, too easy, it would be to just play the part with Jared.

But my heart refused.

I looked over to see Mitch watching us, and quickly diverted my gaze back to Jared.

Jared spoke and broke me from my thoughts. His voice revealed his smile. "You *will* need to apologize to Claire, though. You don't want her to make your life miserable here. Officer Gaudreau is indebted to her after his last affair, so he'll make *me* miserable if I don't get you to show some remorse for embarrassing her like that."

I shook my head. "She doesn't deserve an apology…"

"Charly…" Jared cajoled.

He may have agreed with me, but he was more concerned with smoothing over the situation.

I glanced across the room again, and a familiar face was staring at me from across the bar.

Jared felt my body stiffen, and his head snapped up. "What is it?" His arm tightened uncomfortably around my waist.

"Just need to use the ladies' room."

"You can wait until the song is over."

His arm loosened a bit, and I took a hungry breath, then I nodded.

Joel, dressed in his Class A's, tilted his head and watched me dance with Jared from the other side of the bar.

I knew what he'd seen—the kiss—just by his expression. My heart pounded in my chest, and my stomach curled into a tight knot. A wave of dizziness washed over me.

"A little too much to drink?" Jared asked.

"I'm a lightweight."

He nodded. "That you are."

The song ended, and I pulled away, heading straight toward Joel. But as I walked in his direction, I was just in time to see him slam his highball glass onto the bar top and disappear into the crowd.

I walked from one end of the room to the other, even peeking onto the smoking deck, but I couldn't find him anywhere. My feet ached in the stilettos, but I trekked back and forth, weaving in and out of the droves of people in search of Joel.

"Need help finding the ladies' room?" Jared grasped my arm.

"Yes, please." I smiled, masking my dismay.

He walked me to a small corridor and motioned to the restroom. "Meet me back at the table." He raised his eyebrows.

I wouldn't have much time before he came looking for me again. I ducked into the room to compose myself. I splashed water onto my arms and chest in a failed attempt to calm down as I stared at my reflection and counted my breaths.

"Well, don't you clean up nice." Becca was just exiting a stall. She stared at me gripping the edges of the sink.

Becca's cropped hair was gelled, and she wore her crisp Class A's. She turned on the faucet and washed her hands, staring at me as she did.

"I'm sorry, Becca. I have to go."

I pushed the heavy restroom door open, ready to dart

back to the table. Before I could get my thoughts in order, I was pulled into a small alcove by a firm hand around my elbow.

"We *can* do this without you," Joel whispered sternly. "Your role was included for Sy's sake."

"I don't *want* to be here or near him, but I'm doing what I have to do so Sy doesn't get killed!" I kept my voice in a harsh whisper as I looked around to make sure no one was close by.

"If you're certain, be at the Ground House tomorrow, they open at five. You won't be meeting me, but an associate on our team. Her name is Diogo, and she'll brief you on the plan."

"Becca," I whispered.

"You don't have to do this. Sy's been abandoned by someone he cared about once, don't play along if you're having second thoughts."

I lifted my chin. "I *am* certain. I always have been. I'll be there."

Joel warily searched my eyes for a moment before conceding, "I hope you know what you're getting into." He sighed. "They've moved his jump ahead of schedule. We wake him in 48 hours."

"Jared said he knows you've been researching them." I stiffened. "He went to unplug someone the other day, too. Someone who 'deviated from the mission'."

"Good to know. We're going in blind, now. We can't take any more risks until it's time to infiltrate. Hang in there, Charlotte. It's only a couple more days."

I drew in a shuddering breath. "Yeah, I got this. I can do it." I nodded, unsure if I was talking to him or me at that point. I was relieved this was going to be over soon, that I'd get to look into Sy's eyes again, even if it was just before being killed together, if things didn't go right.

"Tomorrow at five will be your last contact with us before we go in."

I nodded.

Joel darted out of the alcove and straight out the side door marked as a fire exit.

I made my way back to our table, where Jared and Mitch sat together talking. I took a seat on the side of Jared just in time for Mitch to stand. I was hoping he was leaving so I wouldn't have to interact with him, but he offered me his hand. I stared at it, confused, until he impatiently waved it at me. I clutched his hand, and he led me to the dance floor.

I looked back at Jared, who shrugged and smirked, then abruptly turned to converse with some troops who'd stopped to talk with him.

Mitch and I started dancing, and he leaned his head down near my ear to speak to me.

"I hear you've changed for the better, Charly. Jared loved you then, but now—" He shook his head and laughed. "—you've really got your teeth in him. I hope your intentions are pure, because I've been watching, and I will *keep* watching."

"Is that a threat? If anyone should be questioning intentions, it's *me,*" I said through my teeth.

"Huh, I guess he's right. Much improved, not as pathetic as before. You've got some gall to you now. See, Charly? Sometimes it's the pain that helps us metamorphosize into our best self."

"How *dare* you...if you think the accident *improved* anything about my life, you're insane," I seethed. I hadn't broken, I survived on my own not *because of the accident, but in spite of it.*

"You're wrong, Charly. You couldn't even make a simple decision before. You relied on Jared for everything, and were no more than a…distraction. A weakness, a puppet, a pet, a *leech*. But look at you now. You became your own person after losing everything."

"What did you expect? I was twenty-one when he married me, of course I relied on him. That's exactly what he *wanted*."

Mitch nodded. "So innocent you were. Docile. Don't get too smart on us, Charly. We know how to keep you in line. We know where all your *weak* spots lie."

I pulled away from Mitch, my lip curling with disgust. I tried to swallow, my mouth suddenly dry.

He quickly pulled me back to him and kept swaying as if nothing had happened, as if we were discussing the weather and not his assessment of who I was and who I became after he and his son abandoned me. Who I became after losing everything, my sanity included.

"Was losing your grandchild also character building?" I prodded, seeking compassion from him.

"You can make another," Mitch replied coldly, and poked me in the stomach.

A surprised gasp escaped my lips. I hated myself for the tears that stung my eyes.

"See? All. Your. Weak. Spots," he whispered. "You should've died, you know. That was the plan. But the universe had something better in store for us, didn't it?"

My brow furrowed. "W-what?"

"I thought you stood in the way of the plans I had for my son, but it turns out you were inevitably an important piece of the puzzle. I should give Jared more credit," he said thoughtfully.

"You—" I stopped abruptly as his words settled and awareness clicked in place. I had every right to fear him. It wasn't an *accident*. Bile rose in my throat.

I tried pulling away again, but Mitch clutched me tighter.

A soft chuckle indicated he could feel my trembling. "It's been four years, so I've given you a bit of leniency. But time's up Charly. Fall in line. When Jared or I say jump, you're to ask how high. Understood?"

I nodded. Tears streamed down my cheeks.

"Now, Charly, you're going to look up at me and smile."

I did as I was told.

"Look at that, to an outsider, emotional tears of happiness. The general celebrates his son's engagement, and the widow weeps with joy."

I closed my eyes, desperate to stop the tears that brought him so much satisfaction.

"How easily manipulated the world is. Almost unfair, isn't it?" he crooned.

I nodded, and the song ended.

Mitch escorted me to the table while I wiped tears with the back of my hand.

Jared set his drink down on the table and looked up at me. "Do *not* make a scene. Pull yourself together, Charly," he warned.

I stormed away from the table and outside into the humid night air. I sat on a wrought-iron bench that faced the lot, my face aflame with burning tears. My head was swimming from Mitch's words, at how very disposable I'd been. Then, my quick meeting with Joel, who seemed to question my loyalty, not to mention my need to be at the Ground House by five in the morning. And the fact that Sy was probably already in an induced coma. Was he okay? Was he hurt? What would become of us when this was all over?

If Jared or Mitch learned of my intentions, I'd be killed. Slowly and painfully, probably.

I put my head in my hands and struggled to slow my sprinting heart. I dissected Mitch's assessment about who I was now compared to before. I had grown up, for sure, but maybe there was something else. Before, I'd never have put someone like Claire in her place, and I'd have never risked defying Jared or Mitch, or had the boldness to help save Sy while the team took down Quantym, risking my life and others.

I thought about how I'd been struggling to face myself in the mirror, and realized it didn't have as much to do with *me* as it did with facing the hard truth of everything I'd been through. For years I had struggled with survivor's guilt, the evil harpy that tried to convince me my survival was not validated. Jared was worth more because he served the country, and the baby was worth more because he was a new soul filled with promise and hope. My survival was a mistake. I didn't offer the world anything, and my mundane existence for several years after the accident reinforced that.

What I could give the world would never be enough.

But then I met Sy, who helped me feel alive again, and I realized that a part of me didn't die permanently after the accident. I'd died and I'd *come back,* something I never allowed myself to believe before. Maybe there *was* a purpose for me, for my survival, bigger than I could've ever imagined, bigger than just one or two people.

A small truth—not trauma—sat just below the

surface of my jade irises when I stared at my reflection, a truth that I wasn't ready to accept or acknowledge just yet. A truth that meant that everything that happened was part of a grand design far greater than any one of us. Maybe, just maybe, it was an essential part of my journey. But I wouldn't, or more accurately—couldn't—face that truth just yet.

The window of my life was shattering and realigning itself in a new way, now offering a clearer view of things both old and new.

I tapped my heel on the concrete, my shoulders releasing tension as I counted each *tap, tap, tap*...

A breeze and slight movement sounded from behind me. And I didn't have to look to know—Jared was watching me.

Chapter 17

"I know of no better life's purpose than to perish...in attempting the great and impossible." – *Friedrich Nietzsche*

When we got home, Jared headed into the kitchen.

Ice cubes clinked as they were thrown into a glass.

I peered around the corner as I removed my earrings and saw him pouring two glasses of whisky. He held a glass out to me, which I declined.

He shrugged and downed the glass that was for me, and started on the glass he'd made for himself.

I rolled my eyes as I walked away and then heard more liquor being poured into his glass.

I wondered if he was trying to drink away the memories of the past, his father's words, or both. According to Jared, the accident wasn't orchestrated, and Mitch was messing with me.

I slipped out of my heels and started carrying them to the bedroom. I had just one foot on the bottom stair when his hand wrapped around mine, pulling me back down toward him. I resisted, so he grasped my other arm forcefully, causing the shoes to fall onto the tile with a thud.

He stepped into me, then crushed his lips against mine.

I struggled against his bruising grasp, and tried to cry out as his whisky-flavored lips relentlessly devoured mine.

He pulled away abruptly, and my chest heaved with panicked breaths.

He let out a heavy sigh. "Such a terrible accident, and yet not one visible scar." His fingers trailed over my collarbone, featherlight, stopping to circle the area where it'd broken.

I pressed my back against the wall, fear rising in my chest as he circled the healed bone with his fingertips. "I do have a scar."

"Mmm, I know." His fingers trailed up my neck and into my hair, drifting over the left side, feeling for the aberrant skin on my scalp. "But I said visible."

My breaths came in small pants. I stared at him, his fingers now making their way out of my hair and down my chest.

He fumbled for half a heartbeat, searching my ribs, and then he smiled. "Ah, here." His fingers danced across my lower rib.

My throat constricted.

He circled the barely perceptible bump left from the rib that'd broken and lacerated my liver, causing me to bleed out and nearly killing me.

The bump that still ached when it rained, or if I slept on my right side.

He met my questioning eyes.

"I know *everything*, Charly." He continued circling the tender rib with gentle fingers. "My porcelain doll is so *fragile*."

I tried to sidestep away from him, and he pushed the heel of his palm into the rib.

A wince escaped my lips before I could clamp my mouth shut.

"Kiss me, Charly. Don't make me ask twice."

I reached up and touched his face, gently trailing my finger along his disfiguring scar.

His eyes closed at my touch, and he drew in a sharp breath.

I wasn't physically strong enough to fight him. But I knew Jared, and his only weakness was his ego. *Make him think he won, and his guard will crumble. He's not used to losing.*

The only way to escape this fire was to walk directly through it. Even if it burned me to ashes.

I locked my arms around his neck and stood on my toes to reach his lips.

Jared's lips parted immediately, and his body pinned me to the wall.

My rib screamed in protest, but I continued kissing him, my thoughts racing on how to escape him now that he was distracted, vulnerable.

His hands roved over my curves, a deep sound coming from this throat as he reached around to the back of my gown and released the zipper.

I pulled back with a gasp, and he grabbed a fistful of my hair to angle my face toward him so he could again press his lips against mine. I let out a squeal of pain as his grip tightened around the tuft of hair he held, keeping my face at an available angle for his vicious lips.

I twisted unexpectedly, causing him to stumble and catch himself on the first step of the staircase.

He looked at me with fury, his eyes almost black as he quickly grabbed my arms again.

The loosened dress allowed my knee to connect

swiftly with his groin. *"Don't fucking touch me*!" I screamed.

He doubled over in pain, and I kicked his chest, sending him stumbling to the tile.

He scrambled toward me, uttering a string of profanities, but I was already bolting up the stairs.

I ran up the stairs as fast as my legs would take me, missing a step and catching myself at the very top. I scrambled into the office and locked the door behind me. My heart pounded with the knowledge that I couldn't stay here, near him, for another night or another moment. I dropped to the floor and crawled to the back of the closet to grab my backpack. Inside, along with the phone and pistol, were also extra clothes. I pulled on the shorts, tank and sneakers, leaving the gown on the floor in a pile.

"Open up, Charly. I'm sorry, let's just talk." Jared knocked on the office door.

I didn't answer.

He pounded harder, and the wood bowed against his powerful thumps.

I felt feral as I scanned around the room looking for an escape. I wasn't afraid of heights, but when I looked out the window, I knew I'd never make the jump. My hands shook when I realized I was going to need the pistol. I didn't have time to pine over the decision, and my hands were already unzipping the compartment where it was stowed.

I counted the ticks of the wall clock, and my hands steadied. Internally I kept trying to find alternatives to killing him, but as I counted, my hands had a mind of their own as I slid the magazine into the well and pulled back on the slide, loading a round into the chamber. I pulled the backpack onto my shoulders and pressed my back against the wall.

I pointed the gun at the door.

The door bowed again as the thumping got progressively louder and harder.

"Open the fucking door, Charly!"

His voice was completely unrecognizable with anger and ferocity.

I stopped breathing altogether when the door finally buckled under Jared's assault, swinging open lopsided and crashing into the wall. I looked into his black eyes and fired just to the right of his head.

A chunk of wood exploded from the door frame, causing Jared to quickly crouch to the ground as splinters of wood rained down on him.

"Are you out of your damn mind?" he shouted.

I adjusted my position and held the pistol in position to hit him, not the doorframe. "Move, Jared. I don't want to have to do this." I stared at him, ready to pull the trigger if he made another move.

He put his hands up slowly and moved aside to allow a space for me to get through the damaged doorway.

I aimed the pistol at him as I inched closer to my escape. I drew calm strength from the predictable tick of the wall clock. "Move, Jared. Let me by."

He backed a little farther down the hall.

"Charly, you've done it." He laughed, trying to put me off guard. "You've officially lost your mind. I thought you'd emerged stronger. But look at you, bat-shit crazy."

"For defending myself?" I nodded toward my still-throbbing biceps covered in red handprints where he'd gripped me too tightly.

"Defending yourself?" He chuckled, sliding his hands into his pockets. "I'm your *husband*."

"You must be mistaken." I cocked my head. "I'm widowed."

"If this is because of Simon, I want you to know, I'm looking forward to killing him. And I'm going to make you watch, Charly."

"You can't take accountability for anything, can you?" I spat. "I'm not doing this because of him, I'm doing this because you're such an *asshole*." I silently continued counting the ticking clock on the wall.

"Shhh, Charly. Don't you hear that?" He began tapping his foot out of rhythm, interrupting the predictable ticking pattern.

His foot tapping made counting impossible. My hands trembled; the barrel of the gun gave me away.

"All your *weak spots*," he whispered.

I started backing into the master bedroom as he slithered toward me. I didn't have much time, but I needed his spare badge from the safe. I said a silent prayer that the dates of his death and new life would open it.

Jared laughed again.

I hesitated in the master doorway.

"You never asked me *who* is actually buried in my grave Charly. It might interest you to know now that you have a gun pointed at me." He flashed a sinister smile. He paced, sliding his hands back into his pockets. Casual. Unconcerned. He answered his own question when the silence stretched on.

"Adam Cardoza. We did look quite alike. Now, if you think I'd kill my own brother to get my life back, but let *you* get away with threatening *mine…*" Jared fisted his hands and stalked toward me with an evil glint in his eyes.

If he got his hands on me, I was as good as dead.

I slammed the master door and locked it before he could enter. I had only seconds, because he wasn't rapping on the door with his hands this time. I could tell by the sound he was putting his entire body weight into it with his shoulder.

I ran into the walk-in and, with trembling fingers, punched in the dates sequentially, almost crying out in relief when the lock unhitched with a click. I grabbed his extra badge and quickly shut the safe, hoping he wouldn't notice the back-up badge missing before I could put it to use.

I ran to the front window and threw it open. I looked down at the gabled roof that slanted downward toward the front door.

The door exploded open, and I jumped.

I slid down the peaked gable, jumped onto the front porch, and ran to the backyard.

I pumped my legs faster and faster, not bothering to look behind me. I assumed he was chasing me, so I kept running in the dark until my chest burned and legs wobbled. I was able to weave in and out of the thin trees and shrubs and hide better through the back than in the open streets.

When I thought I may have lost him, I rested in a thin line of bushes that separated two large homes. I tried to see if he was out there somewhere, but I couldn't see much, other than the dim yellow lights from the nearby homes.

The night was quiet with only the occasional tinkle of a nearby wind chime floating through the heavy air.

I continued on, this time walking instead of running, trying to figure out which street I was on as I made my way through the thin veil of trees that separated the backyards.

A faint rumble of thunder sounded in the distance.

I kneeled in the damp grass where three pine trees grew up against a tall wooden fence. A breeze lifted my wild hair off my neck, and the coolness was a balm to my burning fear as I cleared the gun, removed the magazine, and stowed it away. Then I looked at my cell and saw Jared was texting me incessantly.

—I'm sorry, come home, we'll talk.—

—It was the drinking, Charly. I would never hurt you. Call me at least.—

—I can't lose you again, come home.—

When I didn't respond, the tone of the texts changed.

—Everyone knows who you are, and everyone works for us.—

—You can run, but you can't hide.—

—I'm going to find you and end you.—

I remembered the night Sy had taken me to Joel's trailer, and how he'd launched my phone so we couldn't be tracked. I powered down my phone and placed it on the ground, then stomped on it until the screen cracked and crumbled. I picked it up and threw it into an above-ground swimming pool at the closest house. The colorful floats left behind in the pool bobbed and swayed.

I pulled the hidden phone out from the backpack and dialed.

Joel answered on the first ring.

"I'm going to need your help." My voice shook. "Things just got a little complicated."

It didn't take long for Joel to find me.

By the time I ran into the street to slide into his passenger seat, I was drenched from the rain that had started abruptly after I'd hung up with him. My knees were muddy and grass-stained, blood caked my arm, and bruises had bloomed on my biceps.

I rested my head on the back of the seat and closed my eyes. When I opened them, Joel's gaze darted from the road ahead and back to me, again and again.

Before he could ask about the bruises, I told him what had happened.

He listened quietly and when I finished, the only sound was the wipers squawking across the windshield. A bright flash of lightning illuminated the neighborhood electric blue for an instant, then a loud crack of thunder followed.

"I'm impressed." Joel stared at the road ahead. "I just wish you'd shot him while you had the chance."

We drove the rest of the way in silence until we pulled up to a large red-brick complex of apartments.

"Diogo was the one who was going to meet you in the morning." He paused and laughed. "But you're not going to like my plan to get you inside." He motioned to the back seat.

I glanced in the back and saw a duffel bag hanging open. I looked at him, bewildered.

How ridiculous it was being smuggled into the apartment like a brick of heroin. I was freed with a loud zip, and I squinted when the bright overhead light hit my eyes.

"Dang girl, you can't catch a break, can you?" Becca held her hand out to me.

I grasped her hand, and she helped me up. My shoulders slumped, and I laughed, looking down and taking in my muddy and bloody appearance.

She smiled and gave a pat on the back as she led me into the washroom to get cleaned up.

Joel poked his head in to announce he was leaving, handing me an envelope before turning toward the door. He stopped with his back facing us and looked over his shoulder as he spoke. "What you've gone through to help me save my brother is brave. I'm going to do everything in my power to ensure the two of you are together, if that's what you want."

I understood what he was implying. "It is exactly what I want."

He nodded and left.

Becca and I talked as she bustled about, pulling out bandages, alcohol, and gauze to clean and dress the scrapes on my knees and elbows.

The adrenaline must've numbed me, I finally noticed my injured elbow was scraped raw from my descent down the roof. My arms were massively bruised, with large handprints from Jared's grasp. The poorly-healed rib throbbed with fresh pain. Plus, my bottom lip was slightly swollen. I shuddered when I realized just how viciously he'd kissed me.

It was well after midnight by the time I cleaned up and my wounds were dressed.

Becca made coffee, and we sat at her small table to discuss the plan for getting me into Quantym. She was certain Jared had everyone looking for me, but she was only able to house me for the night.

By tomorrow evening, I'd be on my own again, as there was a unit returning from a training program, and her roommate would be coming home.

Becca was small but a large presence, and she

wasn't concerned that our plan would go awry. She pulled out a map and started going over the layout of the hospital, pointing to the morgue and the freight elevator I'd need to take as an alternate entrance to Quantym.

Jared's badge would allow me to enter the lower level that most people couldn't access. I'd need to dress as a medical employee and wear a medical mask so I was concealed from the surveillance cameras.

Becca and her team had arranged for her to work security in the ORA wing on the day of my infiltration. She'd help me gain access to the top-secret clearance area.

She placed her finger on the paper and ran it along a small line that indicated a corridor; the old boiler-room tunnels led under the parking lot and into another underground building where the ORA wing was housed. An old freight elevator was one of two entry points into the wing. She explained the landmarks I'd see, and the guards I'd encounter before being able to get into the steel-vaulted wing where Sy was.

She pulled out a bag with scrubs with Quantym embroidered on the breast pocket. "You're a newly hired doctor, enlisted in the Army, with the highest level of security clearance offered by the United States Government."

She proudly held up the fraudulent badge with my photo on it.

I smiled, impressed.

"Hand me Jared's badge."

I dug in my backpack and handed it to her.

She pulled a pocket knife out and began digging into the badge. "Voila." She popped a chip out, then implanted it into my fake badge.

"Where do I go tomorrow? Everyone is looking for me."

"Heh, you ain't kidding."

She pulled a lighter from her pocket and heated the edge of my badge where she'd implanted Jared's clearance chip. She rubbed her finger over it to seal the plastic. "Like butter," she said proudly and handed me the ID.

I put it with the rest of my uniform.

"Tomorrow night." she said, "You need to find a place to blend in."

"Gee, thanks. Now that everyone on base is looking for me, that should be easy-peasy…"

"I'm not worried about tomorrow. Hide in plain sight, always works. What I'm worried about is the day after. And what we *don't* know."

"The day we infiltrate."

She nodded. "Joel will have the team sweep in once we get the call from you that Sy's awake. It won't go down easily; the program is a huge money-maker. They're going to try to kill anyone who goes in, military or not."

"You have the phone?"

I nodded.

"Joel said you have a gun?"

"I do." I tapped my backpack.

"You know how to use it?" She eyed me critically.

"Yes," I assured her. "Becca? What do you think we don't know?"

She drew a deep breath. "A lot. I know you're just coming up to speed with this tech, but there's a program at Quantym that allows people to embed information to bring to the other side, even if they're not jumpers. It

273

isn't the same as, say, you or Simon, who can remember everything. But it's enough to raise hell, the large amount they can have planted before they arrive, and the small amount they can embed to bring over."

"You're afraid the Cardozas already set themselves up on the other side?"

"Yes. They've had years to build up the intel they'd need in case they went there, whether of their own accord or not. We might win this battle, but they've likely prepared for war."

I bit my lip. There was so much I didn't know, and so much more I wanted to ask, but it was getting late.

"So, this whole multiverse thing, you believe it?" Becca asked.

"I do." I shook my head. "As crazy as it sounds, it makes sense."

"Yeah. Maybe life *is* fair." She shrugged.

"What's got me puzzled is the beyond, ya know?"

"Oh, you mean like after a normal lifespan, eighty years or so, right?"

I nodded.

She shrugged again. "That's where faith comes in. Maybe you're reborn, reincarnated, and the cycle continues with your main life in the middle and the multiple peripheral lives happening simultaneously. Or maybe the ultimate judgment comes—heaven or hell. For me, I'm not sure what to believe."

"I'd rather be judged on multiple lives, than just one, though."

Becca nodded, then added, "I couldn't possibly be making all the same mistakes over there." She laughed.

"Don't be so sure," I said quietly.

Becca studied me closely, then pulled my scrubs,

badge, door lock, and backpack into a neat pile. She lifted her Glock, then opened and closed the chamber with a metal chink. "Did Sy mention the bleed-through effect?" She didn't look up.

"No, what's that?"

"I guess they've hypothesized that many dreams or phenomena such as déjà vu or the inexplicable dislike we have for someone we've just met are part of a bleed-through effect. Our subconscious may be aware of events on the Periphery, but they're held so deep within us that we can only experience the *feelings* that bleed through from events occurring on the other side."

"Makes sense I suppose."

"Yeah, or like that chemistry you have with someone when you meet for the first time. Or the fear of someone who gives you the willies for seemingly no reason. Anxiety and depression, too, you know."

"Really?"

"I guess if life over there is bad enough, it's enough to fuck you up here, too. But enough about the Periphery. You need rest."

"Thanks, Becca. For everything."

"Anytime, Charlotte. Anytime."

Becca handed me a pillow and blanket and retreated to her room for the night.

I sat on the couch and opened Joel's envelope, pulling out a folded note.

Charlotte, if you're reading this, I'm probably already under. Or unplugged. If I don't make it back, just know whether I'm in this reality or the next, I'll never stop loving you. You've made everything in my past and present worth it. Please be safe, and please take care of yourself, that is all I ask. I love you. -Sy

275

Determination clawed at my broken heart, and I resolved that, no matter what, I wouldn't let him die. I couldn't.

The next morning, I was alive with adrenaline.

Becca triple checked to make sure I had all of the supplies I'd need—the ID, the scrubs, the pistol, an attachable door lock, and the phone. She went over basic self-defense with me. The compact woman was a powerhouse.

I hugged her tightly before I left just as night was beginning to fall.

She walked me to the edge of the woods. "Charlotte, wait."

I turned my back on the woods to look at her again.

"I can see why Joel's brother loves you." She rubbed a hand over her short hair.

I walked over to Becca and gave her a soft kiss on the cheek. "Thank you, Becca, for walking with me in the dark."

And with that, I pulled the hood over my head and turned to start my silent trek through the forest.

I thought about my journal, and the night I'd burned it, declaring the magic, the supernatural, the vision during death was all a farce. And here I was, about to embark on the most unbelievable mission of my life.

Guess there really is magic, I thought without humor.

When I reached the hospital parking lot, I slowed my gait and waited in the row of bushes. I sat on the wet ground, dozing in my hiding spot. I ensured that the small lock Becca had put on my backpack was fastened. This was the best plan I could come up with to have a place to stay until the next morning when I would be able to wake Sy.

Screeching tires woke me.

A woman wailed and a car door slammed. She stumbled in the direction of the emergency room doors.

I flew from my position. My sweatshirt was over my scrubs, and I looped a mask over my face. I grasped onto the woman's arms. "Let me help you."

"Please, please." She stumbled.

"What's your name?"

"Maria, Maria Lima," she wailed.

"Okay Maria, it's going to be okay. How old are you?"

"Forty-five." She let out another groan and held her stomach.

"You're doing a great job, Maria, almost there. Is that your husband over there, parking the car?"

She nodded.

I braced her arm over my shoulder and held her up. I burst through the emergency room doors and demanded a wheelchair.

I began barking orders. "We have a forty-five-year-old female, dropped off by her husband, acute abdominal pain!"

I pointed to an orderly. "Get your ass over here and put her in the chair!"

He ran toward us and helped the patient into a wheelchair.

Maria cried out again.

"You!" I pointed at a nurse practitioner in a lab coat. "Call radiology, she's going to need a scan, stat!"

The NP crossed her arms. "Who are *you*?"

"Your attending physician this evening." I flashed my fake badge. "Now, *call radiology*!"

She grabbed the phone and began dialing.

I ripped back the curtain of an unoccupied bay with a whoosh. "Bring her in!" I called to the orderly.

A nurse scrambled into the room with a cart. She identified the patient and put a hospital band on her wrist. She began reading the patient's medical history to me.

"Call the lab to come draw her blood, then start her IV!"

The nurse nodded and began pulling supplies from the cart.

"Come on Maria, up you go."

The orderly and I hoisted the patient onto the stretcher.

A young man came in to draw her blood.

"I want a CBC and a chem panel."

I poked my head out of the curtain and pointed at the NP. "Did you hear me? Put the orders in!"

She clicked the mouse on the computer furiously.

"A CBC and CMP?"

"Yes, STAT!" I yelled.

Maria sat up and heaved.

The phlebotomist rushed his vials of blood to the lab, and the nurse handed her a basin.

The patient vomited.

"Get that IV into her, now!" I demanded.

A pang of guilt shook me when I saw the nurse's hands tremble. "And for the love of God, would someone please get me a lab coat?"

The orderly rushed in and handed me a white lab coat.

I pointed at the NP. "Do an acute abdominal pain exam."

The NP scurried into the room to examine the

patient.

"Radiology is ready for her now," the orderly announced.

The orderly unlocked the bed, and I held my hand up. "I'll take her, I want you to get the lab on the line and start getting verbal results."

"I don't think the blood is even in the lab yet," he said, eyebrows raised.

"I don't care! Call them!" I hissed. "And after I deliver her to radiology, I'll be in the on-call suite. If the NP knows what she's doing, she's to take over this patient's care. Tell her only to call me if it's necessary, or I'll have her ass in a vice. Understood?"

He nodded and rushed off to call the lab.

I swiftly wheeled the stretcher into the hallway and followed the signs to radiology. On the way, I grabbed a med bonnet to conceal my hair.

The tech waited for us in the doorway. She pulled the patient's stretcher into the CAT- scan room, and I disappeared down the hall.

I found the on-call physician lounge and dropped my bag onto one of the beds. Fighting the adrenaline rush, I peeled off the lab coat and draped it over the side of the bed, then flopped down. I laid my head back and sighed.

It was hard to sleep, but I was able to get an hour of rest in the uncomfortable bed and scratchy linens. I sat up and dug out the copy of the hospital layout Becca had given me, memorizing the path I'd have to take in just a few hours. I figured out where I was on the map and where the elevator was, so when the sun began to rise, I hopped from my bed and quickly donned the lab coat over my Quantym scrubs.

The change of shift would be happening soon, and the staff would be distracted with their morning reports.

I made my way through the quiet halls and felt the adrenaline course through me like a fresh bolus of epinephrine. I found my way to the freight elevator, and scanned my badge. The lower-level button lit up, and I pressed it. I heard a beep and the light turned green. My stomach fluttered as the elevator descended to the lowest level of the old building.

I concealed my hair in the med bonnet and clipped my fake ID to the breast pocket of the lab coat, then I pinched the wire of the mask over my nose.

I straightened my back, preparing for what came next.

Chapter 18

The elevator jolted to a stop at the lower level, and the door slowly rolled open.

I followed the long, winding corridor that snaked under the parking lot, just as Becca's map had shown me. It was stifling hot. I looked around at the exposed overhead piping and small alcoves where outdated medical equipment was haphazardly stored, noting that each area I walked by was exactly as Becca had described it.

Despite the airless heat of the hallway, the hairs on my arms prickled at the creepy feel of the long underground corridor. The medical clogs I wore filled the quiet hall with a rhythmic *clunk, clunk, clunk,* and as I neared the ORA wing, my heart seemed to be keeping time with the sound.

At the end of the hall, two uniformed and generously armed guards were seated at a desk just outside a heavy steel door.

I ignored the thumping in my chest and focused on the rhythmic sound of my shoes echoing in the corridor. I kept my features calm and relaxed as I approached the guards.

One was looking down at his phone; the other appeared to have noticed me, but quickly looked down at the clipboard on the desk.

I stopped and told them my alias, smoothly hiding

my surprise when Becca, in full uniform, looked up at me with a bored expression.

"We've been expecting you. ID, please." She used a handheld wand to scan my ID.

A loud buzz sounded as the door behind her unlocked.

"Good luck on your first day." She gestured for me to follow her.

The other guard glanced up at me and back down at his phone.

I walked through the door and into the Quantym wing. Goosebumps rose on my arms because the whole place was frigid. I walked down a long glass corridor illuminated with bright overhead lighting that gleamed off the white tiled floors and noticed the pods in the rooms that lined both sides of the hall.

The sensory deprivation tanks. I shuddered at the thought of Sy locked inside of one of the shiny, gray alien-looking pods for days on end before his jump.

Becca walked heavy-booted ahead of me to buzz me through another set of heavy doors. "You'll go down this hall and ask for Dr. Gustav. Good luck."

She held the door, and I stepped through. I was keenly aware of my pounding heart and trembling hands when the door slammed behind me, followed by the almost inaudible click of a lock engaging that echoed through the sterile hall with finality.

I walked over to a large desk and provided my alias to a serious-looking, black-suited gentleman; the clear coil of an earpiece snaked from his ear into his suit collar.

His hands whizzed over the keyboard for a moment, and he asked for my badge.

I handed it to him and restrained myself from

shifting nervously.

"Glad you're here. Michaels, she's with me, I'll check her in." Gustav's accent was unmistakable as he made his way toward me. He quickly took my badge from the man and used a handheld scanner to scan it.

"Doctor, follow me." Dr. Gustav walked me over to another badge-only door.

He smiled at me and announced he'd be giving me a tour before I started my training.

We walked down the hall, and my eyes widened as I took in the glass-walled rooms on either side of us that held sedated and intubated patients. He was talking and walking quickly, and I scrambled to keep up.

He explained the rooms, the room numbers, and where the exits were. He showed me how to get in and out with the badge and the fastest way out of the wing to the outside by going down another long corridor that led to a stairwell that accessed the cancer-care center above us.

Dr. Gustav walked me over to an area where a decompression waking was taking place.

I stood outside the room and watched as the nurses, doctors and counselors prepared to wake a patient.

A tall nurse removed the cooling wraps then stopped the IV.

The room was silent as they monitored and documented vital signs.

A young female doctor extubated the patient fastidiously.

Within moments, the patient started to come to life.

Initially, it reminded me of the ICU I'd worked in, the nurses continually monitoring his vitals and applying heating blankets as his body acclimated to no longer being sedated. But suddenly, it was obvious the patient started to *remember* as a flurry of activity ensued.

The patient was screaming and flailing violently as a nurse angled a camera at him.

I could hear him bellowing but couldn't discern his words.

I was so captivated by the situation before me that Gustav had to pull me by the elbow to get my attention, and we were on the move again. Sy had described waking up accurately, and I wondered how I'd calm him when I woke him from his mission.

We walked back to the heavy door that led to the sedated patients.

"You don't have more than thirty minutes. When Jared's badge registers again when he arrives for work, they're going to know there's been an infiltration, and they'll be looking for you. Simon is in room 312. Be careful," he whispered. Gustav waved his badge in front of the door, the loud buzzer went off again, and he held the door open for me.

"Where will you be?" I whispered in a shaky voice.

"Reviewing the medical data, and ensuring we can minimize loss of lives. Godspeed, Charlotte."

I stepped through the door, and it shut with a loud clang and a quick click as it locked behind me. I was alone again. I wiped my palms across my lab coat and straightened my back as I strode past the glass-walled rooms, the hall filled with the continuous beep of monitors and whooshing of ventilators breathing for the half-dead patients.

Nurses took vitals and checked monitors in some of the rooms, one or two of whom noticed me walking by.

I gave a confident head-nod, but kept scanning each

room number I walked past. My heart rate increased as I got closer. 310. 311. 312.

I looked through the glass, but didn't recognize the man lying in the hospital bed. I scanned my badge and entered the room. *Had Gustav made a mistake?* I pulled the door lock from my backpack and put it at the base of the door and secured it to the floor. I walked slowly over to the bed.

I'd been in ICUs before, but this sterile, clandestine environment was different. I looked down at the man in the bed, and it was indeed Simon. I reached for his hand under the cooling packs and held it in mine.

His chest rose and fell under the pressure of the ventilator tubing taped to his mouth. His large, lifeless body and slightly bluish skin made him nearly unrecognizable.

I discreetly started removing the coolant packs that were wrapped around his large body. I used all of my strength as I struggled to get the cooling packs out from under him. I shimmied and pulled at them, allowing them to fall to the floor with a thump as I freed him from his ice-cold cocoon. He had fluids running into both arms, and I sprang into action. I dropped his hand and ran over to the IV pumps. I recognized the names of the drugs, and stopped each pump, one by one.

I watched his alarmingly slow heart and respiratory rate as the medications made their way out of his system.

Calm. Stay calm. Breathe. You cannot save a patient if you panic. The words of my nursing supervisor ran through my head. I tried to stuff away the intrusive thoughts that were rushing through my head. *Focus, Charlotte. You have a job to do. Slow, steady. Don't shock the system.*

I counted each beep on the monitor that indicated a heartbeat.

Eighteen, nineteen, twenty…

My gaze darted around the room. I didn't see any heating blankets to expedite the body-warming process.

Shit. It's okay. Improvise. Think!

I watched his vitals closely, then looked around the room again, hoping for something—anything—to help warm his freezing cold body. I opened and closed a few cabinets, finding nothing of use.

I turned back to the monitor in time to watch his heart go into a rapid, fatal rhythm—*v fib.*

No, no, no!

I had moments before his brain was starved of life-saving oxygen and irreparably damaged. I started chest compressions.

"Fight, Sy! Dammit, fight!" I yelled at his lifeless body.

One, two, three, four…

I counted compressions while silently begging the universe for a miracle. I was running out of time. Before he died, or before the shit hit the fan and we were swarmed by guardsmen.

Thirteen, fourteen, fifteen…

"Simon! You have to come back, please!" I sobbed. "Come back!"

My arms were sore, my breath ragged as I continued compressions.

Forty-one, forty-two, forty-three…

I scanned the room for hope. No defibrillator to shock him.

Improvise! A voice in my head screamed.

I was taking a huge risk, but I had to do something

to convert his fatal heart rhythm. I stopped compressions and put my ear to his chest. I listened to the ineffective and chaotic quivering of his heart, seeking a pattern in the chaos. I closed my eyes and focused.

Each moment I spent listening he was closer to true death. I opened my eyes and kept the sound of his heart memorized in my head. I straddled him and interlaced my fingers, bringing my interlocked hands above my head, and then bringing them down with a hard blow to his chest.

Precordial thump. Used to produce an electrical depolarization and interrupt fatal rhythms in the absence of a defibrillator.

The monitor started beeping a slow, life-sustaining cardiac rhythm. I let out a wail of relief, but he was still completely unconscious. I knew I was out of time when I heard a loud alarm sound and the hall outside the glass wall lit up red.

Breathe, I coaxed myself, just breathe.

I ignored the clinical voice in my head that screamed for me to wait for more stable vitals before extubating Sy. With fast, trembling hands, I unhooked the tubing from the ventilator, and removed the tape that held the vent tube in place near his mouth. I angled his chin up and pulled carefully on the tube that was down his airway. I released a wail of relief when the removal caused him to cough and gag.

I took his face in my hands and pressed my warm cheek to his cold skin and spoke into his ear.

"Sy, it's me. I'm here, please wake up."

His body remained still, lifeless.

I pressed my warm body onto his to share my body heat. Moment after moment ticked by, and he showed no signs of waking.

Tears streamed down my cheeks, my body trembled, and my heart felt heavy in my chest. I began gasping for air.

I'm going to die, we're going to die. Slowly. Painfully.

My breathing was ragged, my lips numb. This was it. It was over.

I held onto his body and shook with sobs.

"One...two...three...four," Sy's low voice rumbled through me as he counted in time with the heart monitor.

My body calmed; my breaths came more evenly.

"Five...six...seven..." I counted in time with him, with his slow heartbeats.

My heart began to beat in a slower rhythm, calmed by both his voice and the steady counts of each life-sustaining heartbeat. I lifted my head off his chest and studied him. His eyes were squeezed shut, and he shook violently. His hands flexed as his head moved side to side. A painful yell of agony escaped his lips.

I rubbed his arms and crushed my body against his, willing to give him every ounce of my warmth to take away his pain.

He stilled beneath me, and I looked up to meet his gaze. His blue eyes stared into mine with awareness. His arms wrapped tightly around me and I tightened my body around him.

His teeth chattered when he whispered, "Charlotte, you're not supposed to be here. Too dangerous."

His body wasn't ready to spring into action even though his mind was back.

I held him tighter, hoping if I could warm him fast enough, he'd have the strength to stand. I brought my lips to his, and we kissed feverishly at the exhilaration of being together again.

"If I had to die a thousand times just to be with you, I would," he whispered.

"I love you Simon, here, there, wherever we end up. I will always love you."

"I got the servers," he choked. "I have to g-get you out of here." He trembled violently, his lips still blue from his frigid temperature.

"It's ok. Hang on, your body needs to adjust."

"I should've known you wouldn't listen to me. Stubborn."

I choked out a laugh.

A loud buzz in the hall broke us from our trance—the sound indicated an opening door. Loud voices and heavy boots made their way toward us as Sy struggled to regain his strength. I hopped off of the bed and Sy let out another painful groan as he steadied himself on his elbows. I put my arms under his and tried to help him sit up. His large body was too heavy to move, even with my assistance.

I pulled the pistol and magazine out of the backpack and looked up at Sy again. He was sitting, but his shaky arms were barely supporting him.

"Load it." His voice was barely a whisper as he struggled to regain strength.

I looked out the glass into the hall and saw several guards pooled around the door. We were out of time, and Sy wasn't even able to sit unsupported. I watched in horror as the guards stepped aside for someone important, someone who was going to gain access to the room.

Jared.

A loud beep sounded, and a green light flashed. Jared's expression twisted with rage when the door still wouldn't open. The guards were each taking turns ramming their shoulders into it, trying to dislodge the door jammer I'd fastened.

I scanned the room, praying for a way to save us. I pawed through the drawers at the small counter that lined the wall, emptying medical supplies all over the floor. In my haste, I knocked over a metal tray that clanged to the ground.

Sy was sitting now, supported only by one arm. His brow was furrowed in concentration, his body still shuddering and frigid.

I continued riffling through the drawers, looking for anything that could help us.

Simon was sitting up without support, but he wouldn't be able to stand.

Out of the corner of my eye I saw more guards stomping past the window with a battering ram. I diverted my gaze down again, hoping I'd find some miracle in the drawer. I grabbed a handful of epi-pens and ran over to Sy's bed just as the guards hit the door with the battering ram. I uncapped two of the epi-pens and slammed them down into his thigh.

His back stiffened, and he bellowed out a yell, followed by a gasp. He swung his legs over the side of the bed and stood, angling his body in front of me.

The door gave way under the assault by the guards, and they backed out of the room quietly as Jared confidently treaded over the broken door to enter.

Jared looked amused at the gun I held. "Put that fucking thing down, Charly. I'm disappointed. First you lie, then you try to kill me, and now *this?* That's what this was all about, you were going to try to save a *murderer?*" He shook his head and laughed.

I kept the pistol pointed at him.

"And you, don't you know better than to try to steal another man's *wife?*" Jared asked Sy.

"And aren't you supposed to be dead?" Sy countered.

I looked at Sy, who started standing straighter and gaining more strength as the moments ticked by.

"And what now, doll? I have a horde of guards out there waiting. You going to shoot me?"

"If I have to."

"Ah, even if you do, I guess I'll just jump over. I might not remember anything, like you or Simon can, but from what I'm told, I've got it pretty good over there, too. You chose me, *twice.*" Jared chuckled.

The barrel of the gun trembled in my hand.

"Shut him up, Charlotte. Pull the trigger," Sy persuaded.

I pulled the flip phone from my pocket, and hit Joel's number with one hand. He needed to mobilize his team. Now.

"You know what I've learned?" Jared hedged as he sauntered closer to me. "The multiverse may be real, but the possibilities are not infinite. If you don't have it in you to kill, in no reality are you a killer." Jared took advantage of my one-handed grasp on the gun and grabbed my wrist. He twisted it until I shrieked. The pistol fell to the ground with a hollow metal sound, and he threw my body to the side.

"Don't fucking touch her." Sy barreled unsteadily toward Jared, and Jared landed three hard blows to Sy's jaw.

Jared was smaller than Sy, but faster.

Jared pulled his arm back to land another blow, but Sy pushed him off and dragged his body toward the bed to steady himself. He spit blood from his mouth, his body still wracked with tremors from being awakened from the coma.

Jared laughed mockingly at Sy's still-compromised state. "Already did. Many times, in fact."

"Yeah, I saw the bruises. I won't kill you, though. I'll keep you here, alive, where I can break every bone in your body, until you beg for her forgiveness."

"Awfully protective of *my wife*, aren't you?"

Jared barreled toward Sy, ready to attack, but Sy met him halfway with a powerful blow to the jaw. He stumbled back a few steps and held up one hand to the waiting guards, indicating he didn't want them to intervene.

Yet.

Jared straightened himself and cocked his head side-to-side, then rolled his shoulders. Blood dripped from his mouth, but he now had the pistol.

"Wait—" I held my hands in between the two men. Simon needed more time. "Jared, please, don't do this. Just let us go."

He whipped his head toward me. "I bet he hasn't told you a fucking thing, has he? You think I'm the bad guy? Think about it, Charly. If you chose me *here* and *there*, what do you think that makes you? Tell her, Simon. Tell her what she—"

Sy charged at him, and his large shoulder crushed into Jared's stomach, knocking him against a metal tray of medical supplies. White pads of gauze sprinkled around them like confetti as Sy tried to wrestle the pistol from him. He settled for giving him several more blows to the head when Jared didn't release his grip. On the last blow, Jared stumbled backward, and the pistol clanged to the ground.

Jared abruptly kicked, and it slid across the floor and under the bed.

Sy wrapped his arm around Jared's throat in a choke hold. In his rage, he'd become almost unrecognizable.

The veins in Jared's temples bulged as he looked over at me.

I scrambled toward the bed, searching for the gun.

The guards entered the room and started toward both men.

Jared pulled an object from his boot and he plunged the shiny metal deep into Sy's leg.

Sy roared in pain as a dark river of blood began seeping from his thigh.

Jared sprang to his feet and was handed a gun from one of the guards. He held it to Sy's head.

Sy was on his knees, wrapping his hand around the knife lodged deep in his thigh.

Jared looked at me and smiled. "I told you I'd kill him and make you watch. And, unlike you, I keep my promises." He pulled back on the slide, loading a round into the chamber.

"No!" I screamed. "Jared…" I started to beg, dropping painfully to my knees.

Jared hesitated, to savor the moment of pristine control over the situation, or to revel in my begging, I wasn't sure.

Sy pulled the knife from his thigh, and sweat dripped from his temples.

More alarms went off down the hall and the guards

that had been watching the exchange took off running toward the commotion, confident Jared now had the situation handled.

"Drop it," he barked.

The clunk of Sy dropping the knife to the ground awakened me from my stupor, and rage took over me.

I wasn't going to allow Jared to take anything else I loved away from me, not without a fight. In an instant, I grasped the bloody knife and charged toward Jared.

"Charlotte, no!" Sy tried to angle his body in front of me, but I dodged him and barreled toward Jared.

In the commotion a gunshot rang out, and Sy grunted.

I slammed into Jared's hard body, and the knife tore through his uniform and plunged into his soft flesh. Warm blood pooled around my hand, and I looked up when I heard a strangled gurgle emanate from his throat.

His dark eyes held mine, and shock flitted through them as he stared at me for several long, intimate moments. "Charly…" he whispered. He ran his knuckles gently down my cheek.

He adjusted his gaze to Sy. "I'll always win, Simon. Always."

Sy stumbled toward us, bleeding from a gunshot wound to his upper chest.

Jared wrapped his other hand around mine, and slowly pulled the knife from his torso.

Then, he slammed it into me.

"See you on the other side, Charly…" he whispered, then pushed me to the ground.

I was looking up at the ceiling at the long, rectangular fluorescent lights. I looked down and saw the blood spreading over my light-blue scrubs. Instinctively,

I put both hands over my stomach to cover the wound just under my ribcage.

I fought the profound dizziness and attempted to stand. I swayed as I steadied myself, and then fell to my knees. More yelling and gunshots rang out. They sounded hollow and far away, though the hallways lighting up intermittently told me they were coming from just outside the room.

I looked over, muddled, to where Sy and Jared were at the other end of the room. I tried standing, but fell to the slippery ground again. The white floor was now a river of crimson streaks of blood. I must've lost consciousness, because there was a lapse in time from what I last recalled.

Jared's head recoiled from the blows Sy was landing, and his return punches no longer elicited even a small movement from Sy, despite the blood soaking through his shirt.

Jared crumpled to the ground, bleeding from the wound in his torso and the multiple blows Sy had landed.

I wasn't sure if he was dead.

Sy turned back to me with panic in his eyes.

My chest was painfully tight.

He kneeled where I sat and slowly lowered my head to the floor. He grabbed linen off of the bed and pressed the cloth into where the blood was spilling from my torso.

I tried reaching for his shoulder, concerned about the gunshot wound that saturated his shirt with blood, but my hands were too heavy, and they dropped to my sides. I still couldn't wrap my head around the moments I'd lost after being stabbed by Jared or make sense of the panic in Sy's eyes.

"Please just breathe, Charlotte. They're coming. Joel's team has almost secured the wing. Please. Just breathe."

I stared at Sy, but I couldn't talk. I didn't have the desire to keep breathing or the energy to muster a word, but I kept my eyes locked on his.

A warmth came over me, like someone was pulling a warming blanket up over me. It was peaceful looking into his eyes, but confusion muddied the sensation when I noticed the agony in Sy's stare. His large arms wrapped around my body, lifting me onto the hospital bed, and smoke began filling the room. "Hang on, Charlotte. They're here. I'm here. You're going to be ok."

His eyes didn't match the calm of his voice. The warmth that had been crawling up poured over me. It made its way up my neck and to my head, wrapping me in a peaceful, warm blanket that caused my vision to tunnel out and the edges of the room to glow slightly before everything around me went black.

I woke up confused. My back was aching from the position in which I'd fallen asleep. I lifted my head off the large oak table and textbooks were scattered around me. I looked at the photos in the book—multiple views of a spinal MRI—and recalled the paper I spent the morning writing on the fascinating surgical case I'd performed on a young soldier just a few years ago.

I recalled the operating room, the instruments, and the exposed vertebrae that I'd carefully manipulated. I remembered the rush of adrenaline performing such a complicated procedure as a new surgeon. The need to help the broken man was overwhelming.

I saw his eyes for the first time when he woke from surgery. I was checking his pupils with my light, and I was stunned at the color of his irises. Cerulean blue. Something changed inside me irrevocably after that moment. Those eyes, damn those eyes, they haunted my dreams.

His case was complex, but he was able to walk after I completed the procedure. Years after his successful surgery, I was still writing papers and lecturing on the technique our surgical team used.

Something about the soldier captivated me. I kept in touch with him to continually update my data on his recovery, but I knew he was fully recovered. And so did he. But I needed to see him. Each interaction, each interview, each conversation built on the next. And each time we parted ways, I'd count the days, the weeks, the months until I could find a reason to touch base with him again.

Like magnets, we were drawn to one another, but entangled as a patient and a married doctor, ethically it could never be more.

Then muddy memories started infiltrating my newfound awareness.

Simon! Where was Simon, and why was I sleeping in a library and not watching Joel's team take down Quantym? The wrong memories were flooding in— I was sleeping in the library so I didn't have to go home and deal with Jared. I was exhausted from the long night of fighting with my controlling husband over the ethics of the new black-op program he'd involved me in.

I attempted to stop the new memories from flooding my brain; I grabbed a pen and tore a blank page from one of the books. I started scrawling in an unrecognizable script.

Simon. Quantym. Jump to Periphery. Jared killed

me.

    I read the last sentence three times. Jared killed me. And a fourth time.

    I vaguely started to remember what happened. I jumped. My memories were about to fade. I was going to be stuck on the Periphery forever.

    I failed.

    Sy destroyed the data, but I died.

    I'd known dying was a possibility, but my memories made me want to fight. I wanted to go home, back to my life, to my reality.

    I didn't want to forget.

    I looked over at the papers scattered around me and flung open a manila folder. It was the record of Simon J. Donovan, age 32. All of my notes on the technique I used and his injury were meticulously documented.

    I scanned the first and second page and stopped abruptly on the words "Indicative of ability to jump to Periphery, recruitment in progress." I shut the file and drew in my breath. It took an exorbitant amount of energy to stop the gushing flow of memories that exploded in my brain. Equations, space-time, abilities that indicated remembrance of another realm, consciousness relocating to a new realm after death. Being forced to leave my position as a neurosurgeon, and ordered to work on a new up-and-coming project with Dr. Tomas Gustav. Under Mitch and Jared's direction, I was an integral part of the team in a newly formed black-op program, funded by the U.S. Government—Quantym.

    My head jolted when I heard the loud banging and a booming voice calling my name. I looked over to the door that I'd locked and saw smoke curling into the room from the gap under the door.

I flung open the door.

Sy gently pushed me farther into the room and shut the door behind us. When he touched me, an automatic wave of heat prickled over my skin.

The kinetic magnetism existed here, too.

But here, I wasn't his hero. I was recruiting him to build Quantym. I wasn't anyone's hero. I was the villain. This is why I knew so much about physics—I was helping create or destroy Quantym, depending on which life I was in.

Oh God.

"Dr. Cardoza, there's a fire in the server room. I saw you coming in here earlier. The whole place was evacuated, but you never came out."

He was breathing heavily and wearing his military fatigues.

I wasn't scared. I was amazed as I stared at Sy's alternate self curiously. He had no idea. "You came back for me?"

"Yes, of course I came back for you." He stepped closer. "I'll always come back for you."

"The server room is on fire?

He grasped my hand. "Yes. C'mon, let's get you out of here."

I resisted, rooted in place. "Good. Let it burn."

He widened his eyes at my statement, then quickly shook his head. "I have to get you out of here, and we can't go back to the main entrance, the ceiling tiles are coming down…" He reached into his pocket. "This is going to sound strange, but this—" He handed me a small, black hard-drive. "—it's important you have it. Hide it."

"The protocols," I whispered.

"Let's get out of here."

He stalked over to the window, ready to shatter it with a chair.

"It's going to be ok, Sy."

He whipped his head around to stare at me. He'd never heard me address him so casually. So intimately.

I felt strangely vulnerable as I fought the urge to let the new memories take over me, so I let a few memories slip in. Simon and I had discussed books, travel, astronomy, and politics in the encounters we'd had. We had a connection beyond his surgery, but I remained professional due to our patient and provider relationship. How stupid! I scolded myself. Kiss him! He loves you here, too, he told you so on the other side!

I straightened my back and ignored the voice screaming at me to take him into my arms and tell him everything. I tried to stop the memories from flooding in and overwriting what I'd brought with me from the other side, I didn't know how much more time I had.

I looked down at the crumpled paper in my hand.

Simon. Quantym. Jump to periphery. Jared killed me.

Sy swung the chair at the window, and the tempered glass cracked but didn't break. He pulled the chair back again, ready to swing another blow.

"Wait, Sy."

He put the chair down and turned to look down at me.

I was standing so close to him that I could feel the heat coming off of his body. I took a step closer, and my chest pressed against his. I stroked up his arms, and dragged a finger across the dark tattoo on his neck.

I stood on my toes so I could reach my hands around the back of his neck.

He wrapped his hands tightly around my lower back, pressing me closer.

I tilted my chin up toward his face. His blue eyes burned into mine, and I placed a soft kiss on his lips, which he quickly reciprocated with a long, tender kiss. Our first kiss.

"Charlotte," he whispered against my lips, "I have to get you out of here."

I pressed my lips to his again, crushing my body against him while allowing a few more memories to slip through. There was a door, an old exit door in the closet of the library. It had been covered when the footbridge was built.

I pulled away and turned to look at the back of the room. "I know a way out. It'll lead to the footbridge." I pulled Sy toward the closet and showed him the concealed door. "It's plastered over on the other side; we can break through it easily."

I motioned to the metal tools piled in the corner of the janitorial closet. Before Sy could reach for one, I pulled him close again and he shut the closet door, giving us a couple of additional moments before the smoke could penetrate.

"Before we go, I need to tell you something, something I may forget, but I need you to remember. For me, for us."

He looked at me gravely and nodded.

"Do not join Quantym. Whatever you do, please don't sign."

"What?"

"Please, trust me."

"You've been after me to sign into the program for months. Saying no to you isn't easy." He pulled me to his chest and buried his face into my hair.

"Say you won't sign, no matter what. Please, trust me."

"Why?"

"We don't have time, Sy. I'm going to forget."

We heard a crash, and smoke began filling the small space where we stood. Sy grabbed a piece of wood, and I threw the old exit door open to reveal the thin plaster wall behind it. After just a few blows, the wall crumbled, and we stepped out onto the footbridge.

I gently cupped his face, pulling him so close our lips touched as I spoke. "Please, listen to me before I forget. When I forget, you must remember, our lives depend on it. Jared will kill me if I don't get away, please make sure I get away from him."

"That son of a bitch, he's hurting you?"

"Wait, there's something else, the most important thing."

He pulled back slightly to look me dead in the eyes.

"I love you, Simon Donovan. I loved you there, and I love you here. I'm going to forget, but help me remember." I coughed violently, and Sy caught me as I collapsed.

He lifted me, cradling me in his arms.

I loosely looped my arms around his neck and rested my head on his chest as he carried me across the footbridge. "Please Sy. Don't let me forget," I pleaded.

"I won't let you forget." His voice rumbled through me, a solid promise.

Pain seared through me, and my ribs cracked from the force being put on them. I heard the commotion around me, people shouting numbers and beeping and wailing machines.

"She's back! We've got a pulse!" a woman's voice shouted over all the others.

The CPR compressions stopped, and the pain that had concentrated on my right side dulled. I took a breath on my own before losing consciousness again.

Time had passed, but how much time was a mystery. I opened my eyes only slightly to see the IV bags hanging over me slung from metal poles.

The room darkened, and just before I lost consciousness again, I realized: *They got me back.*

Darkness crept in, and I happily sank back into sleep, confident that everything was going to be okay, that here *and there* everything was going to be okay.

Chapter 19

"You must not blame us scientists for the use which war technicians have put our discoveries." -Lisa Meitner

My parents were there when I opened my eyes. I looked out the window of my hospital room to see it was nearing sunset. I looked around the room before they noticed I was awake.

My mother was nervously crocheting something, and my father was sitting on the edge of a vinyl chair staring at the wall mounted television.

I hadn't realized how much I'd missed them.

"Look, look when they show the picture of the shooter," my father whispered.

My mother glanced at the TV. "Turn that off," she hissed. "It does look like him, and you don't want to upset her if she sees it."

"Adam Cardoza. It looks just like Jared. But he was an only child, yeah?" my father whispered, mostly to himself.

"What time is it?" I croaked.

"She's awake!" my mother called to my dad, who quickly tore himself from the images on the screen.

"Hi Mom, Dad…I'm okay."

"We've heard that before. Does the grim reaper have a vendetta?" My father rushed to my side.

"Not anymore. I killed the bastard." I closed my eyes.

"Charlotte! I can't believe you're…*here* again." My mother motioned around us.

"It's time you move down south with us. You're so far away, and so much has happened."

"I'm okay, Mom. I promise. I'm immortal apparently."

"Not funny, I was so worried…"

My mother was speaking, but I couldn't hear her as I stared at the TV and saw Jared's—bloody and bruised—mug shot displayed.

I couldn't make out what the reporter was saying, but the screen split with an aerial view of the hospital and smoke billowing from the Quantym wing. Jared's mug shot was plastered on the other side.

The subtitle under his photo indicated he had been arrested for arson: *Disgruntled soldier Adam Cardoza goes on shooting rampage; sets fire to hospital on base.*

He lived, I noted.

My parents continued talking, but I wasn't listening as I strained to hear the reporter and to read the names that flashed across the screen.

Mass casualties on base. Remembering the fallen.

The TV clicked off, and my father put down the remote.

"Where's Sy?" My eyes widened, and my heart thundered in my chest.

My father stepped closer to the bed. "We sent him to get something to eat, Charly. He hasn't left your side. He saved your life apparently."

"Nice guy, glad we got to meet him," my mother added. "But you should've told us you were coming to

Virginia! We could've met you here, met him under better circumstances. Why on earth were you interviewing for a job in Virginia?"

Sy entered quietly and shut the door behind him. "Charlotte!" He rushed to my side and grabbed my hand.

I lifted my other hand to pull his neck closer, careful to avoid his gunshot wound. I opened my eyes while still holding tightly to Sy and saw my parents gathering their coffees.

My mother winked at me and walked out of the room with my dad.

I fought the effects of the medication to begin questioning Sy about what had happened. He reassured me that Joel was fine, having taken a bullet to the arm, but was treated and released. Becca was completely unharmed, but managed to take out a few corrupt troops who tried to block the exit. Gustav lost his life by jumping on a guard who was attempting to shoot Sy as he carried me out.

Jeff, Max, and Jay successfully hacked into the servers on this side and wiped all traces of the intelligence Quantym used to jump to the Periphery, including the list of jumpers.

The whole ordeal was covered up by pinning it on Jared, making him out to be a wayward soldier intent on burning the hospital down after a mental break. He'd be tried for murder, but was already trying to be transferred under the guise of insanity.

The general always has a plan.

"But don't worry, he's going to prison forever," Sy reassured me. "And the general is busy doing damage control. He won't put his career in the trash for his son. I'll bet he's pinning everything on Jared as we speak."

He leaned down to kiss me, and I clung to him, parting my lips and kissing him with reckless abandon.

A nurse walked in and cleared her throat to get our attention. She checked my vitals and hung another bag on the IV pole.

When she left the room, Sy sat on the edge of my bed again. We held hands for a long, quiet moment. He stared out the window as the sun disappeared beyond the horizon.

"What are you thinking about?" I asked him.

"Quantum entanglement."

"Oh?"

"You mentioned it one night as you fell asleep." A smile danced on the edge of his lips. "I spoke with Jess. She called your parents to check on you, and they blew your cover. I spoke with her and cleared things up, though." He rubbed his hand through his hair.

"I told her you were going on an interview at a hospital in Virginia. It makes the most sense, why you'd hide it from your friends at work and her. And when your parents made me out to be the hero…well, she told me that you had a theory about us, and you know how much I love your theories. Quantum entanglement sums it up very nicely." He smiled.

"The moment I met you here, I knew I'd met you before, and it was the only explanation I could come up with. I knew that in some form or another, I had a bond with you, whether it was from this or another life."

"Gotta love that bleed-through effect." He laughed. "I wasn't kidding the morning you came over and I told you how long I'd been waiting for you. That moment— having you in bed with me—was a moment I'd dreamed about for years."

"You saved me," I said.

He closed his eyes and shook his head. "You almost *died* because of me, I'm so sorry."

"Stop. We did it, right? It's over."

"It's over." He sighed while staring out the window again.

"How is your leg, and your chest?" I asked, reaching toward his collarbone.

"Healing nicely."

"How long have I been out for?" I asked incredulously.

"Just a day. Charlotte, that is something we didn't cover yet about jumping. Every time I jumped and returned, I healed faster and my intuition became stronger. It's almost like the mind-body connection becomes more powerful—" He stopped abruptly and looked at me.

"I knew I wasn't crazy. When you cut your arm and then showed up to the clinic, I thought I wasn't remembering correctly. You could've used stitches just days before, but when I checked you…"

"You aren't crazy. Intuitive, yes. Abnormally so. But you might not have survived this time, if it weren't your second time jumping. Your mind and body are stronger together once they've separated and reunited."

I could see the guilt on his face when he looked down at my IV.

"So, now what?" I asked, trying to break him out of his brooding.

"Well, if you'll still have me, I was thinking maybe we should rent your place out. You've always wanted to live on the water, and the nights without you are too lonely to survive."

I was trying to wrap my head around what I was hearing. Yes. Yes, to all of it. Yes, to waking up in his arms every day in the bedroom that faced the bay. Yes, to putting Quantym behind us.

"That sounds…amazing." I closed my eyes. "Thank you for saving me, Sy. I'm ready for our future. I'm done with the past."

"Why do you say I saved you? This all happened because of me," Sy grumbled. Torment blazed in his eyes.

"You did. You saved me here, but you saved me there, too."

His eyes widened.

I tried to dig up the fading memories of the fire and his return to the building to get me out.

"You didn't tell me I was your *surgeon,* Sy! The server room was on fire, and you came back in to save me. I fell asleep in the library." I sighed. I was embarrassed that he was also aware that I was the one helping build Quantym on the other side, too.

"I didn't know what would happen to you. I knew you were in the library. I planned on getting you out, but you woke me up. I never knew the ending to that side." He ran a hand over his hair and released a breath.

"You saved me."

"And you saved me. Yesterday, and several years ago, too. Remember I told you I wouldn't have met you if I hadn't had my surgery? I was being literal. You saved me first."

"I was trying to *recruit you,* Sy. You should have told me."

"Just because you and Dr. Gustav were working at Quantym, doesn't mean your intentions were bad. You

309

believed in the science."

I shook my head. "I didn't—don't— believe in the science of manipulating life and death. Jared and Mitch, they—"

"I know, Charlotte. You weren't given a choice." Sy shifted and inhaled sharply.

"What are you thinking?"

"I'm thinking I want to be the one to end both their lives, here, there, and in every peripheral life that exists. Somehow, they've entwined themselves with you, manipulated—"

"Stop. Don't use that word. I have choices, and I'm not going to allow them to affect my life anymore. I gave them so much control in the past, maybe that's what bled through to my other lives. I'm not giving them anything more."

He nodded. "I didn't mean to make you sound like a victim. I get it, I'm the product of my choices, too. You're stronger than you realize, Charlotte."

I bit back a smile. "I initiated our first kiss there. I told you I loved you, and I told you not to sign up for Quantym. I hope you listen. You promised you wouldn't let me forget." I stared out the window.

"Well, I hope they live happily ever after over there. Here—" He leaned in and kissed me softly. "—I know they will."

"Thank you for finding me here, Simon."

"I wasn't truly living until I met you. Here, or there. You helped me realize my purpose."

"And what is your purpose, now that you've pretty much saved humanity?"

"To love and care for the woman who saved me, in more ways than one. No matter where life—or death—

takes us, I'll always find you, and love you, Charlotte."

"I'm tired of all the dying. Let's live, Sy, you and me."

"Dying was the best thing that's ever happened to me. It brought me to you."

"Nothing, not even the infinite vastness of the universe, could have kept us apart. You just decided to be dramatic."

He leaned down and slid his fingers into my hair. "The universe knew you deserved no less than someone willing to die to find you," he replied, and then silenced me with another breathtaking kiss.

The End

Epilogue

A loud buzzer sounded, and the large metal cage opened with a grinding whirr. The correctional officer held his elbow and shoved him forward, frustrated with the prisoner's relaxed gait.

The shackles around his ankles and wrists clinked together as he walked toward the seg room where he was to be kept following meeting with the prison's psychiatrist.

Solitary confinement. Abs-so-lutely perfect.

The guard shoved him into the room and removed the shackles. The door slammed shut, and the prisoner listened as the locks clicked and engaged. In the distance, unintelligible shouts from other inmates could be heard. The sound of keys jingling on the guard's belt faded as he walked away from the locked door of the seg room.

He sat on the edge of the bed in the tiny seven-meter room, inhaling sharply. He closed his eyes and bounced the ping-pong ball off the floor, catching it and tossing it again.

Plink, plink, plink.

A testament to how easily people are manipulated, he thought. This one small token from the psychiatrist was going to change everything.

Plink. Plink. Plink.

He smiled as he caught the ball and methodically laid flat on his back on the bed. He fished out the fabric he had twisted from his orange jumpsuit. He rolled up the two small pieces and stuffed the cotton into each ear.

He slid his thumbs along the center of the ping-pong ball, feeling for the weak seam, and pressed his thumbs into the center of the plastic, tearing the ball into two halves.

He placed a half over each eye, and focused on his breathing.

Fools. Sensory deprivation could be achieved without the pomp and circumstance of Quantym.

Just need patience, and absence of sound and sight and touch.

And thoughts to embed, to take to the other side.

So, he thought of *her.*

He thought of all the ways he'd been able to control her in the past, and all the ways he couldn't in the present.

She believed in love, how charming. The myth, the fantasy. It doesn't exist. People joined together for need, necessity, purpose.

Like him and his father. Like him and her. He had done her a favor, marrying her, feeding into her fantasy about love and a happy-ever-after. Not that he didn't reap the benefits of a marriage to someone so docile, so easily manipulated, but—it served an even more tangible purpose after learning she was a jumper. He didn't need to pretend they were an epic love story. Either way, he'd utilize her and her ability—whether she was willing or not.

She just chose the hard way. The painful way.

The thought of her insubordination brought him to the brink of snapping.

But, no.

He was calm, calculated. Methodical. There was always a way. An alternative, even.

So he pressed his hand into his torso to inflict pain on the wound she'd left there. Anger and vengeance flared, hotter than the flames of hell scorching his stomach. He was going to balance the scales. Just a little more pressure would open the wound, cause a bleed.

Unfortunately for her, she wasn't a killer. Could never be, would never be. She'd calculated where the vital organs were, ensured the depth of the wound she inflicted wasn't critical. *He knew that about her.*

So weak. So fucking weak.

But before he could send himself on the mission from *here to there*, he needed to meet with his father. Ensure all the intel was planted and jumpers were ready and waiting for his arrival to brief him. He may not be a jumper, but he didn't need to be. Not with the setup he and Mitch had.

He could handle anything life threw his way. His father taught him that.

Emotions are weakness, resilience is a virtue. Improvise. Adapt. Gain power, gain respect, and allow nothing short of worship.

And what he wouldn't tolerate was being stolen from. Being lied to. Disrespected. Simon stole his disobedient, broken wife. Both were going to have to pay. In this life, and in the next.

He almost felt sorry for them. Almost. They didn't realize just how much they didn't know. How prepared he and Mitch were for this very moment.

And just like that, he drank in the sensory deprivation and embedded what he was going to need for his next mission:

Revenge.

A word about the author...

Born and raised in New England, Amy (AA DaSilva) obtained her degree in clinical laboratory science and brings her love of science and writing together via science fiction. When she's not writing or identifying cells under a microscope, she can be found with a book in one hand and a cup of iced coffee in the other. She resides in Massachusetts with her husband, two sons, and pup Didi. Her debut novel, Periphery, is a science fiction love story that explores fate, strength, and the choices that determine our destiny.

AA DaSilva has completed book two in the Periphery series and is currently working on edits. For the latest updates on new releases and events, visit her at aadasilva.com.

Thank you for purchasing
this publication of The Wild Rose Press, Inc.

For questions or more information
contact us at
info@thewildrosepress.com.

The Wild Rose Press, Inc.
www.thewildrosepress.com

Milton Keynes UK
Ingram Content Group UK Ltd.
UKHW031617231124
451036UK00001B/5

9 781509 257713